THE HOLLYWOOD DAUGHTER

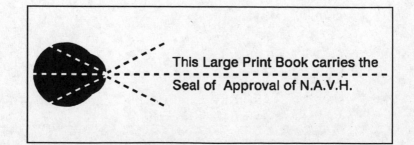

This Large Print Book carries the Seal of Approval of N.A.V.H.

THE HOLLYWOOD DAUGHTER

KATE ALCOTT

THORNDIKE PRESS
A part of Gale, Cengage Learning

Farmington Hills, Mich • San Francisco • New York • Waterville, Maine
Meriden, Conn • Mason, Ohio • Chicago

GALE
CENGAGE Learning®

Thorndike Press® Large Print Basic.
The text of this Large Print edition is unabridged.
Other aspects of the book may vary from the original edition.
Set in 16 pt. Plantin.

LIBRARY OF CONGRESS CATALOGING-IN-PUBLICATION DATA

Names: Alcott, Kate, author.
Title: The Hollywood daughter / Kate Alcott.
Description: Large print edition. | Waterville, Maine : Thorndike Press, 2017. | Thorndike press large print basic
Identifiers: LCCN 2016059273 | ISBN 9781410498267 (hardback) | ISBN 1410498263 (hardcover)
Subjects: LCSH: Large type books. | BISAC: FICTION / Historical. | GSAFD: Bildungsromans.
Classification: LCC PR6101.L426 H65 2017b | DDC 823/.92—dc23
LC record available at https://lccn.loc.gov/2016059273

Published in 2017 by arrangement with Doubleday, a division of Penguin Random House LLC

Printed in the United States of America
1 2 3 4 5 6 7 21 20 19 18 17

FOR FRANK,
AGAIN AND ALWAYS

AUTHOR'S NOTE

This is a story based on the real world of Hollywood and America in the 1940s and 1950s. It's also the fictional world of a girl who lived in this time and place. Some elements come solely from my imagination, while some historical facts have been juggled to serve the story. For example, *The Bells of St. Mary's* was not filmed at a convent school. But for the thrill it gives Jesse, my young admirer of Ingrid Bergman, I couldn't resist.

PART ONE

CHAPTER ONE

New York, 1959

"Dropped something."

A neighbor from upstairs, the man with the sandy-haired crew cut, was emptying the mailbox next to mine. He pointed downward to a cream-colored envelope skittering toward the heating grate.

"Thanks." I scooped the envelope up and scanned it; no return address. It hardly registered; I was holding tight to another envelope, the one from *Better Homes and Gardens.* So maybe they wanted that hasty piece I sent them on a new kind of doll named Barbie? It wasn't one of the stories I labored over at night — this one might actually have a chance of selling. One more glance at the fancy piece of mail, which probably announced the wedding of a classmate whom, after five years, I would only vaguely remember.

The man with the crew cut was closing

up his box and turning toward the elevator. He looked about my age, somewhere in his late twenties. "Good day for you?" I asked impulsively.

His eyes widened. "Uh, yeah," he mumbled. When the elevator door opened, he all but jumped inside.

I truly knew better: you didn't ask questions of strangers in New York. Of course, everybody remained a stranger, but no one seemed to find that a problem.

I started up the stairs to my apartment. For me, it hadn't been so good a day. Too much time now at *Newsweek.* I had managed a promotion to the copy desk, but it was a boring job. It paid the bills, so I stuck with it and wrote stories at night, shipping them off to various magazines. If nothing happened there, maybe the editor's position I had applied for would come through. Today? Well, somebody else got it — a copy boy just out of college. So, yes, I was more tired than usual. I began counting the steps, a favored way of diverting myself from wondering why I was drifting. It wasn't working tonight.

I stopped on the landing and stared into the mirror hung to perk up the light on the stairs. Checking myself out. Blue angora sweater set and single-strand pearls, long

brown hair curled under in a careful pageboy — I looked like every other eager female
marking time until marriage. One of the
copy editors had told me I was a "good-
looking dame" this morning. A compliment,
I guess. But, standing there at the landing, I
wondered just exactly what had happened
to the girl who left Bennington College five
years ago.

Well, I wasn't a virgin anymore.

The usual smells of the second floor
greeted me, especially the pungent but
comforting aroma of garlic and onions from
the apartment next to mine. I didn't know
the people living there, but I heard them
laughing and sometimes shouting at each
other, and I imagined them sitting around a
kitchen table covered in red-checked oil-
cloth, eating some delectable lasagna, while
I was out here in the hall, inhaling the musty
smell of the threadbare carpet mixed with a
faint whiff of fresh dog urine.

Oh, please. Annoyed at my self-pity, I
jiggled open the lock with its ancient key
and stepped inside the apartment, which
felt gloomier tonight than the stairwell. It
was pouring outside, the rain coming down
in exuberant, gurgling rivers over the windows, probably because the gutters hadn't
been cleaned in years.

I dumped the mail on the coffee table, staring at the letter that mattered. Would I feel worse when I found out what was inside? I picked it up and slit it open smoothly with one pass of my fingernail. The article about the Barbie doll fell out.

"Thank you for your submission. Unfortunately . . ."

Okay, no surprise. I glanced at the manuscript of a short story on the table that had come from *The Atlantic* yesterday — topped by a rejection letter with those same exact words. Was there just one typewriter somewhere dedicated to rejecting potential authors? I crumbled the paper tight and tossed it on the floor.

Then, in more leisurely fashion, I opened the fancy envelope.

It was an invitation, yes. Engraved. But not to a wedding.

Jessica Malloy (indeed, me) was cordially invited to attend the 1959 Academy Awards Ceremony at the Pantages Theater in Los Angeles as a guest. Nowhere on the card did it say who was doing the inviting — just a cool request for an immediate RSVP, because attendance was limited.

My heart missed a couple of beats. Me? What was *this* about? There must be some mistake.

I smoothed the polished surface of the invitation with my hand, letting it be, for one second, Aladdin's lamp. The broken gutters, the moldy carpet disappeared.

The Academy Awards. 1946. Once, just once, I had been part of that amazing scene — watching reporters with microphones eagerly search for beautiful people — and feeling my scalp prickle with the excitement of their voices as they grabbed breathless interviews with the stars. Closing my eyes, I walked again down a red carpet, chin up, holding my father's hand, trying to avoid looking at the craning faces of fans searching for celebrities, those whip-thin women in slithery satin gowns and handsome men in crisp tuxedos who filled this world of make-believe. The past was tumbling, all raucous and glittery, into the present. My head suddenly filled with light and color and the thrill of twirling briefly at the top of the world.

Which meant, inevitably, remembering Ingrid Bergman.

The fans had loved her that night, their imploring hands reaching out as she floated by on the red carpet, all hoping her smile would embrace them, giving them something to remember and talk about for years. I could almost see her perfectly sculpted face, even hear her voice again.

And with those memories came the sounds and smells and confusion of my crazy childhood. This invitation — I ran a finger over the engraved lettering — was someone's idea of a joke. Who would be beckoning me back to a city I once swore never to visit again? What was I overlooking?

I reached for the phone and did what I often did — dialed long-distance to talk to Kathleen, my high-school friend, and my strongest link to the past. We had both changed — she sold real estate in Los Angeles, and her voice was now raspy from a few too many cigarettes — but almost everything she said came with either a ring of common sense or a bounce of laughter. Unlike me, she was able to flick away the dictates of rules and orders like so much dust when they became burdensome. Her exit from our shared Catholic upbringing was an easy, casual move, and I envied that casualness. Even after I fled Los Angeles, our friendship survived. It was hard staying in touch at first, but we'd managed pretty well over the years.

I could hear the distant phone ringing. A three-hour difference; please be home, Kathleen, I begged silently. I need you to help me figure this out.

Kathleen did not disappoint.

"An invitation? Interesting," she said.

"What possible connection would I have to that world anymore?"

"Well — maybe it's from a friend of your father?"

"There aren't that many still around, even the ones who went to jail. And none with enough power to send off one of these. I want to know who invited me. This feels phony."

"Call and find out if it's authentic; hey, even if it is, come back out here for a few days. I'd love to see you."

"Well —"

"Anyway, it's good timing — we'd get to catch up — and you get to see the last of Saint Ann's Academy." There was just the hint of a catch in her voice.

"What?"

"They sold our school, Jesse. Bishop Doyle wants the money from the land. They're tearing it down for a shopping mall."

And why did that suddenly punch me in the heart? Our school. That graceful sweep of Spanish mission-style buildings, seasoned by decades of use, settled comfortably among green lawns and lush trees . . .

"Where will the nuns go?"

"An old school dormitory in the Valley. Will you come? One last chance."

"Why would they want to see *me*? I'm the one who messed up our high-school graduation, in case you've forgotten."

"There were extenuating circumstances," she said soberly.

That caught me. I stared out the window, hit now by another downpour of rain. I should hurry and shut all the windows, not waste time digging up the past.

"Okay, will you come? Maybe you'll meet some of those new hotshot filmmakers — you know, people like Bob Fosse." This was Kathleen's teasing voice.

"I don't know who he is."

"Well, you will. And maybe you'll be lucky enough to be around for the next atomic bomb test. They're setting them off every three weeks now."

"But that's in Nevada."

"True. All the tourists head for a front seat in Las Vegas. But if you time it to the second, you can see a burst of light from a few places here. Do you know they're crowning a new 'Miss Atomic Blast' next month?"

"The world is crazy."

"Yep. Crazier than Hollywood." Then a

pause. "Look," she said quietly. "Come back. We'll walk through everything together."

"What if you come here?"

It wasn't just a mysterious invitation at stake; she and I both knew that. I wished she lived closer. But Kathleen would never leave L.A.

"Leave this land of opportunity? No way," she said. "Maybe I'll get rich. Well, maybe not rich," she amended, "but I'm going to be buying a house for myself pretty soon. By the way, speaking of scandals — there's a good one on Errol Flynn in *Screenland*."

"You're trying to tempt me back with old movie gossip," I said, smiling.

"Of course I am; we shared enough of it growing up. Who outgrows gossip?"

"You have a point."

"Ah, you're coming?"

"I'm thinking about it."

"I'll be waiting to hear."

"I'll think about it," I repeated. We said goodbye, and I made my way to the kitchen for a glass of wine, mulling over the mix of glitz and piety that had shaped my childhood in the land of make-believe that was Los Angeles. I had never liked the tall, skinny palm trees.

■ ■ ■ ■

I was something of a split Catholic from the beginning, the product of a pious mother who framed my life within the church rules and a father who provided the shrug, the chortle that helped me breathe easier. I knew we were of some vaguely exotic breed, but that didn't directly affect me. I was a member of the One True Faith, and could feel sorry for all the unfortunate people who weren't. It was sad, but, from what I heard in catechism class, they couldn't go to heaven when they died. Instead they went to limbo, a calm, rather boring place where good people went who weren't baptized. Our parish priest implied we didn't have to feel too sorry for some of them, because they hadn't treated us very well — refusing jobs to Irish and Polish immigrants, and having members of the Ku Klux Klan march around in white sheets with peekaboo eye slits, waving torches, ready to burn our houses in places like the Deep South. The Masons didn't like us, either, and I knew about those "No Irish Need Apply" signs that went up in Boston store windows during the Great Depression. It was all something of a jumble.

I look now on how all this soaked into my soul, and I wonder. But back then, I was daunted by the rigor it took to *remain* a good Catholic in a church that required careful stepping to avoid sin. My father was my protector, mainly with his knowing wink. Mostly he was fun — and that's because he lived and worked in the delightful world of make-believe called Hollywood. He was a studio publicist, which I imagined to be a lofty perch from which he could wave a magic wand and create wonderful realities. I loved hearing about his work at the Selznick Studio, and his jokes about the glamour kings and queens of the movie industry. He lived confidently, and I knew — without having the words for it — that his jaunty jokes would surely prevail over the fears of hell and damnation that dogged me through early childhood.

Not that I would think of testing this assumption. Mother, in her firm, steely way, made sure of that.

My mother — my elusive, haunted mother. Father sometimes jokingly called her the Church's traffic cop; sometimes not so jokingly. Mother knew the moral dangers of life, and had me memorize my catechism before first grade. Hell was a blunt instrument, and she believed in it thoroughly.

It hadn't always been that way. When I was small, she sometimes drew me into the beauty and magic of the Church. I remember one Christmas Eve she took me to Midnight Mass. I knelt before the vividly lifelike image of the baby Jesus in the manger, enthralled by the flickering votive lights and the scent of pine branches, as she whispered to me the story of his miracle birth. Her hand stroked my hair as she talked, and I felt I was sharing with her something spiritual and good.

But there weren't many memories like that. I sensed early that the split between the two worlds my parents represented was a source of constant tension. My father loved talking about the politics of both, but Mother would turn cold at any criticism of the Catholic Church. By the time I was ten, Father had pronounced the Church's influence in Hollywood too powerful. He described to me how Church censors — those arbiters of movies, both acceptable and condemned — kept a cold and ferocious eye on the industry. The industry itself had its own nervous policing, he said, but the Catholic bishops were the toughest. When they condemned what they didn't like, Hollywood sat up straight and paid attention.

"Yeah, we got away with too much in the thirties," Father said when I asked him why. "Too much sex and skin — people got fed up."

"Gabriel" — I remember that warning tone in my mother's voice. I heard it more and more as I grew older — "she's only a child."

"She asked, I answered," he said. "She's a smart cookie."

I treasured that response.

He loved expanding on the topic. Movies could be killed by a speech from the pulpit, he said. Studio heads weren't worried about hell; they tossed and turned at night, worrying about box-office receipts. And it wasn't just movies being condemned. As far as damnation was concerned, even Dante couldn't do better than the emerging political vigilantes in Washington.

"Communist." Father sounded out the syllables slowly. "Nail that label onto the forehead of some writer or actor, and you've killed a career. There are real bad guys in Washington feeding the paranoia —"

"Enough, Gabriel," Mother objected again. She slapped a wet towel against the Formica counter — a sound sharp enough to silence even my father.

I think sometimes these days Kathleen

gets bored when I rail on about how the shabby politics of Hollywood and Washington ruined lives, not to mention the Catholic Church's condemnation of sinners for small infractions, especially for seeing forbidden movies. She would point out that I've always been madder at the moral contradictions that took over my world than anyone else she knows. "You want both parts of your life to work," she said.

"Sometimes I just want to throw them both away."

"Good luck."

No need for dinner. I drank the last of my wine and slowly prepared for bed. So Saint Ann's Academy, that graceful enclave of belief and trust gone sour, was soon to be torn down. Maybe I should show up, to mourn it somehow. I had told myself I would never set foot in Los Angeles again, but this invitation on my bedside table was drawing me in, whispering possibilities. Maybe I should do it. Maybe I could cut through the haze that had enveloped me for far too long.

I had a week of vacation coming to me, plus an extra weekend. I could use it all to make this trip.

I drifted off into restless sleep, listening to

the rain on the windows, thinking of Kathleen's words.

One last chance.

And the floodgates began to open.

CHAPTER TWO

Los Angeles, 1942

My cousin Jeremy once told me you have to choose your heroes by the time you're ten years old. He, a decade older than I, liked to give me lessons about life, which I drank in. He had already read parts of Dante's "Inferno" to me out loud. It was scary — evil popes burning in fire — but I was dazzled, particularly by the spooky illustrations. Jeremy never quite spelled out why I *needed* to choose a hero now, maybe because he clearly preferred instruction to illumination. But I must have sensed that the supply of heroes, like husbands, could thin out if I waited too long. So I obeyed. When you chose a hero, he told me, it was for life. No ifs, ands, or buts about it, you had to stay loyal. And when it came to loyalty, I looked to my father's world.

Jeremy, a baseball lover, chose the Cardinals. I chose Ingrid Bergman.

She slipped into my heart very early, almost before I knew it. It was 1942, and I was still attending Sheldon Country Day School in Beverly Hills. My father was quite artful about making connections that advanced him in the movie business. Surely, that's how I found myself in a Hollywood version of a ride-sharing plan — no mothers driving, just a hired chauffeur in a crisp, starchy uniform and hat — that included Pia Lindström, Ingrid Bergman's little daughter.

I never really knew any of those girls who shared that morning ride. There were about eight of us, all ages; we just wiggled for space every morning, eating frosted doughnuts and scratching away at homework, as the driver made his way up to the winding paths of the super-grand homes where some of them lived. But I looked forward each day to the moment when we pulled up in front of 1220 Benedict Canyon Drive. This was Pia's house.

The car would idle, the driver drumming his fingers on the wheel, until the front door of the house opened. Little Pia, about four years old, all tiny and crispy in her Peter Pan collar, would come rushing out. Her mother would walk her to the car, then wave and smile goodbye, looking sleepy in a blue chenille bathrobe that fluttered around her ankles. Her long hair usually looked like it needed a good brushing; she kept it tucked behind her ears.

I was already enough of a Hollywood kid to know how the light clicks on and off between glamour and ordinary life for actors. But Ingrid Bergman was so beautiful, so queenly — remote and real at the same time. I hadn't seen *Intermezzo,* the movie that first made her famous, but my father raved about her.

"Oh my God," he said to Mother one night, "this new beauty from Sweden can act. She is luminescent, almost ethereal. I guarantee, she's going to be famous."

"Just because she has a marvelous complexion?" Mother responded, with a slight edge.

"No, not just that." Father wrapped his arms around her as she stood by the stove. "She wears flat shoes, too. And you know how I feel about flat shoes."

Mother laughed. That was rare, and I felt warm inside.

Ingrid was tall, very tall; so was I, even in fourth grade. I'm not quite sure why I was so immediately enthralled, but I wasted no time trying to puzzle it out. She made me want to stand up straight, to be proud of

28

my height instead of awkward. She had grace and a beautiful smile, and I wanted to be like her.

I'd peek at her through the car window, hoping she might cast a glance in my direction. No luck — until the morning we pulled to the curb and I dropped my lunch box just as one of the girls opened the door. Horrified, I watched as the box burst open, scattering my egg sandwich and chocolate pudding all over Ingrid Bergman's velvet-smooth lawn.

I scrambled out of the car, acutely aware of the giggling behind me, and tried to clean up the mess before she came down the path with Pia. Suddenly I felt her long, graceful fingers gently pulling me up. "It's all right, child," she said, "the gardener will clean it up." She put her hand to my forehead, and I smelled lilacs.

"Are you okay?" she asked.

I nodded, voiceless.

"Don't be ashamed," she said. "I once dropped an egg-salad sandwich on David Selznick's lap, and he got over it."

She hugged me and laughed, and I loved her forever.

Somehow Ingrid became the gentle, joking, loving mother I longed for. She floated through my days, punctually at seven-thirty every weekday morning, as much a part of my comforting routine as my bowl of steaming oatmeal at home.

The only flaw was, she wasn't Catholic. She was Swedish, so she had to be Protestant; I knew that much. Still, I imagined her as someone like me in one way or another.

I knew being Catholic was what separated my family from the families of my friends at school, and my father from the studio mainstream. It wasn't just that we still lived on the wrong side of Wilshire Boulevard; it was the fact that non-Catholics seemed awkward when the subject of religion came up. My father explained that some people thought we paid first allegiance to an Italian pope and wondered what went on in the confessional, and how we could believe in something called the Holy Trinity. I don't think there were any other Catholics at Country Day, which seemed fine with my father. Religious mandates rested lightly on his shoulders, like feathers he could shrug off at will.

One day, Cousin Jeremy told us all on a visit from college that he didn't believe in God anymore. And he certainly wasn't about to drag himself out of bed at his dormitory on Sundays — after a hard week studying — just to go to Mass. My father didn't seem upset; he actually chuckled that Jeremy was more likely to spend his time out partying, but standing on his own two feet was good for him. Mother was scandalized.

I was aware of her watching me much more closely afterward. And I heard my parents at night in bed talking in low tones. My name kept getting repeated, which put me on alert. My safe life had jiggled a bit at Mother's reaction to Jeremy's declaration of independence. It jiggled more the day my father asserted his.

One Sunday morning, missal in hand, I waited more or less patiently by the front door to head for Mass with my parents. I took a quick peek in the hall mirror, which never reassured this ten-year-old. All it told me was I had dull sandy-brown hair and eyes a nondescript color Mother called "hazel." Worse, they seemed squinty and small, and my ears looked like they belonged to Clark Gable. And was I really getting, as Mother put it, a little "chunky"?

Mother came briskly into the hall, high heels tap-tapping. She leaned close to the hall mirror, the way she usually did, one slender hand applying energetic swipes of creamy red lipstick, looking as fragile as a reed of grass bending with the wind. I wasn't quite sure why that thought crossed my mind, but I knew to be quiet when she had her nervous headaches, and I felt a stab of muddled protectiveness. At the same time, I knew she was always watching me — seemingly afraid.

I caught a glimpse of my father through the dining-room arch, slouched down in a chair, smoking a cigarette. The chandelier cast a light onto his thick head of dark hair, giving it a rakish shine. Why wasn't he up and pulling on his coat? I liked it on Sundays when he laughed and whispered funny asides to me about whether today would be the day tottering old Monsignor O'Hara wouldn't make it through Mass.

"Your father isn't coming with us this morning." Mother's voice sounded thin and scratchy.

"Why not?"

"Ask him."

He swiveled in his chair and faced me. "Okay, Jess. The Legion of Decency makes everybody swear today they'll never see any dirty pictures for the whole year. We've talked about this, right?"

I nodded tentatively.

"Well, you know what? I make my living

in the movie business."

"Gabriel —" my mother warned.

He ignored her. "And that means I see so-called dirty pictures all the time, and my job is to get other people to see them." He turned to Mother. "I'm not going to stand like a lying ass in that church and be a hypocrite."

"People will notice," Mother fired back.

"You care too much what other people think."

"Gabriel Malloy, you care too much about —" Mother stopped, bit her lip.

Her words just kind of hung there, floating free.

"Making it?" His voice softened. "I guess I do." He stood up and moved toward us, but Mother wasn't having any of it.

"Catholics have to take this pledge," she said.

His gaze on her was steady, oddly regretful. "Vannie, do you really believe that?"

I saw determination in her eyes. "Of course I do," she replied.

She grabbed my hand and yanked me toward the door. "Let's go, Jesse. We'll be late."

She had the engine turned on as I hopped on the running board, opened the door, and climbed into our buckety old Ford — there was a war on, and nobody could buy a new car in America until we licked the Nazis, my parents said. It was a mortal sin to miss Mass, wasn't it? You had to be careful of mortal sins. I had this hazy idea that they sneaked up on you if you weren't vigilant. The lessons I absorbed from catechism class were taught simply and briskly: one careless stumble and you could be on your way to hell. Was my father going to hell?

It was not a question to ask Mother that morning.

A buzz of excitement swirled in the air as Mother and I walked into Saint Paul's and took our seats. An elderly woman whispered the news: Bishop Francis Doyle was here; she had seen him step out of his black limousine. He was going to administer the Legion of Decency pledge this morning to all of us personally — an incredible honor. Weren't we lucky? Mother and I opened our missals. I looked at her hopefully and gave an exaggerated sniff, remembering one of my father's jokes. He insisted the wooden pews smelled of wet diapers and whatever else little kids had probably ground into them over the years. Mixed with incense.

She smiled, but it was a tired smile. "No jokes today," she murmured.

I looked up to see Bishop Doyle walking slowly from the vestry out to the communion railing. He faced the congregation.

"My dear brethren," he began. "Greetings. Today we jointly raise a banner against the evils of Hollywood."

Would that include a new movie called *The Outlaw* that my father was trying to help launch? The censors thought the ads were indecent. I had asked him why, and he said it was because Jane Russell had breasts the size of melons. He thought that was stupid, and right then, in church, I did, too. How could it be a sin just to glance at a billboard and see an actress with big breasts? I wondered. If it was, and you stepped off the curb and got hit by a car right after taking a peek, were you going to hell or purgatory? I thought of my father, safe at home, and couldn't help being glad he wasn't here. He might laugh again, and that would have mortified Mother.

"All rise, please." The bishop's voice cut sharply into the air.

As one, feet shuffling, throats clearing, the congregation rose.

I couldn't move. It was as though I was nailed to the pew.

"Jessica, get up," my mother whispered.

I stared straight ahead, feeling dizzy. What

if I didn't?

"Get up," Mother pleaded again. "This is *required."*

The bishop was looking straight at me, waiting.

There wasn't a sound in the church. Everyone was standing, and I don't know why I kept sitting there. I had no rational reason, but I had some confused idea that my father would applaud me.

"Jessica —"

I glanced up into Mother's horrified eyes. No, not horrified. Frightened. That unfroze me. Slowly, I stood.

The bishop's gaze shifted outward. He cleared his throat. "Now raise your right hands and repeat after me," he said to the congregation. He paused until all shuffling stopped.

"I condemn all indecent and immoral motion pictures, and those which glorify crime or criminals," he intoned. We dutifully repeated the words, and I spoke out, loud and clear. "I acknowledge my obligation to form a right conscience about pictures that are dangerous to my moral life," I chanted with the others, wondering what exactly a "right conscience" was. When the bishop finished, I felt restored to pious invisibility. What had gotten into me?

His work done, Bishop Doyle bowed and turned to the altar, preparing to offer an unusually brisk Low Mass. After all, Mother murmured, he was a very busy man. Mrs. Gunther, a parishioner who served on the Altar Society with Mother, the one with the wrinkled skin that Father said came from spending too much time at Malibu, leaned forward from the pew behind us.

"And where is Mr. Malloy today, Vanessa?" she stage-whispered. Her breath smelled like Listerine.

"He's feeling under the weather this morning," Mother replied. She really didn't like Mrs. Gunther, who, the gossip went, had a nephew who had played the chauffeur in one of Cary Grant's movies. That gave her a touch of glamour, though no one seemed to know the nephew's name.

"Do give him our best wishes. It's nice to know we have good Catholic men like him in that nasty business."

Two thoughts — the kind I had learned to keep to myself — raced through my mind: Mrs. Gunther's nephew mustn't be getting any good parts these days. And how could anybody describe the glamorous world my father worked in, with all its glitter and excitement, as a "nasty business"?

A quick glance at Mother's clouded face

confirmed the wisdom of keeping my mouth shut. I didn't retain that luxury very long.

"Why didn't you stand up?" Mother asked softly as we settled into the car.

"He was going to criticize the movies too much."

"Were you trying to be loyal to your father?"

"Yes."

"Then please try also to be loyal to me."

Confused, I said nothing. Until that moment, I thought being loyal to both of them was one and the same thing.

"Have I got a movie for us." My father, whistling as usual, came bursting through the front door as Mother was setting the table for dinner the next night. With both hands, he held aloft two metal canisters. He swooped down and placed a kiss on my mother's cheek, a stray lock of hair falling over his forehead. She lifted her head tentatively and gave him a small smile — a little stiff, but I hoped it meant she wasn't mad anymore. Tension in our home often went unexplained, though it eventually evaporated, and I was counting on that.

"What is it?" she asked.

"It's Jesse's favorite actress in a new movie, and who might that be, Jesse?" His voice was teasing.

I was confused for an instant or two. I liked Dale Evans — she played in cowboy pictures — but I didn't really have a favorite. I looked at my father.

"Well, you talk about her, about how stately and wonderful she is —"

"Ingrid Bergman?" I wasn't old enough to see her movies, Mother said. Anyway, most of them were in Swedish.

He nodded. "You girls ready to visit an exotic town named Casablanca?"

Mother turned back into the kitchen to bring out the pot roast and potatoes, and I couldn't see her face. But I heard her words: "Is that the one you've been talking about? It sounds too grown-up for Jesse. Don't push this, Gabriel."

My father cast me a regretful glance. "Sorry, kiddo."

After dinner, I watched as he set up the projector in the living room, swearing under his breath at the spindly screen that kept sagging in the middle. He explained how he had talked the director into letting him take a copy of the movie home, how he had promised to bring it back the next morning. This one was slated for the big time.

Mother scraped globules of fat and gristle from our dinner plates into the garbage pail with such speed that one of the plates chipped. "Why did they let you bring it home?" she asked as she removed her apron, then smoothed her hair in a primping motion, almost as if she were about to head out to a party.

"Kind of a bonus gift, I think."

She turned to him, eyes wide and questioning. He stood in place, shoving his hands into his pockets, looking oddly shy. Mother reached out and touched his cheek with her hand. "A promotion?" she asked.

He nodded.

Mother leaned close to him, her cheeks suddenly flushed. The expression on Father's face as he hugged her tight was a mix of relief and triumph, and for a few seconds, I felt they existed only for each other. But then he thrust out an arm and pulled me in. Soon we were all three laughing.

What happens now? Mother asked with excitement.

It meant he would be handling publicity for some pretty big stars and working on some big movies, he said.

"Who, Gabriel?"

"Well, my first job is selling Ingrid Bergman in this movie. But the one she's excited about is *For Whom the Bell Tolls*. That gets released next year."

"You'll work with her?" I asked, awed.

He smiled a slow, sweet smile, the smile of a man who knows how to gear down and savor a moment. "My job is to make sure that lanky Swede who doesn't wear makeup becomes famous. And the studio is putting up the cash." He tickled Mother under the chin. "This means we can buy a new house in Beverly Hills — just what you want, right, honey?"

Mother nodded, eyes suddenly dreamy. I looked at the clock; it was getting late. Soon I would be sent to bed, and I wanted to be part of my parents' excitement for as long as I could. They were victorious, and I could take my universe for granted when times were good with them. I loved the sense of us as a family, and wished I had a brother or sister, too.

I didn't have the words to express the anxiety I felt when they snapped at each other. My world was shaped around certitude — bedrock certitude. That's what being Catholic did for you. There were rules, and if you broke them, there were sins, and, yes, some of those sins sent you straight to hell. The point was, stick to the rules, never question, and all would be fine. Simple, really. That's what Mother said, every day. I felt suddenly ashamed of having been so stubborn at Mass yesterday.

"Please let me watch," I pleaded. "I want to be here with both of you."

They exchanged glances. Mother sighed, but it seemed such a happy moment, she nodded consent. Something in her seemed to relax, and I knew with a sudden cramp in my stomach how much I had wanted her to be less rigid. The usual lines pulled tight around her mouth had vanished. She was so pretty right now, as pretty as any movie star. I told myself we could both be proud of my father.

I can't say I understood the whole context of *Casablanca* that night, as we watched the wavering images on our sagging screen. But I knew it was a love story, and I saw Bergman's sadness. I couldn't take my eyes off of her face. She glowed in almost a holy way, and tears tumbled down my cheeks when Humphrey Bogart's Rick told her on the foggy tarmac of the airport that she belonged with her husband. *When that plane leaves the ground and you're not with him, you'll regret it. Maybe not today, maybe not tomorrow, but soon and for the rest of your life.*

"But she loves *Rick,*" I blurted. "Not the other guy."

My father chuckled. Mother's brow promptly settled into its usual furrow.

"Don't worry," my father stage-whispered to us both. "This is Ingrid. She'll do the right thing. She knows her route to stardom."

The movie reached its close. I was mesmerized by every shot of Ingrid's beautiful face. And I knew in my heart at the fade-out that Ingrid would do no wrong, no matter how much I wanted her to choose the man she loved. She might not be a Catholic, but she had a strong moral compass; surely, even Bishop Doyle would agree.

"She never liked him," my father said as he turned off the projector.

I blinked. "Rick? She didn't like Rick?"

"No, Bogart." He was talking more to Mother than to me. "It's complicated sometimes. He was having marital trouble — his wife was jealous, sure he would end up having an affair with Bergman."

"But she's married," I broke in, astonished.

Father shrugged. "He played it safe. He'd show up for a kissing scene, then shoot off to his dressing room, keeping a distance from everybody. He wasn't a very friendly guy, not with those rumors."

"You mean . . ." I blushed, but was determined to get this straight. "You mean, you know, going all the way?"

Father threw back his head and laughed. "Well, well, our little girl is growing up."

"Gabriel —" my mother cautioned.

"Vanessa, she's old enough. Anyway, he wasn't too genial. With Bergman or anyone else."

I felt emboldened. "I know all about that stuff," I said.

My parents cast glances at each other, and I saw Mother stiffen up. In that instant, I knew I should have kept my mouth shut.

"Don't be ridiculous; you know nothing about sinful behavior," she snapped. "Now go to bed — right now."

I lay under the covers, sleepless, straining to hear what my parents were saying, catching a word here, a sentence there. They were arguing hard. Mother was furious, saying I was growing up too fast and her job was to protect me from evil. That movie tonight had been a mistake; I shouldn't be watching movies that implicitly condoned adultery.

"Vannie, Vannie, what's happening to you? You're so busy guarding her virtue, you're forgetting to love," my father protested. "For God's sake, it's just a movie."

"She drinks them in, and it's too much.

And that school she's in doesn't help, either."

"Look, Country Day is the best school in the city —"

"It's a Hollywood school, you know it is. And being too wrapped up in the movies isn't healthy."

"Why shouldn't she fantasize a little?"

"Because she'll act on it."

My father at that point just groaned. But a few tense days later, I learned which parent had prevailed.

"We are transferring you in the fall to a Catholic school," my father said gently that morning, watching as I spread a liberal dollop of butter on my toast.

"What?" I was stunned. "Why?"

"Your mother feels you need better moral grounding than you're getting now. Too much Hollywood creeping into our lives." He stared at a spot on the ceiling above my head. I remember him taking the time to pat his mouth with one of Mother's scratchy Irish linen napkins.

"But you always said I'm at a wonderful school."

"You are," he said, chopping the words into two sharp syllables. Mother shot him a glance both brisk and placating. She had won, after all. "This isn't something out of the blue, Jesse," she said. "I've felt for quite a while that things are too free and easy in the older grades at your school, and I think you will do better with the nuns."

I stared at my toast, already getting cold. My heart was chilling just as fast. Mother was talking about those sophisticated girls with long golden hair and wise eyes whose parents were directors and producers, and who were very happy to share the gossip of Hollywood with their younger classmates. They made sure we knew all about sex, who put what into whom; it seemed disgusting when I first heard it, but they made it sound funny. A new school? That meant making new friends and losing old ones. And having nuns as teachers? My only experience with nuns was at church on Sundays, where a few in full habit regalia taught a perfunctory catechism class. They were nice, but mysterious, and I wondered if they had any hair under their black veils.

"What school?"

My parents glanced at each other. "To be determined," Father said dryly.

"I like Saint Ann's," Mother said. "It has as good a reputation as Country Day."

"About the only church school that does."

"That's not fair."

Father closed his eyes. "Okay, we're thinking of Saint Ann's."

"Where is it?" Another worry was growing.

"On the Westside, out Sunset. It's an excellent school."

"How will I get there?"

"I will drive you at first, and you'll take a city bus home," Mother said.

I protested. It wasn't that I had *that* many friends at Country Day. Leaving there meant I would not be sharing the morning ride anymore, but how could I tell my parents why that mattered? I would never again be able to watch Ingrid Bergman, in person, float out to the car filled with girls, giving — or did I imagine it? — one of them, *me,* a comforting smile, a tacit acknowledgment of our special bond.

So there it was. My connection with Ingrid was being snatched away, just as I had seen her soul open in *Casablanca.* I sent a pleading glance in my father's direction, but I already knew this had been decided and wasn't negotiable. Especially when he put an arm around my mother in a show of solidarity. Their two heads came together — Mother's eyes, slightly wet and as blue as the sea; his, the color of warm chocolate, sending me a signal to concede.

Well, at least they weren't arguing.

■ ■ ■ ■

School wasn't the only thing changing. Mother around this time stopped coming into my room at night to read bedtime stories or sing a song, and when I asked once if she would stay, she told me I was too old for that kind of thing now. Oh, she would come in, give me a crispy kiss, and then ask if I had said my prayers. Sometimes we talked about homework. I would try to think of things to say that would keep her there longer.

But something was disappearing. I liked being considered too grown-up for childish things, but that wasn't quite what was going on. I knew instinctively I shouldn't bring up things like the exciting fact that I had budding breasts. Mother would tense up, I was sure. It would mean talking about sex, and I had already stumbled on *that* one.

I puzzled it out, bit by bit. Mother didn't just fear bad things would happen, she was *sure* they would. It was part of her faith. Sin was everywhere. That's what the confessional was for, wasn't it? As for sending me off to a convent school, she was protecting me from succumbing to the glittery hedonism of Hollywood — and what safer place to put me than that?

CHAPTER THREE

Los Angeles, 1942

Mother didn't waste much time. Within a week, she had me enrolled at Saint Ann's, starting in the fall, and had notified Country Day that I wouldn't be coming back after summer vacation. In the last week of school, my teacher told the class that Country Day was "losing" me next year and everybody should say goodbye. I remember my cheeks burning; she had caught me by surprise, and I had no time to figure out how to arrange my face, or how to field inquiring glances. But that, of course, wouldn't have changed the fact that I didn't know *what* I felt.

Well, that's not completely true. I brooded over all sorts of terrible things that might be ahead. What if I wasn't smart enough? What if the girls at Saint Ann's didn't like me? Would I have to pray all the time? While my parents discussed the war news, the Nazi killings and bombings in Europe, I brooded more. It was like being sent to an alien country, going to that Catholic school, and no one cared what I thought — that's what was happening.

"I've heard about those secret tunnels they dig," one of the blond girls who already wore lipstick said one morning. Two of her friends stood waiting for my reaction, giggling.

"What secret tunnels?" I asked.

"You know, the ones between the convents and the monasteries."

"Why would they do that?"

All three girls broke into laughter. "*You* know, silly!"

When I came home one afternoon, Mother was sitting at the dining-room table, searching the "Houses for Sale" ads in the *Examiner.* She looked up long enough to give me a buoyant smile and inform me there were fresh chocolate-chip cookies waiting in the kitchen, still warm from the oven. That was a treat these days, now that the government was rationing sugar. And butter, too. Mother bought margarine as a substitute, with a little button of orange food coloring in the middle of the package. My job was to knead the package, spreading the food color, until it was all a respectable yellow. Then, as my father put it, we could play a game of Let's Pretend. And, Mother said, we were helping the war effort.

Mother had a peculiar lightness of being that afternoon, and it was clear she wasn't puzzling out how *she* felt, which made me grumpy. So I pretended not to hear her when she told me to tidy my room, and got grumpier when she didn't seem to care that much. I realized I knew two things: She wanted a new house, and I didn't want anything to change at all. Especially not by being trapped in a dreary new school.

Later, after I was in bed, Father came in and sat down heavily on the floral bedspread that Mother had chosen for me — it was some kind of purple and pea-soup green, and I hated it. One of the best things about getting a new house would be getting rid of that bedspread.

"Your mother said you were kind of a pill today, Jesse," he said quietly. "Maybe I can guess why."

I waited. I could use any help he could give.

"You were maybe trying to thumb your nose at us for yanking you out of your school."

"I don't care much for Country Day," I blurted. "Everybody's a snob."

"Then?" He raised an inquiring eyebrow.

"I'm not going to like Saint Ann's, either. I think nuns look creepy. And I heard about the tunnels they build."

"Tunnels?"

"*You* know." I held my breath, waiting for the revelation of one of those jarring grown-up secrets that might provide a stepping stone to being an adult.

A small smile pulled at the sides of his mouth. "Oh, *those* tunnels. Guess what? It's not true, and anybody who says it is, is pretty dumb. But I think you're going to be very happy about something that *is* true."

"What?"

"Your favorite actress is signing up to play a nun. Secret information."

Ingrid? Yes, he said, he meant Ingrid. But he would tell me no more.

"I'm going to miss not seeing her every morning," I confessed, surprising myself.

He cocked an eyebrow inquiringly. It occurred to me that he might really be listening.

So I told him about the school driver's winding up the hill every morning to Ingrid's house, and how beautiful she was, and how I imagined her to be. And how I wished I could *be* her. And how that was the most special thing I was about to lose, though he probably thought I was being silly.

His face turned thoughtful and he squeezed my hand. "Some things do get lost and stay lost," he said. "But there are big adventures ahead for you, and you'll feel better soon. You don't have to lose the people who will matter the most in the future." He frowned, his handsome, angular face sagging slightly. "Well, most of the time you won't."

I was too tired to try and figure out what *that* meant, but I did feel somewhat comforted. I turned over on my side and shut my eyes to the world of purple-and-green bedspreads and drifted off to sleep.

It was the last day of school. The town car was winding up Benedict Canyon, and I was concentrating on seeing Ingrid again. I wondered if I had the nerve to tell her I thought she was wonderful in *Casablanca.*

"You're going to a *Catholic* school?" said Debbie, a seventh-grader who liked boasting that her father wrote *Gone with the Wind,* though my father said that maybe forty screenwriters took a whack at it, and only one of them ever made the credits. She also wore false eyelashes, which was very impressive. "Why?"

"We're Catholic," I said.

"You *are*? I thought you were Jewish. I knew you weren't like us. I was wondering, but Jews don't usually go to Country Day."

I didn't answer. My father worked with Jews, I knew that, and he said a lot of idiots who didn't know anything thought they were worse than Catholics. I never had liked Debbie. Changing schools didn't seem quite so terrible all of a sudden, and I figured her father probably never wrote a word of *Gone with the Wind.*

Debbie said something, but I wasn't listening anymore.

As we rounded the last corner, I caught my breath in surprise.

Ingrid Bergman was standing at the curb, Pia's hand in hers. When we stopped, Pia jumped into the front seat. But Ingrid didn't smile and float away; she leaned forward and peered through the back window.

"Jesse? Are you there, Jesse Malloy?" she asked in a soft, almost musical voice.

I raised my hand.

"Ah, the egg-salad girl." She giggled. "Well, I've heard from your father that you are leaving Sheldon, but he says you are going to a wonderful school, and that is exciting. I just want to wish you all the best."

I thought I would faint. I barely managed to croak out a thank-you before she stood straight and moved back from the car, blowing a kiss to her daughter, and gifting me with a wave of her hand.

The car was dead silent as we drove away. We were pulling back onto Sunset Boulevard before anyone spoke.

"*Your* father is a friend of Ingrid Bergman's?" Debbie finally said. She sounded cross.

I nodded, stunned. But somehow I knew — my father had orchestrated that little moment as a goodbye gift, so that everybody at Country Day who cast me sidelong glances, wondering if I was being punished for something, would realize they were wrong. He let me pretend for a moment I was sort of a pal of Ingrid's. I could think of her by her first name now — because he believed giving me a touch of Hollywood stardust on my way out the door was just fine, and no threat to my morality.

"You let her believe that actress was her *friend*?" Mother said sharply that night. "Gabriel, what got into you?"

"What's wrong with doing that? The poor kid gets to feel part of things, the glamour stuff —"

"That's exactly what's wrong with it! It's all fantasy, not reality, and that's what we need to shield her from."

"Damn it, Vannie . . ." Father shook his head and walked out of the room.

I could never quite construct in my imagination how my parents fell in love with each other and got married. They weren't the fairy-tale prince and princess types. Father was Dick Tracy–handsome without his glasses, but with an easy smile that broke the sculpture of his face and welcomed me. He grew up in Los Angeles, somewhere out in the San Fernando Valley. I never knew his parents; they ran a pharmacy that went bust early in the Depression, and they were killed in an auto accident when he was in high school. He had an older brother, my uncle David, Jeremy's father, but they didn't see each other very often, and I wondered sometimes if he had been lonely.

He laughed when I asked. "Not me," he said. "I always knew, after that crash, that I was going to have to take care of myself." He had an ingrained geniality, a way of looking at the world that drew people to him. When he met a new person he would find some connecting history between himself and that person almost immediately.

Maybe someone had the same last name as a great-uncle (we're probably related, he would say), or maybe the person played poker at the Los Angeles Athletic Club (let's put a game together next week). And he'd be off and running with a new pal. People loved it. He warmed a room, and I loved *that*.

He met my mother when she was working in the ticket booth at Grauman's Chinese, and always said it was her shy reserve that drew him. He liked the fact that she wasn't just one more peroxide blonde hoping to be discovered by the movies. She had wrists as thin as a bird's wing, high Hedy Lamarr–type cheekbones, and a smile she held in reserve, even from me. But when she gifted him with it, he liked to joke, he couldn't help melting.

It was harder to figure out her history. She grew up as Vanessa Corrigan — a fancy name chosen by her dreaming Irish mother, she always said — in a town called Somerville, outside of Boston.

"Why don't we ever go to visit your family?" I asked. "Are my grandparents living?" I thought, sometimes, it would be nice to have one or two. Everybody else did, it seemed to me.

She was standing with her back to me at

the time, ironing a tablecloth. "No," she said.

"What happened to them?"

"Bad luck, mostly." I waited for her to shed a tear, but it didn't happen.

"That's awful."

She gave only a few details. Her father had died in a lumber-mill accident, and her mother was left to clean houses in Cambridge. She had little time for her daughter, and work wore her out early.

"If it weren't for the nuns at my parochial school, I would have had no moral guidance at all," she said. "They were stern taskmasters, and they were my true family." She folded the tablecloth briskly. "That's all the questions for tonight, Jesse."

She must have realized early on that getting my father to feel as devoutly as she did about the Church wouldn't work. But she did love Gabriel Malloy, and since she saw no apparent crisis of faith surfacing in my young heart, she just made herself busier with the Church. Until we moved, she was a longtime member of Saint Paul's Altar Society, which meant, from what I could tell, she had the privilege of laundering the altar linens for the priests every week. My father would shrug and say, "Well, at least it keeps you busy."

We spent the first month of that extra-hot summer of 1942 touring big new homes, and I liked the smell of fresh wood and all the polished doorknobs, and imagining what my bedroom would look like in each one. Mother finally found the house she wanted. It was on the edge of Beverly Hills, really — a comfortable, sprawling stucco with a red tile roof, shielded from the road by eucalyptus trees. It sat near the bottom of one of those winding streets that undulate up into the hills above Sunset Boulevard, promising treasures of celebrity behind every privacy hedge. There was a large kidney-shaped pool in back that took my breath away, a pool hewn out of a sloping hillside lush with bougainvillea and exotic-looking shrubbery. Mother worried that I might drown, of course. I was awed by its size. I was sure Esther Williams, Hollywood's glamorous swimming star, could emerge from that pool. It was worthy of her.

It wasn't long before we moved in, a joyful day with Mother running back and forth, breathlessly directing the Bekins man unloading the van as to what boxes went where — and, oh goodness, where are the pots and pans? And Father standing by, looking so pleased with himself, telling her,

60

Forget them, we'll buy new ones. Everything new.

After the Bekins van pulled away, my father and mother stood in the living room, their arms wound around each other. My father kissed my mother with such tenderness. I watched her close her eyes, those long, long eyelashes, tipping her face up to his, and they seemed to melt into each other. We all three inhaled change, and I was dizzy with it.

Father insisted on hiring a maid. Mother seemed shy and ill at ease about that at first, not sure quite how to carve out enough for the new maid to do. Fueled by my father's enthusiasm, she finally decided that, with such a big house, Mandy — that was the maid's name — would have plenty to keep her busy.

Anyhow, Mother told us both one night, now that her workload had disappeared, she was considering signing up for a volunteer job. She said it a little nervously, but with a bright smile.

"Job? What kind?" Father looked surprised. I think he expected Mother to run any plans of hers that took her out of the house by him first.

"Saint Clare's. Just helping out a couple

of afternoons a week."

"The place for unwed mothers?"

"Yes. The ones with no place to go."

He nodded casual approval. "A place for them to hide, right?"

She nodded. "It's doing good work," she said stiffly.

I wanted to ask her: Did the pregnant girls have to hide their faces? What happened to them? How did they keep their sin secret? There were all those whispers and giggles I had heard about Loretta Young's baby, and how it was a girl who had Clark Gable's ears. I had tried to ask Mother about it, but she called it malicious Hollywood gossip. This time I kept silent, because my parents had moved on to deciding what restaurant we would dine at that night — somewhere fancy, my father insisted. They were absorbed only with each other at that moment, and there was nowhere for me to break through.

But mostly that period was full of hope and promise. I got a new bike, a bright blue one, and Mother began to relax about that pool. She never had to worry again about my picking up polio or something at the local municipal swimming pool, which made her fret less.

I loved eavesdropping on my parents that

summer, on those golden late afternoons when they sipped cocktails before dinner. My father's job was exciting. He talked casually about famous people, tapping a finger against his glass — the only sign of a new restlessness. I didn't hear him and Mother arguing at night, but he only went to church with us now every other Sunday. When he started joking about becoming a "C and E Catholic" — Christmas and Easter only — Mother reverted to disapproval. She didn't talk to him through a whole evening.

But all was good. So good, I was jolted when I realized that the first day of school was upon me.

We came, Mother and I, for the first time to Saint Ann's on a foggy morning, one of those dreary days when nothing seems to reflect light. Nothing sparkled or bounced. My first impression of the school was of an expanse of mud-brown masonry buildings peppered with winding walks and heavy arches that soaked up all color, swallowing it. I knew the school would be large. I was prepared for that. It was a "lifer" school, after all, from first through twelfth grade, and there was a convent here, too. But it was still intimidating.

We walked up the path to the main entrance in silence. On both sides of the walkway, tall, graceful palm trees, precisely placed, swayed with each puff of wind like dancers in a chorus line. Everywhere, lush expanses of freshly mowed grass. I saw a nun, in black garb wearing one of those cardboard collars, walking slowly, silently, about the grounds, a rosary wound through her fingers.

I felt near tears. "Mother —" I said urgently.

"Welcome, Jessica."

We had reached the steps to the entrance of the school. I looked up into the alert, very blue eyes of a slightly stooped nun standing at the top of the stairs. Her hands were clamped in front of her ample stomach, and there was a somewhat stitched smile on her weathered face. She looked as immovable as a rock.

"Sister Teresa Mary?" my mother said. She took my hand and we started up the stairs; I felt like some kind of Aztec sacrifice.

The nun nodded. "I am delighted to welcome you to Saint Ann's," she said. She and my mother appraised each other, in that kind of benevolent, alert way that people have of signaling preparedness for the unknown.

Her eyes shifted back to me. "I suspect you are feeling nervous about changing schools," she said.

"Jessica is very much looking forward to her new school," Mother lied, fingering the clasp of her purse with lacquered nails that clicked against the brass. "And she's well prepared academically."

"Is that true, Jessica?"

What? That I was looking forward to being in this strange place? Or that I got good grades at Country Day?

"My name is Jesse, not Jessica, please."

"But that's a *boy's* name," Sister Teresa Mary said, a touch of amusement in her voice. "This is a *girls'* school, dear."

"She enjoys English and is exceptionally good at math." My mother's voice had hardened.

Sister Teresa Mary was quite adroit at sidestepping small confrontations, as I would later realize. "I'm sure she will be an excellent student. I thought we could take a little tour of the campus before introducing Jessica to her homeroom teacher," she said to my mother.

The three of us set out across the green grass, following the threaded pathways that led to the main campus, past a shrine to the Blessed Virgin. Two nuns in sheer black veils knelt there, heads bowed. They did not look up.

"Two of our postulants," Sister Teresa Mary said. "We are gratified that some girls each year choose the convent."

"At what age?" my mother said in an interested voice.

"We don't allow such a choice to take place before the age of sixteen."

For some stupid reason, I was counting the years between me and sixteen in my head when I saw a pool emerging through all the foliage. It was good-sized, and a tall girl with slender, muscular legs had just sprung from the board in a graceful dive as we arrived. She certainly wasn't a nun. I felt immensely cheered; this was somebody about my age.

Sister Teresa Mary's reaction caught me short.

"Kathleen, just what are you wearing?" she snapped at the girl in the water.

The girl looked up and froze, her face — framed in a white rubber cap that couldn't fully hide copper curls at the nape of her neck — alert, but as rosy as an apple.

"My bathing suit had a rip in it," she said. "I'm sorry, I borrowed my mother's."

"Do I have reason to believe that?"

"Well, Sister . . ." The girl seemed to be

66

contemplating her answer as she drifted in the water. "I guess I have used that excuse before."

Sister Teresa Mary let out an exasperated sigh.

"Two-piece suits are not allowed, as you are well aware."

"Yes, Sister. But they are more comfortable." She glanced at me, and I saw her eyes dance.

"I believe we will have to discuss detention, Kathleen Cochran."

"Yes, Sister."

"Now, please come out of the pool."

Kathleen pulled herself out of the water, flashing a quick glimpse of a pale, bare midriff before she wrapped herself in a towel. She stood obediently before Sister Teresa Mary, waiting for further instructions.

"What do I do with you, Kathleen?"

The girl looked up with a quick grin. "Forgive me?"

"Not yet," the nun replied coldly. "You will not be allowed to play basketball for two weeks. Enough of these infractions. Now, go."

Kathleen glanced at me with casual indifference. She turned, the towel swinging around her hips, and strolled slowly into a changing room.

But not before I noticed that the bright blue two-piece Rose Marie Reid suit she wore was exactly the same as the one I had been trying to convince Mother to buy me.

Mother and I exchanged glances, but said nothing.

Sister Teresa Mary marched briskly onward, past peaceful expanses of lush grass, her black robe swishing back and forth, the rosary beads at her waist clicking in cadenced rhythm, queen of the elegant campus over which she presided. Mother and I followed, nodding and hmmming in agreeable harmony, as our guide pointed out the functionality of various stolid buildings: the gymnasium, the school auditorium, the new study hall named after a liberal grant from — surprise, surprise — Bishop Doyle, who was clearly a friend of the school.

And then we arrived, inevitably, at the door of the classroom that would be mine.

In front of me, through that door, was a phalanx of classmates in identical black rayon uniforms, all taking me in quite coolly; I could see the coldness of their eyes. I took a deep breath. I said goodbye to my mother and walked in after Sister Teresa Mary, not quite absorbing her introduction, my brain scrambled between two conflicting worries — the stares of a classroom-full of strange girls and the argument ahead at home, when I would try very hard to talk Mother into buying me that new bathing suit.

CHAPTER FOUR

Los Angeles, 1942–43

It was not an easy transition. I was reasonably up-to-date on history and civics, but daunted by theology, especially after I saw the size of the book I was supposed to master. I thought of protesting that I was not yet twelve years old — this was surely for the older girls, right? Wrong.

And it was unnerving to move from classroom to study hall to lunch, wondering if I was supposed to say hello to the grave-faced nuns gliding like silent blackbirds around the campus grounds. I usually settled for a nod and a tentative smile.

Our schedules were a mix of ordinary school and religion. Every Monday, all students had to attend morning Mass in the school chapel. I would get there early, yawning, my mandated beanie on my head, and doze a bit as the priest prepared to celebrate the Eucharist. Though I complained at home, in truth I came to like those quiet mornings. The hymns playing softly on the organ were soothing, and the fragrance of the candles and altar flowers made praying every day less boring. The chapel itself was a tiny jewel box of gilded statues and burnished wooden pews and railings. I particularly liked the melancholy paintings of Christ carrying his cross up to his death on Calvary. I began to feel a knitting together of the stories and the rules, a deepening of belief, especially during those brief moments when I actually *thought* about what those paintings depicted.

I also soon realized my classmates were not devout nuns-in-the-making, as I had feared. They chewed bubble gum and read comic books just like me; some of them became my friends, and some treated me from the beginning as the snotty Beverly Hills kid they assumed I was.

I was slowly relaxing into the rhythms of Saint Ann's world as the months went by. I even managed to finish an assignment on how God's existence could be proved through study of the natural universe — everything from trees and animals to the rhythms of day and night. It was called "intelligent design." I wasn't really sure what I was saying, but I got a B.

I was curious about Kathleen Cochran. She was my age and on the school tennis team, but I couldn't figure out a casual way to get to know her. When I tried a few times, she looked right through me. I wondered whether she didn't like the fact that I had been witness to Sister Teresa Mary ordering her out of the pool — but I honestly didn't think so. She hadn't acted embarrassed at all.

She was popular at Saint Ann's, probably because she was something of an aerialist when it came to breaking the rules, walking the high wire, while people like me watched and held their breath.

How did she get away with not bothering to put on her school beanie when we gathered in the school chapel for Mass? We always had to cover our heads in church; I wouldn't dare to question that. Kathleen didn't actually defy; she just went her own free, breezy sort of way, and yet the nuns loved her. Even Sister Teresa Mary.

I took to sitting in the tennis-court bleachers to watch her practice with her teammates at lunchtime. She had a wicked backhand, hitting hard, as her short-cropped, bouncy red curls jumped like bedsprings. "Fifteen–love!" she would yell, and whatever opponent was playing her that day would usually just be waiting for the inevitable "Thirty–love!" that soon followed. She was good-humored, joking with other players after a game, and her reputation for daring never seemed to get her in trouble. I couldn't help wishing she was my friend.

One night in early November, I was doing homework in our new, expansive kitchen — it even had a dishwasher — while my parents, drinking their honey-gold cocktails, murmured and laughed over some funny story Father had brought home from the studio. I could hear pages turn as he scanned the evening paper.

"Holy Jesus," he suddenly sputtered, thrusting the front page into Mother's hand. "The Allied forces have landed in Casablanca."

"That's good," Mother said, a little bewildered.

"Good? No, it's *perfect*!" He jumped up and raced for the phone. We listened, agape, as he ordered a studio operator to connect him immediately to the all-powerful Howard Hughes's private number. "Howard?" he roared into the phone. "Are you listening? The Allies are in Casablanca, and our movie is ready! We can't wait two weeks. We've gotta release it *now*!"

Of course, what could be better publicity for Ingrid's movie? The very next day, Hughes ordered that *Casablanca* should be released to the public. That left us blissful in the knowledge that Ingrid Bergman's movie rode to triumph *with* the Allied forces and was an immediate hit. Slaps on the back, praise, and a fat bonus — all of it came my father's way.

Mother was proud, too — I could see it. When he insisted we go out to dinner to celebrate, she hurried to the bedroom and put on a new dress, a blue print of crunchy taffeta sprinkled with tiny yellow marigolds. She executed a few dance steps as she came out, looking so beautiful that I felt a sudden shyness.

Just that week, Father had insisted she should look every bit as good as the other Hollywood wives up the street. So, ignoring her protests, he had taken her to I. Magnin, the most elegant of the Los Angeles department stores.

There they sat on a sofa while young women with skin as pale as waxed fruit took turns modeling fine wool suits that molded to the body and full-skirted gowns with intricate designs stitched in fine silk. It was, Mother told me later, overwhelmingly exciting. Father chose half a dozen dresses to buy, and when she tried to object, he said, quite seriously, "You will be wearing these, not too long from now, and I want you to be ready."

And now here she was.

At the restaurant, Mother sat erect, self-consciously smoothing down the folds of her skirt, carefully holding her cocktail so not a drop could stain that dress. It was clear, even to me, that she had never worn anything so elegant in her life. She was loving it, and loving my father. And I was getting easy smiles from her, without her usual furrowed brow.

I wanted to bottle that evening, to take it home with me and make it last forever, make it so strong that no tensions could break it apart.

The wave of Father's good fortune had not yet crested. Over the next year he orchestrated a grand flourish of publicity for Ingrid, especially where it concerned the film that mattered to her the most: *For Whom the Bell Tolls*. As I entered sixth grade pictures of Gary Cooper and Ingrid Bergman were pasted on billboards everywhere, and Hollywood columnists were tossing effusive praise like bouquets of roses. I was thrilled that it was my father's show, but I wasn't allowed to boast: bad form, my father said. *Keep your triumphs muted and nobody gets nasty. I've tripped up on that, at times.*

"Would you like to go see Ingrid's new movie with me on Saturday?" Mother said one night as we sat around the dinner table.

"You and me? *For Whom the Bell Tolls?*"

She smiled brightly. "Of course. You're old enough now. And you are doing beautifully at Saint Ann's."

That was important. I was realizing myself that my father's elevated status meant I had to perform, too. Mother wanted everything perfect. This meant dance and even riding lessons, which I got out of by proclaiming myself in terror of horses. But, no question, bringing home a report card sprinkled with A's had helped me along, in my mother's eyes, to maturity. "Yes, oh yes," I said.

She and my father raised their usual cocktail glasses, touching them together with the tiniest of clinks, and glanced into each other's eyes.

"To the pleasures of growing up," Mother murmured.

Again, no question, I told myself: Mother was softening. Not too much; she didn't know *For Whom the Bell Tolls* had just been labeled "Objectionable in Part" by the Legion of Decency. My father had slipped the report of that news — carried in the archdiocesan newspaper, *The Tidings* — under a sofa pillow before cocktail time. He didn't laugh as much these days about the censors' poking away at every scene in every movie, looking for something to condemn. Somewhere along the way, the censors had become too powerful.

She found out the next day, but she didn't back off her invitation. I was dizzy with anticipation. I had never seen a movie that was Objectionable in Part. Thank goodness, it wasn't condemned: I would have pushed to see it anyway.

The line outside the theater was long and filled with excitement. I heard people chattering back and forth to each other: "I've seen it twice already. Wait until you see her face; oh, she's so beautiful, it makes me want to eat rose petals," one woman sighed to another. "Did you know she never wears makeup?" the woman ahead of us in line said to Mother. "Can you believe it? Not even lipstick."

Walking into that darkened theater was one of the most thrilling things I had ever done. Being there with Mother felt strange at first, but she bought me a big box of popcorn and seemed almost as eager as I was. When the music and credits began, we slumped down into our seats, munching away, and she never scolded me about spilling some of it over her new gray coat.

I soon forgot her presence. I was swept up by the violence and the drama of the plot — would the guerrillas be able to push back the enemy by blowing up a critical bridge? But mostly I was captivated by the growing love between Robert Jordan, the American fighting with the guerrillas, and Maria, the Spanish girl played by Ingrid.

Only near the end was I aware of Mother. She was leaning forward, tears in her eyes.

Gary Cooper, as Jordan, lies badly injured. He cannot be moved — he cannot ride — and the enemy is approaching. He insists on sending the weeping Maria away to safety with the guerrillas. And then he cradles his gun, awaiting the enemy — and his inevitable fate.

We emerged from the theater into a soft, balmy evening and walked slowly to the family car, each of us still somewhere off in the mountains of Spain.

"How did you like it?" Mother finally asked.

"I thought it was wonderful."

"So did I," she said.

How could it be, my mother and I feeling

alike about anything? Certainly not about the yearnings of love and romance!

I took a stab at being funny, not sure how it would go over. "I've kind of wondered what Maria was thinking when she and Jordan kissed," I said. "You know, when she asked him where the noses go?"

Mother actually giggled — softly, like a girl. "I used to puzzle over that, too," she said. "You learn."

I felt quite grown-up. We were actually having a *conversation.* In the car, almost back to the house, I took another chance and asked her if I could get my hair cut like Ingrid's. It was so daringly short, kind of free and challenging, and I knew she wouldn't agree.

She was silent at first, as she reached for the ignition key and shut the car engine off in the driveway of our super-grand new home. She turned to me.

"Okay," she said. "Why not?"

It was stunning. And now I couldn't stop babbling. I loved the movie, I was crazy about Gary Cooper, Ingrid was beautiful and enthralling — as usual, of course, but, then, she *was* wonderful, wasn't she?

Mother didn't answer. We reached the kitchen door, and only then did I realize my father's car was not in the driveway. The house was dark.

I kept babbling. Cooper was tremendously brave when he blew up the bridge; I was sure he wouldn't make it, but he did and —

Mother pushed open the door, her face in shadow. "Men enjoy blowing up bridges," she said, flicking on a light in her spotless kitchen. I glanced at her; her mouth was pulled tight.

"It was for a good cause —"

She didn't seem to hear me. "At least as much as they enjoy building them," she added. "And women? We let them do it."

What did *that* mean? I knew American soldiers were fighting and dying in Europe and Asia. I worried a lot that my father might have to go fight, but Mother told me he was too old. Every month we had our paper drives; every month we bundled our newspapers and brought them to the school parking lot, although I was vague on exactly how the papers helped. We would also save rubber bands and bring them, and this was another part of being patriotic. And now Mother was saying men liked destroying things and women let them do it; did that make war our fault?

"Jesse, I don't mean just bridges literally." Mother was reaching out, her voice hesitant. "Sometimes women have to suffer for what men do. I don't mean to sound so angry. And there are men who suffer for what women do to them." She paused, and then seemed unable to say anything more.

And there I was again, feeling in over my head.

I sat in the bleachers on Monday, watching Kathleen trounce her tennis opponent — thinking about the movie, which I knew I shouldn't talk about having seen, because it was classified as objectionable by the Church. It felt quite daring, and I wanted to tell somebody, but I knew it might invite disapproval.

So I wasn't prepared when Kathleen walked over after the game, straight to me, bouncing a bright yellow tennis ball on the strings of her racquet.

"You're always sitting here. Do you play?" she asked casually.

I shook my head. "I'm not the athletic type," I said, feeling stupid.

"Why do you watch?"

I blushed. "Because it looks like fun. And you play so well."

She smiled. "Better to be a doer than a watcher," she said.

"I like swimming."

"So that's why you were at the pool. I

81

remember you staring at me that day." She pulled a ChapStick out of her pocket, twisted it open, and smeared it across her mouth with an impatient gesture. She rubbed her lips together with a slight smacking sound. "Want to learn?"

I nodded.

"Okay." She nodded toward the racquet her opponent had left locked tight in its wooden case. "Take that, and let's hit a few. I've got a couple of minutes."

I felt a sudden need to show her I wasn't just one more callow newcomer. "You know," I blurted as she unscrewed the case for me, "I saw *For Whom the Bell Tolls* Saturday."

Kathleen flashed a quick grin and set her bright red hair in motion, then shrugged her shoulders and raised an eyebrow. "So did I. Ingrid Bergman was swell."

I figured then we were going to be friends.

I was right. We each gave the other a link to a needed, but different, plane. It was Kathleen who helped me navigate the tiptoeing necessary in my muddled world of glamour and religion. To be a product of Hollywood meant learning how to play the right part at the right time so you looked perfect. To be a Catholic was different. Once you were baptized into the One True Religion, you didn't just have to *look* perfect, you had to abide by a stiff book of rules that you couldn't ever ignore, not if you intended to make heaven. But it was more than that. It was mystery and beauty and the pageantry of the Mass, and it was the hunger to believe. If that hunger faded? Well, you were on your own then. A tricky journey, reaching the point of knowing your own heart and brain.

Kathleen reached that point long before I did.

CHAPTER FIVE

Los Angeles, 1943–45

I couldn't muster the courage to look in the mirror, so I concentrated instead on the sound of the snipping scissors at the nape of my neck. Mother waited in a chair, glancing up now and then, saying nothing, then going back to flipping through some magazine with a picture of a man shooting a deer on the cover.

We were at the barbershop, not the beauty parlor where she usually had her hair done. Not where women with deft hands sculpted and combed and wound hair into elegant pompadours and chatted, where everything purred and all the walls were painted in some soft peachy color. This place was hard-edged, with heavy metal chairs and flat wall mirrors that didn't look very clean.

"I couldn't get an appointment at Heidi's," Mother explained. "But your father says Jim is a fine barber, and he certainly can do short hair."

I wanted to ask the man named Jim if he had seen *For Whom the Bell Tolls,* but I figured he probably wasn't a moviegoer, and I didn't know how to describe the kind of haircut I wanted. So I stayed quiet.

"There you are, young lady," he said, whipping the white cotton sheeting from under my chin and shaking dark hair — gobs of it — onto the floor. "That should last you a while." He turned to a man waiting on a bench. "Next," he barked. My haircut had taken all of five minutes.

I slipped out of the chair and only then looked into the mirror. I couldn't believe it. I truly looked like a boy, not Ingrid. It was too short, too straight, too cropped. Hers was saucy and daring; mine was awful. I turned to Mother, whose eyes widened as she looked up from the magazine.

"Well," she began, then saw the tears welling. She stood and patted me on the shoulder, looking distressed. "Oh dear. It will grow out," she said.

I refused dinner. I went to my room and cried, vowing I would wear a bandanna every day to school until my hair reached a respectable length. I grabbed skinny fistfuls of it and yanked and yanked, wondering if I could make it grow faster, and soon I was crying as much about my sore scalp as about the haircut.

Somewhere around eight o'clock, the bedroom door cracked open; my father was standing in the doorway.

"Hey, I've got an idea for Saturday," he said.

"So what?" I snapped. He was pretending everything was fine; did he think that would make me feel better?

"I'm going to the studio — lots of work piled up." He walked in and sat down on the end of the bed.

"What's new about that?" I didn't care if I was rude; I was mad at everything and everybody. But he didn't reprove me.

"I thought you might like to come along."

"Me?"

My father didn't like mixing work with personal life. I had been to the Selznick Studio just once, when I was about eight, and had only glimpsed a few extras dressed as cowboys, looking bored, puffing on cigarettes in front of one of the soundstages, before we had to leave.

"Somebody else with short hair will be there," he said quietly. "And I thought the two of you could commiserate."

It took time for me to digest this. "Ingrid?"

I ventured.

He nodded.

I threw my arms around him, inhaling the fresh soapy smell of his shaving lotion. I remember he laughed and teased, and I begged: Are you sure her hair is still short? You mean I will get to talk to her? Now I could say something knowledgeable about her beauty and graciousness to my class-mates, instead of having to admit I didn't really know her.

"She still looks like a helicopter cut her hair," he said cheerfully. "Just through the publicity tour for the movie, mind you. But she knows how it feels to look a little like a bald eagle. A great time to meet."

It was early morning when we arrived. A bandanna covered my hair — no matter how Mother pleaded, I had worn it all week. I pulled my sweater tight against the sud-den chill as we stepped into the cavernous embrace of the soundstage. The place was huge; the people running about looked so small. I glanced questioningly to my father, and he nodded in the direction of a lone figure at the far end of a platform cluttered with cameras and floodlights.

"Go, tiger. Say hello."

And there she was. Ingrid Bergman. Not

a floating image, viewed by a girl peering through a car window, but a quite beautiful woman in a gray wool skirt and a plain white cotton blouse, sitting alone in a canvas folding chair. She had a small frown on her face, and it took me a second to realize she was concentrating on a pair of flashing knitting needles in her long, tapered fingers. I blinked. Ingrid Bergman was knitting? Yes.

I moved forward slowly. Was I supposed to talk first?

She glanced up at me, smiled, then held aloft what looked like the half-finished sleeve of a child's soft blue sweater. "Nice shade of blue, don't you think?" she said, surveying her work critically. "Angora flattens out too quickly on the needles; I have to work fast."

"Is it a sweater?" I managed. Of course it was — what an idiotic comment to make.

She nodded. "I'm knitting it for Pia." She looked at me with sudden interest. "You have the same liveliness in your face that she does. You make me think of what she might look like in a few years."

I was tongue-tied at first, then blushed. I wanted to say something intelligent, but I was staring at her hair. Oh, it looked nothing like mine; what was my father thinking?

It was a halo of curls gathered artfully to her jawline, whereas mine hung as lank and dreary as a man's. I started to turn away, but her voice stopped me.

"I hear you aren't too happy with your haircut," she said companionably. "I felt the same way about mine at first, but it will grow."

"That's what my mother said."

"I also hear they're calling it the 'Maria cut.' All you pretty girls out there are going to despise me for a while." A smile played at her lips as she rested her knitting in her lap. "It's nice to meet you again, Jesse," she said. "And I'm delighted that you liked *For Whom the Bell Tolls.*"

"Oh yes, I loved it. And it's wonderful to meet you again, truly," I managed. Was this really happening? Ingrid Bergman had called me a pretty girl. If only for that, she would have been my hero for life.

A sudden bustle of activity; my small bubble popped.

"Ingrid, sweetheart," an urgent male voice cut in, "we need some new head shots of you — we're almost out of photos for your fans. And we've got people waiting for your autograph. Can we get you to tuck the knitting away for a few minutes?" A lean-looking man with sharp eyes was maneuvering himself between me and Ingrid.

She laughed. "Here we go again," she said. She stood, leaving her knitting on the chair. "Don't push the makeup again; I won't do it," she said. "So what's my image today, Rodney?"

He frowned, clearly devoid of humor. "We'll shoot you looking up into the light — as the beautiful, noble, pure-at-heart woman we all know you to be."

"The one who had no idea which man she was supposed to end up with in *Casablanca*? Is that what makes me pure?" she teased.

"Miss Bergman!" A matronly-looking woman was standing on the sidelines, bouncing with excitement. "Please, can I have your autograph?"

Rodney leaned closer. "She's a cousin of Selznick's," he whispered. "Ten more of them waiting over there." He nodded in the direction of a cluster of people by the door, peering in. They looked almost hungry, I thought.

Suddenly Father materialized behind me, a protective hand on my shoulder. "The penalty you pay for success, Ingrid," he said with a grin. "Look, I've got a pile of questions here from Hedda Hopper; just give me one quick answer, and I'll manage the rest. So who's your favorite leading man?"

She giggled, color rising in her face. "You know who, Gabriel. Gary Cooper."

"You were wonderful together in *For Whom the Bell Tolls*," I burst out. I wanted to tell her my mother had cried when Gary Cooper was dying, but it felt, confusingly, like maybe not the best thing to say.

"Jesse is a great fan," he said, squeezing my shoulder gently. "Time to go, honey."

I reached out my hand, which she folded into hers. "Thank you for talking with me," I said.

"Oh, by the way," she said before letting go, "try pin curls. You know, for volume."

"I will," I said fervently. That was all, but it was enough.

I turned toward my father, and saw a pretty woman in a bright red dress, holding a thick notebook, plucking his sleeve. "Gabriel . . ." she said with quiet intensity. He bent toward her, and for just a second or two, they murmured to each other. She glanced over at me with the strangest expression, then smiled apologetically and walked briskly away.

"Who's that?" I asked as we left the sound-stage.

"Just a script girl," he said. "She wants a quick read of a new story draft."

"Her rouge is too pink for her dress."

"Anything wrong with that?"

"It's a shade or two off." I tried to sound knowledgeable. "That's what Mother would say."

He was silent for a few seconds. "So how do you like Ingrid?" he asked finally.

"I love her, she's perfect. And you know what? She told me I had a lively face, sort of like Pia's." I couldn't help a sudden, wistful thought: what would it be like to have Ingrid as *my* mother?

He laughed and gave me a hug.

I took the bandanna off as we drove home and tossed it out the car window.

I learned pretty quickly that the "Maria cut" was indeed about to become the most requested haircut in beauty salons all over the country: Ingrid was right. I wouldn't be the only one winding my hair each night into tiny dime-sized pin curls before bedtime, praying that it would grow fast. And — to my delight — I noticed that the "Maria" was showing up on the heads of dozens of my classmates at Saint Ann's, even though none of us were supposed to have seen the movie.

Once I made it to seventh grade, Saint Ann's got considerably tougher academically, which meant I didn't have quite as much roaming time — not when I was struggling with math. I was proud my school had high standards, and Mother was pleased that our teachers pushed us to do better than the public schools. Periodically, Sister Teresa Mary would announce over the classroom loudspeakers our latest test performance records. The most delicious part of her reports came when she compared our test results with the *always* inferior performance of the public schools.

We liked the feeling of being superior. It made up for being out of step with Protestants, for being "different." A lot of us gave off the whiff of coming from immigrant stock; all it took was a name like O'Brien or Romero. Our priests baffled everybody with their vows of celibacy, and it was pretty strange not to be able to eat meat on Fridays. And weren't our schools really ghettos that went against the grain of true Americanism?

Well, you couldn't be rejected if you were better than those who didn't like you, could you? So we made sure we were. We studied hard and played hard, and whether non-Catholics noticed or not, we took pride in being winners.

We also lived in a sunny town bathed in

moral contradictions, which made it a little hard to sort things out neatly. Especially when it came to "real" life.

I had made the naïve assumption that Kathleen had a family pretty much like mine, and we didn't talk about that at first. It was enough to find out that she was able to sneak into any "Objectionable in Part" movie she wanted to see: that made her the worldly one. We would swim together in the school pool at lunchtime, rush out of the water and dry off quickly, then throw on our uniforms and hastily looped ties and barely make it to history or Latin before the bell rang.

Once, as we sat at an outdoor picnic table, munching roast beef sandwiches from the lunch cafeteria, she said abruptly, "I don't have any sisters or brothers, either. Like you."

"Just you and your parents?" I remember thinking, Here's something we share in common.

"No, just me and my mother."

I stopped eating. "Your father died?"

"He ran out on us. Three years ago. He just left, and my mom doesn't want to talk about it. She wants people to think she's a widow. So this is a secret."

"Oh, that's awful," I breathed. "I'm so sorry."

She seemed to relax. "There, I've told you." Her face was uncharacteristically solemn.

"But — how do you —"

"My mother sells hosiery at the May Company. She's their top seller — she was named employee of the month a few weeks ago." She smiled, lifting her chin.

We didn't discuss it again after that. With Kathleen, it was all play and energy and fun on the surface, but I knew we were best friends now.

She became my teacher on several fronts. Tennis, of course. I came to love the game, even though I wasn't very good, but Kathleen was usually patient. After a few months, we started playing actual games and keeping score, which made me nervous.

Like that time I kept missing an easy backhand. I was furious with myself. Couldn't I do anything right? "I'm sorry," I bawled. I missed a second one. Another apology. And then I missed a *third* backhand. When I had again wailed out my contrition, Kathleen shocked me by throwing her racquet to the ground and yelling,

"Stop saying 'I'm sorry' after every shot you miss!"

I was stupefied. Nothing fazed Kathleen. She must hate me now. I felt terrible.

"I'm sorry!" I bellowed in anguish.

She plopped down on the court, shook her head, and started laughing. "Your backhand wobbles like Sister Teresa Mary's backside!" she yelled.

"She could've walked by the tennis court just as you said that," I scolded as we abandoned our game and sat down on the tennis-court bench.

"Not likely. Anyhow, you're something of a scaredy-cat," she chided.

"No, I'm not," I said.

"Well, you're a bit literal about the rules, you know. You should take more chances, like me."

She wasn't just talking about tennis. "Like what?" I parried.

Without answering, she opened a geography textbook next to her on the bench, and I found myself staring at last month's *Photoplay* magazine, the one I had flipped through at the drugstore as fast as I could. Shirley Temple was on the cover, and inside, all the gossip about Ginger Rogers and Errol Flynn's love escapades and —

"Does your mother let you read it?" she asked.

"She says it's a waste of time."

"What do you think?"

"I love the stories."

"Guess who's on the cover this month?"

I stared at her. "Ingrid?"

She grinned, nodding. "Let's go get it," she said. "I've got fifteen cents."

"Sister Teresa Mary doesn't allow —"

"That's why geography books are so big. Let's go."

We did. We locked our racquets into their wooden presses, left them on the bleachers, and rushed over to the drugstore. There it was, fresh out on the racks, the new *Photoplay* with a gorgeous Ingrid posing as Maria, gazing out at the world through what looked like a field of wheat. Kathleen put down her money, and it was ours. We folded it into her geography book and hurried back to the school tennis court. Hardly anyone would be around this late; we could enjoy it together.

The story inside was entitled "Candid on Bergman," and we couldn't read fast enough. Ingrid wore slacks at home, but never in public. She liked to read sitting on the floor. She had a horror of open-toed shoes. She didn't smoke and she didn't drink, but she liked to chew gum.

"How tall is she?" Kathleen asked.

I thought of her figure floating down the driveway of the house in Benedict Canyon and tried to guess. "I think close to six feet," I said.

"Really?"

"Really."

"Says here she won't wear a bathing suit for any photographs, but she'll wear one on the beach as brief as the law allows." Kathleen giggled. "She's never met Sister Teresa Mary."

Oh, we had a good time. We learned all about Ingrid's fairy-tale marriage to a doctor named Petter Lindström. And it was true, David Selznick had seen her in the Swedish version of *Intermezzo,* and was the first one to bring her to Hollywood.

We devoured that issue over the next couple of afternoons. Laraine Day told us mustard yellow was the important color for casual fall wear. Margaret Sullavan, in a piece about Hollywood parents called "Minding Their Minors," declared her three children would go to public schools, because private schools gave too much attention to Hollywood children whether they deserved it or not.

"My mother would like that," I said. "Unless she's Catholic."

"Well, her name *is* Sullavan," Kathleen said knowingly.

The story about glamorous parents riveted us. Joan Bennett's six-year-old daughter enjoyed ordering the family car and giving orders to the chauffeur over the intercom. Norma Shearer made a practice of changing nurses every few months so her children wouldn't become too dependent on any one person for their comfort. Joan Crawford, on the other hand, believed in spoiling her little girl and giving her everything she wanted.

I thought of Ingrid, knitting the sweater for Pia. And I suspected, deep down, that she was the best mother of them all.

From then on, each Friday, Kathleen and I played a quick game of tennis, stored our racquets, and hurried out to the drugstore to pick up the latest movie magazines. We would hide them, of course. And well that we did, since Sister Teresa Mary walked onto the tennis court one late afternoon and asked what we were doing, huddled together on the bleacher bench.

Kathleen waved her geography book. "I'm helping Jessica with her geography," she said.

In truth, I was learning a lot. Sitting there

together, Kathleen and I talked one afternoon for a couple of hours about sex and
unhappy marriages after reading an article
entitled "White Lies — the Truth About the
Stars' Deceptions." Claudette Colbert was
probably getting a divorce, and Errol Flynn
was a downright rake, and Jennifer Jones
was ordered by the studio not to confess
that she had been married and had two
children when she played a devout village
girl in *The Song of Bernadette.* Her fans,
they said, would be shocked.

"Do you think lying is a mortal sin?" I
asked Kathleen.

"No," she said. "Otherwise, I'm going to
hell — and I don't think hiding a movie
magazine in a textbook is so bad."

Kathleen's confidence intrigued me. We
talked about God and the universe and what
was a sin and what wasn't and who got to
heaven and who didn't. Kathleen, to my
astonishment, didn't think much of the
concept that non-Catholics would be locked
out of heaven. "So why should they sit
around in limbo or purgatory?" she demanded. "If they missed out on belonging
to the One True Church, why is it their
fault?"

Put like that, it made sense. As we sat
there, our heads bent over those magazines,

we discovered a clandestine world to share. With whom else could I have ruminated over all the tampon ads (how, please, were you supposed to get one into the *right place*?) and why Lysol was necessary for feminine hygiene, and what you were supposed to do about embarrassingly wet underarms.

Even then, I sensed I was learning as much from Kathleen as I was from *Photoplay.* We were equals, poised for everything ahead — everything, that is, except tennis.

There was another gravitational pull operating in my life that year. I stumbled for some lucky reason into a class on drama and public speaking, an elective presided over by a middle-aged teacher with a lofty smile who doled out approval in small, fixed doses. Her name was Miss Coultrane. She wasn't a nun and she wore no wedding ring, but other than that we knew very little about her. She had the high mono-bosom of the stern-faced suffragists in the early part of the century, and dressed each day in a properly buttoned wool tweed suit that was always carefully pressed. Those of us who took her class made up stories about her: Why was she an old maid? Had she suffered the tragic loss of a lover? She gave no clues.

101

But she understood theater — she *was* theater — and we who took her dramatics class three times a week were riveted by her style. You never quite *liked* Miss Coultrane. She reminded me a little of Gloria Swanson when she disapproved of a reading. Her head would tip upward, her eyes would widen, and she would demand that whatever luckless girl was reciting take a deep breath and try harder. I grew to love her class so much, I prayed I would never trigger a frown.

How had she found a place for herself in a quiet convent school staffed by nuns? I never knew. But Miss Coultrane was an institution at Saint Ann's by the time I got there. She took drama and public speaking seriously. She had managed now for more than ten years to coax performances out of those of her students who were good enough to put on an annual play or musical — a real one, for which the school charged admission, even though buyers were mostly parents and friends of the school.

I didn't know all of this at the time. All I knew was that Miss Coultrane — who patrolled the classrooms, looking for talent — heard me give an oral report in English and suggested I take her dramatics class.

"Dramatics?" My mother had looked

somewhat dismayed. "You don't want to become an actress, do you?"

The thought had never seriously crossed my mind, even if Ingrid Bergman had called me "pretty." But I was flattered by Miss Coultrane's attention.

"Your father and I don't really approve of acting."

I already knew there was something wrong about that assertion. I could tell that my parents and their friends loved the reflected glamour of working with stars, even though, at their parties, they would roll their eyes and speak disparagingly about them.

"That's not what I like the most," I said. "It's public speaking, too."

And so I gained permission to sign up for Miss Coultrane's class. Within a week, I was fully immersed in the challenge of turning words on paper into words sent floating through the air. Plays, speeches — my voice their "vehicle" — that's what Miss Coultrane called it. She would sit, straight and forbidding, fingers tapping the surface of her desk, as each of the fifteen girls considered talented enough to deserve her coaching groped her way through that week's assignment. It might be Shakespeare or it might be — she really did this — a grocery list. "Enunciate!" she would bellow, her own voice so deep it made me quiver inside. We learned. We enunciated.

While I was growing and changing at Saint Ann's, Ingrid's career was soaring ever higher. Her next performance was in *Gaslight,* a spooky movie that captivated audiences. Kathleen and I saw it together and clutched each other at the tense parts — but I couldn't take my eyes off the beautiful young wife on the screen whose mysterious husband was trying to convince her she is insane. The gaslight would flicker. Ingrid would look up, her eyes conveying deep terror of the unknown. Her face was mesmerizing. She was so alone, so fragile. I wanted to reach out a hand to comfort her, push through the screen into that lonely house to assure her she was loved and sane and her husband, Charles Boyer, was evil.

Me, and everybody else.

"Hey, guess what, ladies," Father yelled out one evening as he walked in the door. "Ingrid's been nominated for best actress for *Gaslight* — damn, this is great news. Are you impressed?"

Yes, oh yes, we were impressed. The night of the awards ceremony, we huddled close around the brand-new Packard Bell in the living room. "She's going to win this time," my father predicted, with a sweep of his hand that could have been taking in the whole world — or at least that's the level of confidence his gesture conveyed to me.

"What if she doesn't?" Mother worried. "Will people feel sorry for you?" Mother had a thing about pity; that's what she called the whiffs of condescension she had endured from her early years. She hadn't graduated from high school. I only learned that when I was a teenager, but I had noticed her wariness, the way she held her head high, when she and my father started going to Hollywood parties. I loved watching her dress for those parties, loved the dazzling array of crystal perfume bottles that had seemed to appear overnight when we stepped into our new house. She would stare into the mirror, smoothing her hair into place, mostly without smiling. It was as if she was wondering what she saw — her old self or her new.

"Feel sorry for me?" He laughed, leaned close, and kissed her nose. "Never, babe. Never."

It turned out there was no reason for anyone to pity Father. When Ingrid Bergman's name was called out as best actress of the year, our living room filled with the radio's explosion of applause. Father scooped up Mother from her chair, then reached for my hand, and soon all three of us were laughing and hugging.

"Okay, you two, you think this is wonderful?" Father said, stopping for breath. "Well, have I got news for you." He beckoned Mother and me to sit down and turned off the radio. He sat down himself, circling the rim of his Scotch and water with a finger, looking almost solemn.

"Is anything wrong?" I asked, feeling anxious.

He looked up with a vaguely bemused expression. Mother and I waited.

"Sorry," he said. A smile spread across his face. "My mind was elsewhere. But I've got news I think you'll like. It's been in the works for a long time, but now it's real." He lifted his empty glass and winked at Mother. "Another hit, honey?"

He said it just like that: "news I think you'll like." The most extraordinary thing was about to happen at Saint Ann's, and that's how he told us.

Ingrid, *my* Ingrid, was already filming a movie in which she was to play a nun. That was exciting enough. But *now,* Father announced, she was actually going to film scenes at *my school.*

"What?" I gasped.

"It's true," Father said.

Ingrid Bergman would walk in her black robes, hair covered, rosary beads in her fingers, through the halls and on the pathways and around the shrines of Saint Ann's in person — actually in person. And not only would *she* be at Saint Ann's, but so would Bing Crosby, who would play a priest, wearing a Roman collar for the second time in his career. Was I hearing this right?

"Yep," my father said. The movie was Leo McCarey's *The Bells of St. Mary's* — and McCarey, a stickler for authenticity, wanted location shots at a real convent school. Ingrid was enthusiastic. "I told him about Saint Ann's — told him it was picture-perfect; it's what a convent school *should* look like. I gave your yearbook to Ingrid to look through. She loved the palm trees and those leafy little shrines, and insisted this was where we should shoot some scenes from the movie."

"How have you managed to stay so quiet about it?" Mother asked, looking proud, as she poured more Scotch into his glass.

"The studio had to explore the site first. That school principal of yours? Sister — what's her name? Sister Teresa something?"

"Sister Teresa Mary."

"She's a bit of a tough nut, but a healthy donation to the school and it was decided pretty fast. What Ingrid wants — now especially after *Gaslight* — Ingrid gets."

That rakish grin of his — he so loved astonishing me. And he had; oh, he had. This was happening at my school? Saint Ann's would be famous. All those girls at Country Day would feel jealous when they found out.

But the most amazing thing? This time, I wasn't going to Ingrid. She was coming to me.

It was spring before anything actually began happening. That was when small squads of squinty-eyed men with notebooks and pencils behind their ears started roaming the campus, choosing the most picturesque sites, even asking Sister Teresa Mary if they could move one of the statues of the Virgin Mary to a different location: "Better light, you see." She stared them down and said no, not under any circumstances, that statue had been in that grotto for fifty years and no movie people were going to . . . Well, they got the message and backed off. The whole deal was suddenly in jeopardy when Sister Teresa Mary realized the fictional convent school in the movie was supposed to be depicted as poor and dilapidated. It took some soothing sessions with Leo McCarey, my father reported, to calm her down.

I got *that* information directly from Kathleen, who had been in the school chapel when the argument began outside one of the stained-glass windows.

We were thrilled when Father brought home a copy of the shooting script. We memorized it, poring through the pages after tennis, agreeing that it was a wonderful story, a story that unspooled without a single scene in it that could, surely, be objectionable to anybody. Not even the pope.

. . . Father O'Malley, a warmhearted and gentle priest, is sent to evaluate whether a run-down school should be closed. He meets Sister Mary Benedict, a wise and dedicated nun hoping to convince an irascible property developer to gift Saint Mary's with a new building to save the school from that fate. Father O'Malley and Sister Mary Benedict spar, becoming friends. The script turns dark when Sister Mary Benedict becomes ill and has to be sent away from Saint Mary's for treatment — but no one tells her the reason why. Until . . .

"Bing will be perfect as Father O'Malley," Kathleen said, rubbing her eyes. She wore glasses now, but kept taking them off and losing them, which made my tennis game seem slightly better than it was.

The weather was changing, in that imperceptible way it does in Los Angeles — the days get warmer and longer with fresh blooms popping up each day, but nothing drastic, and we barely noticed as we sat huddled together. Change was sneaky in our town.

"For Bing, it'll be *Going My Way* all over again," I agreed authoritatively. We felt empowered with that script in our hands, like full partners in this Hollywood venture. Bing and Ingrid were coming into our domain, telling a Catholic story: our Catholic story.

So when were they going to start? *Why* was it taking so long? The whole school spent the month of April holding its collective breath.

Finally, the morning came when trucks, huge ones, began rumbling into the school parking lot. Workers with muscular arms began unloading stacks of mysterious equipment as girls and nuns giggled and watched — until Sister Teresa Mary got on the

110

loudspeaker and ordered us all back to our classrooms.

It was three more long days before the actors began to arrive. Enormous portable dressing rooms had appeared overnight — and even Sister Teresa Mary couldn't stop the peeking and clustering as black limos drove up, depositing familiar faces onto our ordinary piece of the city. When I looked up at one point, I was sure I saw some of the cloistered postulants in the convent windows peeking out, too. Those windows, so dark and gray.

I felt a heavy hand on my shoulder just as I saw Ingrid Bergman step from one of the limos, wave to all of us, and disappear into her dressing room.

"Jessica, you have class this period, I presume." It was Sister Teresa Mary, and now her leaden hand pressed harder.

I wanted to say it was just dramatics, which surely didn't count as a class, did it? I was supposed to be learning Portia's speech from *The Merchant of Venice,* but I couldn't concentrate on that now. And, after all, dramatics was *play,* not work. Of course, that would not have been a wise comment.

"I need you to set an example," she said. "Go to class."

I dragged myself reluctantly away, glancing back, hoping for just one more glimpse of Ingrid. But the bell had long since rung, and I half ran down the stairs to Miss Coultrane's classroom.

She stared at me, the webbing of tiny wrinkles around her eyes magnified by owlish glasses, as I slipped into my seat and tried to keep my head down.

"You're late," she said.

Being late was almost unforgivable in that class. And even though other classroom teachers were quietly giving their students permission to skip out that morning to watch the excitement, I knew Miss Coultrane would not do the same. When the hour was over and all the others began packing up notebooks and pencils and rushing for the door, she stopped me.

"Jessica, stay here. I want you to practice Portia's speech. You haven't been giving it your full attention."

For the next fifteen minutes or so, I stumbled my way through the speech. I didn't care right now about Portia's argument.

"You are enunciating *without meaning.*" Miss Coultrane's eyes were fierce. *"What is this speech about?"*

I was her favorite, I knew that, but I was losing my preferred status. All I could think of was that Ingrid was somewhere on the grounds of Saint Ann's, and I wasn't able to see her.

Only slowly did I become aware of a commotion out in the hallway that connected the drama classroom with the school auditorium. There was a knock on the door. Miss Coultrane, frowning, walked over and opened it. She stepped outside and I stood there, listening to the murmur of voices.

And then the door opened again. Miss Coultrane moved aside and beckoned the person behind her to come in. Ingrid Bergman, wearing slacks and a dark sweater, stepped forward, a retinue of people clustered behind her, hovering, looking anxious.

She gracefully apologized to Miss Coultrane for interrupting, as if any apology was necessary, and looked around the room, voicing regrets that she hadn't been able to visit earlier — she wanted to meet as many of the girls at Saint Ann's as possible, and what a wonderful school it appeared to be.

Miss Coultrane never lost a moment of her own dignity as she greeted the actress, nodding gravely. "I'm delighted to have you here, Miss Bergman," she said. She nodded in my direction. "From what I understand, you and Jessica have met before."

I blushed scarlet. What if Ingrid had forgotten?

"Yes, indeed, we have," Ingrid said. "And I see your hair grew out, too." This, with a faint smile, was enough to make me guess that my father must be among the cluster of people waiting out in the hall.

"Jessica is working on Portia's speech," said Miss Coultrane. "She has a way to go, I'm afraid, but she is a talented speaker, all the same."

"I know that scene," Ingrid said directly to me. "It's one of Shakespeare's greatest speeches. May I hear you?"

My mouth went dry. I swallowed, glanced at my teacher, and saw something in her eyes I hadn't seen before. She was nodding. She wanted to be proud of me. She thought I could do it. Well, I would try.

"The quality of mercy is not strain'd, / It droppeth as the gentle rain from heaven / Upon the place beneath. . . ."

I faltered.

"Think of what was at stake in that courtroom," Ingrid volunteered. The polite commotion at the door was getting louder, but she ignored it. "It is a man's life against the twisted logic of justice. This is Portia's plea for the truth about salvation, taking it to the core. Taking it to *mercy*."

114

"Please," I managed. "Let me hear you."

She smiled faintly. "If you want," she said.

Her face began a slow transformation. What was changing? Her eyes widened, filling with dignity and resolve — she was becoming someone else.

"It is twice blest; / It blesseth him that gives and him that takes," she began, picking up from where I had left off. " 'Tis mightiest in the mightiest: it becomes / The throned monarch better than his crown. . . ."

There was no supplication, no tearful pleading. Ingrid's voice, her presence, grew in strength, expanding through the room. Without histrionics, she swam deep into the soul of Shakespeare's scene. And, finally, to Shylock: "Though justice be thy plea, consider this, / That, in the course of justice, none of us / Should see salvation: we do pray for mercy: / And that same prayer doth teach us all to render / The deeds of mercy."

I blinked as she continued, finishing the last lines. Then — just silence. Shakespeare's Venetian court of law and all the players in it shrank back into my copy of *The Merchant of Venice.*

"Miss Bergman, that was wonderful. I am stunned. Thank you."

Miss Coultrane had regained her voice before I regained mine. I saw tears in her eyes. She looked — what was it, transported? I wondered briefly if she had ever hoped to be an actress like Ingrid.

She rose, opening the door to the auditorium as wide as it would go. At least a couple of dozen people stood there, eyes wide, raning for a view of Saint Ann's dazzling visitor.

I vowed I would never allow myself to forget that brief visit of Ingrid's. She took me, without the artful help of film, to a place of imagination I had never been. I couldn't know then how Portia's eloquent plea for mercy would fare in the real world ahead. But I had truly heard it for the first time.

CHAPTER SIX

Los Angeles, 1945–46

The cast and crew of *The Bells of St. Mary's* transformed Saint Ann's into something of a fairy-tale place for the brief span of days they were there. I watched the filming as often as I could, any concentration on my classes tossed to the winds. I had to pinch myself more than once. She was *here,* at a *Catholic* school, of all places — at *my* school, gliding down the meandering paths, looking saintly in her black robes.

We were all starstruck, of course. It might have been my imagination, but I thought I saw the real nuns stand straighter, and I could swear a couple of the younger ones were trying to emulate Ingrid's walk.

Even Sister Teresa Mary fell under the spell. She was seen several times smiling and nodding as Bing Crosby whiled away the time between takes, unspooling one of his lazy, ambling jokes. He was a languid sort of man, I thought — always smoking his pipe, asking the older girls for a light when it went out, then laughing at their flustered responses.

"Oh, of course, you young ladies don't smoke; I should have known," he teased, with a knowing wink. Even Sister Teresa Mary smiled. My father said everyone from the studio was under strict orders to cater to her and keep her happy. If she grew restive with the chaos of cables and lighting equipment that seemed — briefly — to devour our school, it could cause trouble.

There was one worrisome moment.

"Doyle is making waves," Father muttered at the end of the first day of filming. Mother automatically glanced around nervously, even though we were in our house and no one could possibly hear him.

"What's wrong?" she asked.

"He's complaining that the nuns didn't have the right to give permission for the filming — as bishop, only *he* has the right. We've got people over at the chancery showing him the script now. Even the Legion of Decency couldn't find anything wrong with this one."

"He just wants his power acknowledged," Mother said quietly. "To keep movie people a little afraid of him."

"Very astute, Vannie," Father said, raising an eyebrow as he looked at her. All was smoothed out by morning, and for a few days, my father glanced at Mother with an extra edge of respect.

The coming of Hollywood to Saint Ann's stirred up the neighborhood in ways that Kathleen and I thought were funny. The raspy-voiced clerk who worked in the hardware store across the street sauntered over every day, peering at all the movie equipment in the parking lot with lustful melancholy; I wondered, What had he wanted out of life? Young mothers in flowered housedresses from the little stucco bungalows on the next block wheeled their sleeping babies as close to the action as they could, trying to pretend they weren't yearning for a glimpse of Bing or Ingrid. They looked frazzled, most of them. They often had a toddler or two on the back of their baby buggies. It took me a while to realize how young they were — maybe only five or six years older than me. We students in our drab black dresses and class ties were given bright-colored badges by the movie crew so we could move freely around the school, even when they were filming. We stored up every little morsel of movie gossip we could, to pass on nonchalantly to all the neighborhood watchers still hanging around after school.

The atmosphere was wonderfully relaxed. Between takes, Ingrid would put her feet up on a canvas chair and laugh and tell jokes with the crew members. "I can't actually say I *enjoy* being a nun," she said once to a Hollywood reporter visiting the set. "The best part of it is, nobody complains about my weight when I'm in this habit."

We giggled over that, enjoying this little peek into our heroine's sense of humor, and repeated it around the campus. "It is one of the advantages," Sister Hildegarde, my Latin teacher, murmured to another nun with a faint smile. That was impressive: Sister Hildegarde had never been known to respond to a joke.

All the sideline vignettes were, to tell the truth, more interesting than the actual filming. A few minutes of watching the cameras turn, of standing on tiptoes, craning to see past the other girls, the nuns, and the crew members, and then long waits. And then shooting the same scene, again. And again.

"Grass grows faster," we all told each other in a newly discovered weary way. Ten, maybe fifteen takes would consume hours. Kathleen and I agreed that each version of Ingrid floating across the main courtyard, appearing troubled as she worried about her beloved school's financial future, looked pretty much like another.

Oh, we loved being jaded.

But not on the last day of shooting.

. . . Sister Mary Benedict kneels before the chapel altar. She has been told she is being transferred, and she thinks it is because of her efforts to save the school. "Remove all bitterness from my heart," she prays as she struggles to accept the decision.

Father O'Malley and Sister Mary Benedict face each other in the courtyard; it is time to say goodbye. The tenderness they share, the respect . . .

As I watched, I had the most confused feelings; suddenly, irrationally, I wanted them to end up in each other's arms.

. . . Sister Mary Benedict walks away. Father O'Malley is struggling: he can't let her go like this. He calls her back, they stand face-to-face. "I can't let you leave like this," he begins. "I have to tell you the truth. When Dr. McKay said you were perfect, he was right. But he didn't mean physically."

What was wrong with me? What was I hoping for? I knew the script, I knew how this ended. What made me suddenly yearn for it to turn into a love story?

. . . "You have 'a touch' of TB," Father O'Malley tells her gently. That is why she has to leave, to get proper treatment.

Relief and joy spread slowly across Ingrid's luminous face. She is not being banished for trying to battle against the closing of Saint Mary's. It is only health, after all, that has brought this forced, painful departure.

"Thank you, Father O'Malley," she says gratefully. "Thank you with all my heart." . . .

"Cut," Leo McCarey said quietly.

The spell we were all under did not snap immediately. First, there had to be a mass exhalation of breath. I stared at Ingrid, hardly believing that Sister Mary Benedict was fading before my eyes. In her place was this real person, turning to McCarey, a sudden mischievous look on her face.

"Please, can we do one more take?" she pleaded. "I know I can do this better, convey more."

"We don't need it," McCarey protested.

"Please."

Who could refuse Ingrid? McCarey bent to her entreaty, and the cameras rolled again.

. . . Ingrid lifts her face to Father O'Malley. "Thank you, Father, thank you with all my heart," she begins. Suddenly she moves close to her costar, and flings her arms around him. Bing Crosby, startled, has no time to move before she plants a lusty, wet kiss on his lips, and then —

"Cut, cut!" yelled McCarthy. A priest assigned by the Legion of Decency to monitor the making of the movie jumped up from his chair, yelling, "No, no, Miss Bergman, no, this cannot be done!"

Her laughter burst out, a wonderful, rollicking sound that soon had the entire assembly laughing with her. I laughed, too, hardly able to admit to myself that whatever wave of erotic emotion had come over me, I had fantasized that second take in the first place.

"Thank you all, you wonderful women and girls!" Ingrid called out, then embraced Sister Teresa Mary as we all cheered. Even the representative of the Legion smiled, albeit a bit warily.

Yes, it was over. The next day, all the trucks were loaded up, and drivers, shouting at each other, roared out the gates. Ingrid presented Sister Teresa Mary with a splendid Waterford glass bowl, etched with a thank-you from the studio, commemorating the dates during which Saint Ann's had briefly become the fictional — and surely soon to be famous — Saint Mary's.

The bowl was given a place of honor in the formal, slightly shabby parlor of our school, and the students of each class were allowed to file by, one by one, to admire it. We were all very proud. We had been given a touch of the magic wand of Hollywood. For the space of just a week, we had been granted membership in the secular world, a very special membership that would become part of the history of our school.

From the moment filming was finished, all the way to its Christmas release, there was a drumbeat, a sense of waiting for a winner, one that was inevitable. How could we be so sure? We just knew.

We were right. *The Bells of St. Mary's* was enormously popular, fulfilling all of my father's hopes. Ingrid was hailed in a national movie-magazine poll as the model for American womanhood, to great acclaim. Oh, we Catholics were proud. She had single-handedly changed the nation's idea of a nun as a pokey old spinster to a strong woman, wise and kind.

Mothers would stop Ingrid on the street, pushing their starry-eyed little girls forward. "Miss Bergman, will you say hello to my daughter?" each would ask. "She wants to grow up to be just like you."

"Surely, you mean like Sister Mary Benedict," Ingrid would gently correct as she signed autograph book after autograph book. But she gave up when they stared at her blankly.

The adulation soared on and on. Even before the film premiered, *Look* magazine put Ingrid on their cover that fall, dressed not as herself but in full religious habit.

It wasn't just Catholics elevating Ingrid; it was everybody. Protestants and Jews and atheists — we were all rooting for her.

"It's amazing," my mother said.

"You know what it is?" Father said, in one of his happy, pontificating moods. "Think about it — the war is over; all those American soldiers pouring home are getting married, buying houses, starting families. People want warmth, sentiment from Hollywood, after all the fighting — stories of grace and nobility they can believe in," he said. "And who better to deliver that dream than Ingrid? Through my masterful efforts, of course. We're giving them what they want, and isn't that what the movie business is supposed to do?" He grinned. Within his question was the answer, and it made perfect sense to me.

Life on the surface at Saint Ann's seemed

about the same. But for a while, telling someone what school I attended brought eyes widened with curiosity. "What was Bergman like?" someone would ask eventually. Or "What is Bing Crosby like?"

As if we had the faintest idea, to tell the truth of it.

There were so many people peeking through the fence around our school during the filming, I hardly noticed those who seemed to linger in the aftermath, still straining to see some hint of Hollywood here. So, one afternoon, when Kathleen kept pacing the tennis court and glancing over at the fence, I was puzzled.

"What's wrong?" I asked. "Are we playing or not?"

She nodded toward one figure standing by the wire-mesh fence. "That's my father," she said in a strained voice. "I want him to go away. I've seen him here before."

I could hardly believe it, there were tears in her eyes.

"Are you sure?" I asked, pushing back a sudden romantic scenario of a reunion between father and daughter.

"Yes. I can't talk to him — I don't want to. Ever."

"Shall I go get Sister Teresa Mary to order

him away?"

She shook her head violently. "No, I don't want anyone to know."

I stared at my friend. Those tears in her eyes were so unnerving. I could see she felt trapped. "I'll tell him to go away," I said, though I was instantly afraid of my own bravado.

The look of relief on Kathleen's face put my feet in motion. I was actually doing it, walking over to that slumped figure by the fence. No one else was around. And then I was right there, staring at a haggard-looking man with doleful eyes. His face was flushed; I figured he was a drinker.

"She wants you to go away and never come back," I said.

"I just wanted to see her," he said in a pleading voice.

"Go away; she doesn't want to see you." I was scared. What if he stood his ground? Was the fence strong enough to hold him back?

But this was a defeated man. I couldn't suppress a guilty thought — how awful it would be if this were *my* father.

"Just tell her I'm sorry. I won't come back." He turned and trudged away slowly.

I walked back to the tennis court, still shaking. Kathleen was leaning against one of the benches. She reached out a hand and grasped mine.

"Thank you," she said.

I squeezed her hand back. "Let's play," I said.

Both Ingrid and Bing Crosby were nominated for Academy Awards. The day the nominations were announced, my delighted father declared it was time for both Mother and me to go dress shopping for the awards ceremony.

I could hardly believe it. "You mean, I really get to go?" I asked.

"Of course you do, and I want my girls looking glamorous," he teased.

"Where is it going to be?" I put my fork down. I was too excited to eat another bite.

"Grauman's Chinese — this is a very splashy event," he said.

I glanced at my mother, hoping I would be able to talk her into getting me high heels. Going to Grauman's Chinese Theater? It was the exotic center of Hollywood glitter, the place outside of which actors and actresses sank their palms into wet cement, leaving handprints for the ages. It had to be one of the most famous places in the world.

And, of course, this was where my father had met my mother. Not that she liked talking about it. I always thought it sounded so romantic — this handsome man courting my beautiful mother, right in the midst of the glamour of Hollywood stars — but she would give a quick smile and change the subject when Father tried to coax her to tell the story.

I had never been inside. Kathleen and I, like any tourists, had wandered the famous sidewalk, giggling and placing our own hands into the imprints, including those of an actress, Carole Lombard, who was married to Clark Gable and had died in a plane crash a few years ago. Kathleen had stared at the Lombard handprint with a pensive expression on her face. "Nothing lasts, even when you think it will be around forever," she said.

It was times like this, in small flashes, when I had some insight into Kathleen's fists-up approach to the world. The sight of her father's face at the school fence was etched in my memory. There really were things that none of us could change, no matter how much we fought against them, and maybe my mother's forebodings were right — which ones were waiting out there for me?

But there was always Hollywood.

■ ■ ■ ■

I dreamed my way into the magic world of the Academy Awards. Yes, there was a cream-colored envelope sitting in a place of honor on the fireplace mantel of our grand new home. I would finger it, awed by the elegance of the expensive paper and the elaborate script of the address.

I don't think I quite believed I was actually going to the ceremony until the day arrived. That is, until, as I hummed and twirled in my new gown, I heard a new sound. I peeked out the window and saw a glistening black studio limo gliding sleekly up the driveway.

It was really happening. I was about to float into a fairy-tale evening in my beautiful new silver high-heeled shoes. I hoped the neighbors would notice, but, of course, they might be going, too. This *was* Beverly Hills, after all.

Before I knew it, I was bathing in light — the radiant, glittering swirl of sparkling jewels and gorgeous gowns, my own included. Mine was all frothy satin and tulle in a beautiful shade of blue, a color I knew I would always love. The only shadow over the evening was Mother's insistence that I wear a stupid white bolero to cover my strapless shoulders, which I resented. I was thirteen now — almost fourteen. I was growing up. But of course that was the problem as far as she was concerned, I told myself.

I stopped brooding about the bolero when we got to the theater and saw the crowds of people crunched into a small roped-off space, craning their necks to see each new arrival, smiling, clapping. "We want Ingrid, we want Ingrid," chanted one group, holding up signs, waving them, cheerfully bumping into each other.

And then came the reception. Waiters walked around handing out little sausages wrapped in crispy dough, politely offering them to me on silver platters, but I kept shaking my head. If I dropped one of them on my dress — or, worse, the carpet — I would die.

I recognized many of the actors and actresses in their sleek glory. There was Gregory Peck, signing somebody's cocktail napkin, and I heard some people whispering that Joan Crawford was so afraid she wouldn't win the Best Actress award for *Mildred Pierce,* she wasn't going to show up. But the most chatter was about the Best

Picture race, which was clearly between *The Bells of St. Mary's* and *The Lost Weekend,* which was all about drunkenness, I knew, though Mother would never let me see it.

Everyone seemed affable and hearty as they greeted one another. But my father had reminded me at home, "Don't forget, everybody's an actor at the Academy Awards." I thought of that when I saw Bing Crosby and Ray Milland — his rival for Best Actor — lounging against the cocktail bar, laughing over a shared joke. I sipped a ginger ale, trying to make it last. My father led my mother around, a hand on her elbow, introducing her, so clearly proud. I thought she looked perfect in her apple-green silk gown with her hair swept high, even though her smile seemed strained and nervous. And if she was nervous, what was I doing there? I tried to pretend I belonged, although no one actually talked to me.

Just before the lights blinked, signaling us all to take our seats for the show, I made a rush for the coatroom in hopes of checking the white bolero. This would have been a futile act of defiance under any circumstances, and I had thought better of it and started to turn back when I saw Ingrid Bergman standing half in shadow in the narrow corridor. A man stood close to her, a man with a carved, almost gaunt face and thinning black hair. He was talking rapidly, his tone sharp, his words clipped, lecturing urgently about something; I couldn't tell. She wasn't resisting but kept her head averted, saying nothing. Her eyes were blank, as if she willed herself elsewhere.

I hesitated, shocked. I was seeing something that was private, surely. But this couldn't be — were they rehearsing a scene? I had never seen Ingrid expressionless. More than that, there was a detached look in her eyes, whereas his seemed to be straining for dominance. I was seeing detachment winning over passion for the first time.

But something was ordinary, pedestrian. Real. What should I do — go past them? Pretend I didn't recognize her? Or go back? I cleared my throat.

Ingrid looked up. "Hello, Jesse," she said calmly.

The man next to her turned and stared at me as if I had done something wrong.

"I'm sorry, I was just —"

"Petter, this is Gabriel Malloy's daughter," Ingrid said.

"That publicist of yours?"

"Yes." She moved herself lightly away from him to touch me on my shoulder. "You look lovely tonight," she said. "Jesse, this is my husband, Dr. Lindström." The lights flickered; she glanced up with a smile. "It's time for the show to begin; we should go."

I nodded and managed a few words, still trying to absorb what I was witnessing. Ingrid's husband made no pretense of saying hello. He simply followed his wife, managing to look intent and irritated at the same time.

At a loss, I started back. I did not want Ingrid to have an unscripted reality. I did not want her to be anyone other than the role model I adored. I stared after the man she had identified as her husband and saw only an ordinary person who should not be in this scene. Or any scene bred in my imagination.

"Lindström is something of a cold fish," my father said when I told him about the encounter as we took our seats in the theater. He stared straight ahead, a sober look on his face.

"Were they fighting?" I asked.

He waited a moment before replying. "She isn't a fighter," he said. "He rules in that marriage."

How strange it felt to think of Ingrid Bergman being ruled by *anyone.* "Do you like him?" I asked.

Father laced his fingers together, clearly

biding his time. "I'm not in the business of selling Petter Lindström, I'm in the business of selling Ingrid Bergman," he said. And then, with an audible snort: "I'll tell you this. He isn't as smart as he thinks he is."

The lights dimmed; the show was beginning. And that was the extent of the glimpse I was given into the marriage of an intense, dour man to the actress I adored. How could any man rule a woman like Ingrid Bergman?

Neither Ingrid nor Bing Crosby won an Oscar that night. And Best Picture went to *The Lost Weekend,* which clearly dismayed my mother. But my genial father wasn't upset at all. "Why should I be?" he said with a grin as he strolled out of the theater, exchanging waves and air kisses with Jennifer Jones. "Ingrid is doing just fine on the Oscar front. She won for *Gaslight* and Crosby won for *Going My Way;* it's all gravy from here."

He was right. *The Bells of St. Mary's* remained hugely popular, garnering plenty of awards, and Sister Teresa Mary announced them all during Assembly — including the fact that it was well on its way to being the top-grossing film of 1945. For quite a long time, we felt a collective owner-ship of that movie. The nuns even approved a new ritual: we older girls, as guides for selected first- and second-graders, were al-lowed to bring them to the parlor to show them the bowl on display that marked our school's place in cinematic history.

I had chosen my hero well. Now she was everyone's hero.

Reality, of course, reasserted itself with finals at the end of the school year. I came out with an A in drama, but only a B-plus in geometry. Mother sighed over that; but, after all, girls weren't supposed to have the same flair for mathematics that boys did. My other grades were a mix of A's and B's — sometimes with a plus.

All the chatter and preening about *The Bells of St. Mary's* began to fade. But there were still regular single-file visits to the Wa-terford bowl in the front reception room. The younger children weren't sure what it was all about, but they knew Ingrid was important.

"My mama says she's going to become a saint," one third-grader announced.

Kathleen gazed after the little girl as she left the reception room and said, "When you think about it, saints tend to get sacri-

ficed sooner or later, don't they." There was
no question mark at the end of her sentence.

CHAPTER SEVEN

Los Angeles, 1946–47

Kathleen and I played as much tennis as we could the summer before we entered our sophomore year at Saint Ann's. She was working now, dishing out sandwiches and ice-cream sundaes at the soda counter of the Thrifty Drug Store across the street from Carl's Drive-Inn, on the south side of town. I thought that was exciting, but Mother shook her head when I told her, murmuring that poor Kathleen shouldn't have to work at such an early age. But she obviously had to help her mother make ends meet.

My friend shook those springy red curls of hers and laughed when I told her what Mother had said. "Your mother's smart; she probably shops at the May Company," she said. "Anyway, I *like* having a job. And with this one, I get free hot-fudge sundaes, so what could be better?"

I nodded agreement, wishing I could get a job, too. Anyway, she had weekends off.

"Look," she said one Sunday at our pool, pulling a stack of magazines out of her canvas gym bag. "I get these, too — just to borrow."

My eyes popped. There they were, crisp and inviting, all the latest movie magazines — one copy each of our favorites, and they wouldn't cost us a penny?

"My boss said they've got to be returned in perfect shape," Kathleen said, grinning. "Great, huh? Much better than dozing over *Silas Marner*."

"Great" was hardly a big enough word. The magazines would cut into our weekend tennis playing, but for three sunny months, my friend and I had free access to every bit of gossip about Hollywood that we could ever want.

We sat together on weekends by the side of our blue-tile-lined pool, flexing bright red toenails, smearing thick dabs of white zinc oxide on our noses and plenty of shiny baby oil on our arms and legs.

I paid little attention to my mother. She would sit at the opposite end of the pool, wearing a dopey-looking black bathing suit, with a floppy hat covering her eyes, reading the newspaper and listening to some symphony on her portable radio. She seemed somehow to be fading, I thought once, and sleeping more. Father had brought the radio home for her when she told him she'd rather listen to broadcasters than talk to people during the day. She wasn't making many friends in our fancy neighborhood — I knew that. I didn't realize at first that the social ascendancy both my parents were hoping for probably wasn't going to happen anyway. My father's role in the industry was vital, and his efforts could make or break careers, but he said it best. "Actors will kill for a publicist as good as I am," I heard him say to Mother, "but they won't invite us to their dinner parties."

"Doesn't your mother swim?" Kathleen asked curiously as we emerged from a dip in the pool one afternoon.

"She doesn't want to get her hair wet. Can you imagine?" I said, rolling my eyes. And then I would forget her. Kathleen and I would settle into our beach chairs and begin inhaling the stories brought to us by *Photoplay* and *Screenland* and all the other magazines — including the names of the bright-faced, handsome, or beautiful stars who filled their pages. Here we were, considering ourselves almost grown-up, and it was like playing with paper dolls again.

I remember, one hot day, chortling with Kathleen over a breathless account of a party billed as the Paper Costume Ball. Arlene Dahl, we learned, dressed up as a papier-mâché señorita and then worried all night that someone in the crowded room would get too careless with a match. Betty Hutton wore a dress made out of playing cards, and Paulette Goddard had fashioned her dress out of milk cartons. Jeanne Crain wore a "priceless white mink" lined with wallpaper. "Be nonchalant," advised her designer. "Don't wear it, Madam — drag it!"

We found that hilarious. "I'd like to see what Ingrid would wear," Kathleen said. I shook my head. "That's not *her* kind of party," I replied. "Not somebody who can play Saint Joan."

Kathleen nodded agreement. Ingrid, after all, would next year be taking on the part she had dreamed of for her entire career; that's what my father reported. "Going from playing a nun to playing a saint," he announced, almost rubbing his hands together in satisfaction. "Nobody can beat her at this point. She might as well convert now; Catholics already feel they own her."

■ ■ ■ ■

But there was something going on, some new undercurrent. One lazy Sunday, my father, clutching the newspaper, came over to my mother at the pool, leaned over, and murmured something. Mother's hand went to her throat. "Oh no," she said, her eyes wide with what looked like fear. "Gabriel, I —" They both saw me watching at the same time and swiftly pulled apart. Father strode back into the house, ignoring me. His expression was strange — dark and still.

I wanted to ask what was going on. But Mother buried herself in her newspaper again, clearly in no mood for questions. That annoyed me. But pretty much everything about Mother was annoying me at the time. And that odd expression on Father's face stopped me from asking him.

Kathleen and I sat rapt in a dark theater a few days later watching Ingrid in *Notorious,* a story that presented moral ambivalence in a way neither of us had seen on film before. I wanted to talk about it with my father, but he still seemed tense. I finally got up the courage to ask him if anything was wrong, given that he had taken to pacing the house late at night. His eyes widened. He laughed and ruffled my hair. "Something wrong?" he said. "Nothing important at all, worrywart. Just that, on this movie, Ingrid's got a tricky sell."

Even I could see that. Playing the daughter of a convicted Nazi spy, Ingrid is recruited after the war by a U.S. agent, Cary Grant, to spy on Nazis in postwar Rio — and instructed to reignite her romance with a top Nazi, played by Claude Rains. Even though she is in love with Grant, she follows orders — pretending to be in love with Rains — and helps destroy a dangerous spy ring.

When Kathleen and I went for sodas afterward, I was wondering, soberly, how Ingrid could do such an awful thing, even though all came out right in the end.

"But that's really not *Ingrid*," Kathleen reminded me.

"Well, I know that," I said hastily. We agreed that life was about compromise, maybe even moral compromise. How sexual compromise fit in, we weren't sure, but what mattered most was the greater good. It sounded right at the moment, as we sat there on the bar stools at the drugstore, sipping chocolate sodas. We were working now at trying to figure a lot of things out, and not spending all our time just poring over the movie magazines.

It was true, our country had dropped the atomic bomb on Hiroshima and Nagasaki. But the A-bomb ended the war, didn't it? The reason we did it was to save lives that would have been lost in an invasion. So did that moral good cancel out the moral evil of killing so many people?

Cautiously, I ran that reasoning by my mother. Mistake. Just as I figured, she wasn't interested in exploring morality in any free-range way. Plus, she had seen *Notorious,* too, and her instruction was not about bombs. "Marriage was flouted in that movie, and you know marriage is a sacrament," she said quietly. "And moral compromise is a sin, and God will punish it. Don't ever lose sight of what you've been taught, Jesse."

"But what if I have trouble believing all of it?" I asked.

Mother stared at me. She said not a word, just got up from her chair and vanished into the kitchen.

I thought a lot about that. I wanted to talk about it with my father, but it was becoming harder to get his attention. Lots of money was flowing in, and he was usually very busy. But it wasn't just his job, I was sure now. He was attending meetings late at night, mostly of the Screen Writers Guild, coming home tired and strained. I started paying more attention to the news, especially stories about fights between the labor unions in Hollywood and the movie producers. The papers were saying that communism was secretly taking over Hollywood; that people with the power to write important movie scripts were dangerous, that they could send hidden messages to moviegoers, no matter what the movies were about.

I wondered — wouldn't they be dangerous, if they were out to overthrow our government? I raised my questions timidly one night.

Father's gaze was weary but patient. "They're getting to you, too?" he said. "Look, there are people too afraid of boogeymen to remember that this country, damn it, is a democracy that values free speech. It's right-wing types here and in Washington who don't want anything getting in the way of their gaining power and money who are feeding that fear. If anybody speaks up for giving ordinary Joes a better break these days, he's a communist." He stopped, looking at me closely. "Am I loading you up with too much here?"

"No," I said. "I'm learning."

■ ■ ■ ■

A few days later, I heard the front door slam. Father walked in, frowning, and threw a copy of *The Hollywood Reporter* on the dining-room table with such force it knocked over a candlestick. "It's wide open now. They're naming names, these spineless jerks."

"Who are they accusing?" Mother asked in a tight voice.

"Dalton Trumbo, Lester Cole, Howard Koch —"

"What happens now?"

"Hearings in Washington, in front of the House Un-American Activities Committee. You want a moral issue? This is the one to think about now." He sat down and stared directly at me. "If Hitchcock were making *Notorious* in today's climate, it wouldn't be about Nazis, it would be about some of the people I work with. If these red-baiters keep it up, there won't be a Bill of Rights anymore. Did you see what Adolphe Menjou said? He wants all communists sent back to Russia. And Gary Cooper? He says he's rejecting scripts that have 'communist ideas.' At least he didn't name any names." He slammed one fist into the other palm, and I jumped.

He turned to my mother. "Vannie, I have to go talk to these guys —"

She gave him a brisk nod. "I'll keep your dinner warm."

I sat there, deeply shaken. Was this going to hurt my father? Why was he so involved? Perspiration was breaking out on my forehead; my heart was thudding. Staring after him as he left, I asked Mother the only question that, for me, mattered.

"Father isn't a communist, is he?"

"No, Jesse." Said firmly.

I took a deep breath. Finally, a much-craved black-and-white answer from Mother.

Days later, the blacklist was initiated. And the ten writers — the Hollywood Ten — who had resisted HUAC were indicted for refusing to testify.

I kept trying to push worries away, even as my family's old exuberance faded. Mother was still sleeping a lot, but she would mix the cocktails each night when Father came home, and we would sit together, as usual. I could sometimes convince myself that all was well.

Kathleen and I tried hard to take a break from puzzling over the political issues swirling around us, turning instead back to the movies. We went from talking about the Hollywood Ten to sighing over the erotic kiss shared by Ingrid and Cary Grant in *Notorious*. What better example of playing by the rules and breaking them at the same time?

We thought the joke Alfred Hitchcock played on Joseph Breen was hilarious. That pursed-lip enforcer of the Hollywood Production Code had decreed no kiss on screen could last longer than three seconds.

"Three seconds?" my father chortled. "Look, Jesse," he said, pulling Mother toward him. "I'm going to demonstrate. Isn't this romantic?" He touched Mother's lips with his for exactly three seconds and pulled away. "That's a hummingbird kiss," he said, laughing.

Alfred Hitchcock dutifully adhered to the rule in *Notorious* by having Ingrid and Cary Grant brush lips, then obediently pull back after three seconds — only an inch or two, with an assistant director standing nearby hoisting a stopwatch to call a halt.

A few murmured endearments . . . then Ingrid and Cary moved close again, to share another three-second kiss. Parting; a whispered exchange; then another kiss. And another . . .

I was dizzy when it ended, that kiss — because it lasted almost three full *minutes.*

"Look," Kathleen said, pointing to her copy of *Photoplay.* "Hedda Hopper is calling it the longest kiss in film history."

She turned the page, and we scanned the lingerie ads. Kathleen told me the trick to wearing a rubber Playtex girdle was to turn it inside out first and sprinkle it with talcum powder. Best not to wear it on a hot day, she advised: you could smell the rubber.

We did learn a lot from each other — and from our magazines, which we continued to devour throughout high school.

We were sitting outside one day toward the end of our sophomore year, flipping through *Screenland,* and suddenly we stopped. "Look," Kathleen breathed.

We were staring at a full-page, full-color photo of Ingrid encased head to foot in medieval armor. She was gazing resolutely into the distance, holding her sword high. *"Coming:* Joan of Arc, *starring Ingrid Bergman."*

That was all the ad mentioned.

"She looks beautiful," I said. Soon we would be able to see her in what would surely turn out to be her greatest role.

"And determined," Kathleen added softly. "She knows how to be what she wants to be better than anybody."

She closed the magazine and gave it to me. I stacked it carefully, almost lovingly, with all the others. We stayed silent as we stared out over the rippling water and lush bougainvillea vines lining the flagstone path around the pool. We didn't have the language for it then, but Ingrid was more to us than just a revered star — it was her ease, her naturalness. Her ability to make decisions on her own, the idea she seemed to embody of what independence for a woman could be. We mulled that over, an idea half formed.

My brain felt peaceful, blank for the moment; I was taking a pause from growing up. Those magazines — those deliverers of the raw material from which we were building our own stories — comforted me with their proximity. To open one was to gain access to the personality quirks, the likes and dislikes, the sexual allure of the stars. We could safely ignore or celebrate them. We could wish we had Ava Gardner's sultry, smoky eyes or sigh over Clark Gable's muscular arms, or talk about which brand of tampons we should try next. But there was one star we could count on to see us through.

"She looks great in armor," I said. "But it

must be hot to wear."

Kathleen giggled. "Probably not as hot as a girdle," she said. She glanced at her watch. "Gotta go," she said. "I've got night shift this week."

"Maybe some famous director will discover you, like Lana Turner at Schwab's."

"Famous directors don't buy sodas at Thrifty's in my neighborhood."

"Well, if they saw you, they would," I said loyally.

My father agreed one Sunday to join us at Mass if Mother didn't insist he wear a tie. She was pleased; she thought he spent too much time brooding over the movie censors' banning the newly realistic movies coming in from Europe. Joseph Breen had denounced *The Bicycle Thief,* refusing it entry, calling it glorified theft.

"I don't know whether to laugh or cry," he said to me as we waited. "But I'll tell you this — the battle lines with the Legion of Decency are growing wider. Though some of it is still funny." He rattled off a list.

A dog wetting on the floor in *The Best Years of Our Lives* had to be cut from the film. A commode in a jail cell could be glimpsed in *The Paradine Case* — out it went. The word "brothel" couldn't be used — it had to be "a high-class roadhouse" or "speakeasy." Joan Crawford couldn't be the mistress of a politician in *Flamingo Road* — she had to be married. And on it went.

Darryl Zanuck was even ordered to alter the script of *Gentleman's Agreement* — the heroine could not be a divorced woman. That would be "tacit justification for divorce." In the ensuing uproar, Zanuck refused, and got away with it.

"So he won, right?" I said as Mother adjusted her hat. I loved the fact that, more and more, Father talked to me like an adult.

"He won one round," Father said. He looked distracted. He was rarely without a cigarette clenched between his lips anymore. "But people aren't going to the movies the way they used to."

"Why not?"

He shrugged. "They're moving to the suburbs, maybe going bowling or to the racetrack — we don't know. And the censors are making it worse. They're too powerful; they can break any studio that doesn't comply with their rules."

"Gabriel, don't forget your Sunday missal," Mother said soothingly.

He stared at her with a blank expression, and I wondered if he had even heard.

"What do people like Breen think the world is *about*?" he muttered in the car. "It's absurd — according to the damn censors, nobody is divorced. Nobody has an abortion. People who are married don't have affairs, Christians never marry Jews, and even married couples sleep in separate beds." He ground the cigarette out in the already jammed car ashtray. "Where does the Legion of Decency think their next generation of Catholics is coming from?"

I laughed and glanced at Mother. A frozen smile — there were so many like that now — tugged at her lips.

Mother pulled her Persian lamb coat tight, almost protectively, around her frame as the three of us entered Saint Ambrose, our new, much fancier church in Brentwood. A towering brick edifice, it blazed with modernity — beautiful but, to me, cold. All the marble statues of the saints and the Holy Family held their arms straight by their sides, like soldiers ready to march off to war.

"Gabriel, promise to be civil," Mother whispered.

"No problem," he said.

Father Nolton, one of the younger priests, strode out onto the altar, gave the tabernacle holding the Holy Eucharist a brisk nod, genuflected, and got down to business. He was a stalwart conservative who preached against loose morals, condemned birth control, and scoffed at the idea of anti-Semitism, declaring it didn't exist. He deplored any question of modernizing the Church. And he had been known to suggest that clergy who supported more liberal views were flirting with communism and endangering their immortal souls.

Father Nolton moved quickly through the opening prayers. In record time, he was ascending the pulpit and opening his Bible to a page marked by a red velvet bookmark.

Today it would be the Gospel according to Saint John. Something benign, about good works and loving God.

He began calmly, soothingly, thanking the good ladies of the parish who had carried off a successful campaign to raise money for a new church organ. He made a gentle joke about how much better the congregation would sound once the new organ was installed. A few smiles; a titter or two.

"And now let's talk about the misconception that we are no longer at war — that, because the Allies defeated Nazism, we are at peace," he began. "I wish with all my heart I could say that is true." He paused, looked down as if to muster strength, then up, directly at the congregation. "The truth is, we *are* at war. We, the Catholics of America, are at war with the vulgarity, the immorality, and the *sinfulness* of a grotesque land of perverted entertainment — the land we call *Hollywood.*"

My father's expression didn't change, but his entire body stiffened. So much so that I feared that if I touched him it might be like poking cement.

It was time to unsheathe our swords, Father Nolton said. Time to fight back. "Know this: Hollywood is flinching. The cowards of the industry, the communists, quail before the Legion of Decency, and *we will win.* Keep your hard-earned cash at home. Don't dig in your pockets to sit in a grimy movie theater showing actors and actresses engaged in filthy —"

Father sighed, an almost imperceptible sound. He cast a glance of regret at my mother, stood up, stared at a startled Father Nolton, then walked out of the church. People gasped. Mother bent her head forward, and I didn't know whether to be ashamed or proud. Not everything from Hollywood was immoral. And I didn't like Father Nolton anyhow. I started to get up, to follow Father, but she cupped her hand gently over mine and I felt her plea. I stayed put.

He was sitting in the driver's seat of the car, slumped down, looking exhausted, when we left the church after Mass.

"You *planned* to walk out," my furious mother accused him as we got in the car. There were tears in her eyes. "You shamed me, Gabriel. You underscored your superiority by showing contempt for Father Nolton. You set us up in there. Have you thought about *that*?"

"Vanessa, I'm sorry, I had no intention of hurting you. But don't you see what these people are *doing*? This is about a lot more than cleavage and calling a whorehouse a whorehouse. Didn't you hear him call us communists? You know what that's a cover for? They hate the Jews; they fear anything and anybody who isn't like them. And Washington? The House Un-American Activities Committee — look what they're doing to writers —"

Mother clapped her hands over her ears. "Stop it," she screamed. "It's my church, it's my pastor, so go walk out on somebody else. Don't leave me trying to look people in the eye who feel sorry for me!"

Father sat back, stunned, as if she had

physically slapped his face. "Vanessa?" he said.

"You do not respect me."

"Oh God, not true."

"You care about the people you are in charge of tarting up at the studio, not me."

His voice sharpened. "I've been a good provider; give me that."

Mother, stop, I pleaded silently. *Stop. You know how; he doesn't.*

"You wouldn't bother staying home on the weekends if there weren't a swimming pool."

"Fuck it," he said.

He waited, but there was no response.

With a sharp thrust, he pushed in the ignition key and the car engine rumbled to life.

I tried to make myself as small as possible in the backseat, wishing I could disappear. This was not a real place; surely, what just happened was a scene that would be recut immediately.

I wanted no contradictions, no puzzles to be voiced and hurled by my parents. Are we all like this, we children who would give anything to hold the structure of family together — with tape or string or paper clips; with tears or kisses or acts of loyalty? And how do we choose sides when all choices carry both truths and lies?

I waited for Mother to reach out to him, to put a hand on his shoulder, to suggest we stop for a Frosty Freeze or something, so I could breathe deep again.

She stared straight ahead all the way home.

CHAPTER EIGHT

Los Angeles, 1948–49

My mother's migraines began shortly after that. I would come home from school to a still house, and her bedroom door would be closed. I remember staring at that door, wondering if it was permissible to knock. Neither of my parents said anything to me about the scene in the car. My whole world felt shaky, and they pretended that nothing had happened at all, which stopped me from asking questions. They forced me to pretend with them.

After a week of facing that silent house all by myself, on a day when Kathleen had the afternoon off, I coaxed her into coming home with me by promising fresh chocolate-chip cookies. "We'll bake them ourselves; they'll be hot," I said.

So she came. We pulled out the blue mixing bowl, the flour, and the butter and laughed about finding the sifter in the refrigerator. It was good to be part of a normal conversation again. For a brief time, as we mixed the batter and folded in the Toll House chocolate chips, life felt back on track.

"This stuff is good," she offered, licking one of the spoons. I took a bite; it was delicious.

"So is your mother sick?"

"She has headaches."

"Does she spend all day in her bedroom?"

"I don't know."

Kathleen nodded, as if this were a perfectly normal thing to say. I told her about my father's walking out on Father Nolton at Sunday Mass and the fight in the car. She nodded again, more thoughtfully this time. "Nolton's a jerk. If you listen to the priests, you'd think everybody in Hollywood was either a spy or a communist making dirty movies. No wonder your father got fed up." She said it in such an offhand way, so matter-of-factly, that I felt the tension inside of me ease slightly. I asked her a question I had wondered about for a while:

"How do you . . . just decide what you believe?"

"You mean thumb my nose at the rules?"

"More than that."

"Like, what's going to send me to hell?" A

small smile played across her lips.

I thought of the rosaries I had whispered my way through from a darkened church pew. "Nothing is going to send *you* to hell," I said.

"Okay, I have bad thoughts, too. And you know what? I think it's part of growing up. And I'm not confessing it, and I'm not reciting any rosary for penance. What do you think now?"

"Wherever you go, I'll go, too."

Silently, Kathleen picked up a spoonful of cookie dough and held it out to me. "This one has lots of chips," she said gently.

We never did bake the cookies that day. We just ate all the batter, and it was delicious. I was scraping the almost empty bowl with a spatula when I looked up and saw my mother's startled face appear in the doorway.

"Girls," she said in a perfectly normal voice. I clung to the fact that she wore a bright smile and her hair was combed. "What are you thinking? You'll ruin your appetites for dinner."

"Yes, ma'am, we'll make up for it tomorrow," Kathleen said.

Mother laughed — actually laughed. She was back.

Just as Kathleen got on her bike to ride

home, my father pulled into the driveway. He hadn't come home until after ten o'clock all week, and it wasn't even dark yet. I let myself consider the possibility that, finally, with him home and Mother smiling again, things might be tipping back into place.

"Hi, kid," Father said as he climbed out of the car. "Rough week all around, right? Sorry."

Just like that. To the point. His eyes looked hollow, and I could see sweat marks on the cuffs of his dress shirt.

I couldn't pretend. "Are you still fighting?" I asked.

"The war is over," he said. "We talked."

"Whatever that means."

"Okay, you're worried. Do you want to know more?"

I shook my head vigorously. No, no. I strained to keep my departing friend — hair flying, pedaling away down the hill — in sight. I didn't want to know anything about my parents' lives, not then and maybe not ever. I just wanted to think about sitting in the kitchen eating cookie batter with Kathleen.

"Okay," he said again, his voice tired. Together we walked back into the house, where Mother had already set the table for dinner and poured their usual cocktails into their usual glasses, and Father gave us an update on studio news, and it all felt strange, so it barely registered that Ingrid was thinking of making a movie for an Italian director off in Italy.

I wasn't spending much time pondering any of that. I had landed a part in the school play. We were doing *Pride and Prejudice,* which I was thrilled about, but unfortunately I had to play Mr. Wickham. I protested that this was unfair, but Miss Coultrane argued that it would test my dramatic skills in a way that playing a female role would not. I didn't buy that for a minute, but we had no boys at Saint Ann's and I was the tallest in the class even though I was only a junior, so I was stuck. Our production was in full, semi-frenzied rehearsal. Kathleen wasn't interested in dramatics, so I saw little of her as the shadows of winter began lengthening. Long rehearsals were filling up the after-school daylight hours. No time for tennis.

I loved learning my lines, loved the feeling of creating a part that involved a person I could bring to life, even if I had to play a male lead. I took it as a challenge when Miss Coultrane insisted I learn how a man walks — the stride, the posture, the chest thrust forward, demanding the easy command of a room.

"Spread your legs when you sit," she snapped from the darkened theater during one rehearsal. "Now place your palms on your thighs. *That's how a man takes charge.*"

Strange, to do that. And yet, when I did, I caught a glimmer of what Miss Coultrane was telling me. It felt freeing; that was the truth of it.

Playing Mr. Wickham in general felt comfortable enough, but I hated the uniform I had to wear. The pants were obscenely tight over my too-generous hips. The heavy military coat felt like armor over my proudly developed breasts. My hair was cut short again, and the fake sideburns and mustache made some classmates snicker.

So, okay, I told myself, I didn't have the body to play a man. But if Ingrid Bergman could stand straight and proud in a full suit of armor, I could manage Wickham.

That worked until the handsome brother of one of my classmates came to pick up his twin sister after rehearsal one afternoon. I had seen him once before, at a church hall mixer, and knew a few things about him. His name was Philip, and he was a junior at Thomas Aquinas, the Jesuit school for boys, but I hadn't noticed until now that his eyes

164

were a brilliant blue and he had an engaging, lopsided smile that flustered me.

I didn't see him at first. I was practicing my lines in the fountain garden outside of the auditorium, striding back and forth, trying to deepen my voice, waiting to be called for my scene, when I heard a startled exclamation. I looked up, straight into Philip's handsome, shocked face. "Who are you?" he asked.

At first I thought he meant what *part* was I playing, and I had opened my mouth to tell him when I realized he might really, truly wonder if I was a *man*.

"I'm Jesse, a junior, like your sister," I blurted. "This is just a costume, I'm playing Wickham —"

He was backing away, looking at me as if he had swallowed a peach pit. "Sure," he said. "Yep. Hey, you look — swell." He turned on his heel and exited the garden, leaving me briefly devastated. I wanted to tear off the sideburns and the stupid mustache; how could I ever have let myself become an object of ridicule? And that's what I would be; I knew it. Philip would laugh and tell his friends and —

"My dear Jesse." I looked to my left, at the path by the fountain, and saw Miss Coultrane standing there, her straight-up-

165

and-down body as erect as a soldier's. "What a wonderful thing — you actually convinced that young man that you were Wickham. It takes a good actress to become her part. You should be proud."

I must have looked unconvinced.

"You do know Miss Bergman plays a woman playing a man in her new movie," Miss Coultrane said in a voice unusually gentle.

"Yes." Of course. I felt a glimmer of comfort.

"And you do remember that Portia, in Shakespeare's world, had to be a man playing a woman playing a man?"

I smiled, still a little grudgingly. Yes, I knew that.

Then Miss Coultrane — steely, demanding Miss Coultrane — touched my shoulder and gently guided me into the auditorium.

"You can quit, you know," she said. "Or you can play your part. You're an excellent Wickham."

I had a fleeting thought: how many parts was I to play in a single life? Probably not as many as Ingrid. "I'll stay," I said.

The production was a success. All our families dutifully attended each weekend performance, and several of the local Catholic schools packed the house for our two matinees. I tasted the fear and joy of waiting in the wings for my cue, saw how music and lighting and costumes could create magic, and wondered: did Ingrid feel something transporting like this every time? How exhausting and thrilling that must be. I felt a kinship with her as I peeked through the heavy velvet curtains in Saint Ann's auditorium. Perhaps she had once been in my shoes, whispering her lines, straining to be ready for the moment when, in character, she had to stride onto the stage and take a rapt audience into the palm of her hand. That possibility was exhilarating. And I was proud to play Mr. Wickham. Even when I spotted Philip sitting in the third row.

Just before Christmas 1948, with great fanfare, *Joan of Arc* was released. Kathleen and I saw it together, and I was enthralled. Who could not be moved, watching Ingrid as the Maid of Orleans bravely lead the French army into battle — and just as bravely meet her fate at the hands of the dreaded English? It was the noblest of sacrifices, I said to Kathleen.

"Well — if it really happened that way," she responded. Was she hinting that my reaction was excessive? I didn't care. I felt elevated, somehow more splendid myself.

Ingrid Bergman's acting had a way of making that happen, and I was sure lots of people must feel the same. She did what heroes were supposed to do: she *enlarged* me. Into what? I wasn't sure, but I knew she would point the way.

True to their mission, every movie magazine carried a story. "All my life I dreamed of playing this incredible woman," Ingrid told *Look* magazine. "And now I have."

Maybe Ingrid wasn't one of us, but she was the closest thing to it in the secular world, and we were proud. Sister Teresa Mary took to the school loudspeaker on the movie's opening day to urge every high-school girl at Saint Ann's to go see Ingrid Bergman "bring to life a saint of the holy Catholic Church." We felt bathed in the reflected light of her courageous character, somehow part of it. How easy it turned out to be, this conferring of sainthood on the real person under all that armor. Even Father Nolton knew enough to keep quiet for a while about the danger of the movies.

It was my father's idea to install a plaque at Saint Ann's to commemorate the filming of *The Bells of St. Mary's.* After all, it was part of the school's history, he told Sister Teresa Mary. There was no opposition. Sister

Teresa Mary was quite pleased with the idea, especially when Ingrid agreed to come for the installation ceremony.

"We might as well get all the publicity mileage for *Joan* that we can," Father said offhandedly, out of earshot of the nuns. That gave me pause, but, really, generating publicity was his job, and nothing was wrong with that.

So we crowded together, this time near the chapel, where, in an enclave lined with roses, a bronze marker had been set into the earth. Etched into the metal:

The Bells of St. Mary's —
starring Ingrid Bergman
filmed on this site in 1945

And we waited for Ingrid.

A half hour passed. Forty-five minutes. Sister Teresa Mary's welcoming smile was getting strained.

Finally, a polished black Cadillac drove up. It stopped, and our star stepped out, giving us a warm smile. Her dress was navy blue, cut short, with sleeves and a crisp white collar. She looked almost like a schoolgirl herself.

She strode forward and embraced Sister Teresa Mary, who had regained her welcoming smile. Cameras flashed; aides poured from the two following cars. I saw one glancing at his watch, catching the eye of another, and shaking his head. "She's probably got six more events she's supposed to show up for," Kathleen whispered.

Ingrid made a short speech applauding the nuns for their good work and thanked them all for their hospitality. "This is a lovely, serene home for those in communion with God," she said gracefully. "And I thank you for honoring me by allowing *The Bells of St. Mary's* to claim your school as its real-life counterpart."

I was sitting in the front row, straight and tall and proud, listening to every word. No one clapped harder than I did, and I was thrilled when she spotted me and actually winked. There were some who murmured that she could have talked about goodness and holiness, but I thought they were ridiculously picky.

"She looks almost ethereal," breathed one of the younger nuns, staring after Ingrid's departing figure as she worried the polished black beads laced around her waist. "Do you think she'll convert?"

My father laughed heartily when I relayed that wistful thought. "People will believe whatever they want to believe," he said.

I did wonder, even then, with the serene presumption of the intellectually superior, how people could be so naïve as to believe such a thing. Ingrid was a Protestant, after all. Anyone with any level of sophistication knew *that* didn't work.

Joan of Arc was a failure. No, that is the wrong description. *The movie that took Ingrid to sainthood was not a box office success.* Somehow we at Saint Ann's found ourselves suddenly bumping down a rutted road instead of flying, and it was a sour review by Bosley Crowther of the *New York Times* that did it. He said of Ingrid, "While handsome to look on, [she] has no great spiritual quality. Her strength seems to lie in her physique rather than in her burning faith."

Was he calling my hero a phony? Or somehow incompetent at playing the role she had dreamed of all her life?

The atmosphere at school the day that review came out was universally glum. We couldn't help taking it personally: Ingrid was our link to the world beyond our parochial selves. So we made contemptuous remarks about Crowther and went about our day. Kathleen brought over the latest movie magazines to the tennis court, and we soon put the criticisms of *Joan of Arc* behind us. Ingrid would emerge triumphant in her next movie, whatever it would be.

When I came home that afternoon, I had my first sense that there was more to the failure of *Joan* than I realized. Yes, it had come as a surprise. I could tell that it was a *great* surprise by the deepened lines on my father's forehead. Home early, he sat smoking at the kitchen table. His mood was cranky, with an edge of something else.

That night, I awoke, fully alert, when I heard my father's rumbling voice through the bedroom door, talking to Mother. I never paused to wonder why I would come back from the deepest sleep any time his voice pierced my dreams.

"Not a good sign, those box-office receipts," he said.

"What went wrong?" Mother murmured.

He sighed; I heard him exhale. He kept two packs of Lucky Strikes next to his side of the bed now. "Too long, and it cost too much," he said.

"But Ingrid can save any movie —"

"Not with the route she's taking. She's off to make that movie with Roberto Rossellini, the Italian who did *Open City*. On an island."

"But surely —"

"Vannie, oh, Vannie." He sighed again.

"She's going to find out sainthood is a curse."

CHAPTER NINE

Los Angeles, 1949–50

The first part of my senior year at Saint Ann's was rigorous, with plenty of history tests, English essays, and late nights spent studying. But somehow I had become a very good student. I even mastered chemistry, getting pretty good at fiddling with test tubes and memorizing formulas.

Yet what I loved most was knowing I had become one of Miss Coultrane's favored pupils when — Mr. Wickham safely behind me — I focused on public speaking. I spent long hours working on diction, orating; I grew to like the sound of my own voice. Miss Coultrane entered me in a few local school tournaments, and I won second place in debate at Loyola High, which pleased my parents. "Stay away from debating communists in labor unions," Father warned half jokingly. "You'll have the government on your tail."

174

Politics, for me, stayed vaguely on the horizon. Kathleen and I worried over what would happen to the world now that Russia had the atomic bomb: would we all be blown to bits? But such concerns floated out somewhere on the horizon; even small hints in the papers that Ingrid was maybe involved in a romance didn't rise to the top. We dismissed them. I somehow managed to table my worries about my father. I was much more interested in a coming citywide speech tournament and the pamphlets from faraway colleges that had begun slipping through the mail slot at home. I daydreamed over them. Bennington College: So "back east." Girls wearing pedal pushers riding bikes around a bucolic campus of green grass and winding paths. Stanford University: So serious and important. A girl could even major in math there. I filled out applications, discussing them with my father, feeling unsure of myself — until Sister Teresa Mary announced one day that Saint Ann's was not sending out *one single additional transcript* of mine unless I applied to a Catholic college.

"How can she dare do that?" I railed to Kathleen.

"Does your mother know?"

"Why would she understand? She never

went to college."

"Apply to a Jesuit college and shut up. You don't have to go there."

When you were pragmatic like Kathleen, you could cut through all the thorny tangles. I did — and set my heart on Stanford.

That was how my last year at Saint Ann's began, all orchestrated comfortably and according to script.

The biggest change was Philip. Maybe watching me onstage had helped him understand that my pretending to be Mr. Wickham was an acting challenge, or maybe I just wasn't that convincing in the role. Whichever it was, he eventually asked me out. So there I was, linked to the star athlete at Thomas Aquinas.

Other girls told me that some boys gave wet kisses, which were sloppy, and others gave dry kisses, which were better. Philip was a dry kisser. I tried to be coy and pull away that first time, remembering Ingrid's three-second kisses in *Notorious,* hoping it would make me sexier. But when he flushed and started to back off, I thought maybe he hadn't seen the movie. It was a bit disappointing — I could hear his breath whistling through his nose — but I discovered that the mechanics of kissing were not as complicated as I had feared. And when his hand moved to my breast, I fervently thanked the falsies I had stuffed into my mother's bra. Maybe he would think they were real.

Was letting him touch my fake breasts a venial or a mortal sin? I would go to confession tomorrow.

There were to be a series of earnest confessions as we moved further into our senior year in the fall of 1949, but really, I told myself many times, kissing Philip couldn't be a ticket to hell, because we never went All the Way.

How could I possibly concentrate on *anything* important when I was busy agonizing over sex? Philip took me to his school's winter formal, which I remember mostly for its textures — the soft tulle and scratchy net of my blue dress, the dancing glitter Mother sprinkled over my carefully sprayed hair, the feel of the orchid he brought for me to wear on my wrist. And then the secret textures — parking in the dark oil fields above L.A. after the dance, fumbling, tongues locked. Even the Church couldn't stop sex forever. Everything heaved with possibility.

"Did you hear the news?" Kathleen shouted to me as we biked down a steep hill toward

Westwood on our way to a movie. The afternoon was beautiful, one of those sharp, tasty days in Los Angeles when you actually believe that, yes, the seasons do change, even in California.

"You mean that stuff about colleges making the faculty sign loyalty oaths?" I yelled back. I was pleased to be up on the news. Outrageous, my father had said. "They're hunting for communists everywhere, and this violates freedom of speech."

"Are you kidding? I mean Ingrid falling in love with that Italian director and living with him in Italy!"

I slammed on my brakes, almost pitching over the handlebars. "I don't believe it," I yelled.

"Have you seen the latest *Photoplay*?"

I shook my head. "They're making a movie, that's all," I said. "It's just rumor."

"She admits it."

Something churned inside of me — a roller coaster of shock and surprise. Hollywood gossip was always about somebody else, *not Ingrid*.

We pulled over to the curb and tried to put it all together. The details had been collecting, of course: those sly little hints in Louella Parsons's columns about a possible romance, not naming names. But to Kathleen and me — no fans of Hollywood's nasty and lugubrious columnist, though we read every piece she wrote — it pretty much seemed the usual kind of made-up scandal thing. Everyone knew Ingrid was happily married. A shadow passed quickly over that thought as I remembered the tightly stitched husband I had seen with her at the Academy Awards. I hadn't liked him; I could go that far.

"My father would know, and he hasn't said anything of the sort," I reasoned.

"Are you going to ask him?" She was so infernally direct.

"No, why would I have to do that?"

"Because he might tell you if it's true."

"I don't believe it."

Kathleen sighed. "Maybe you've been too busy with Philip," she said.

It was the closest thing to an admonishment I'd ever heard from my friend.

We decided to pass on the movie. It was just another Roy Rogers Western, the kind of thing we were mostly too grown-up for now anyway. Instead, we got back on our bikes that sunny fall day and pedaled to a nearby park, where we settled on a bench. Kathleen dug into her book bag and came up with her copy of *Photoplay*. We stared at the cover: a head shot of a smiling, winsome Ingrid in a high-necked white blouse filled the page. Glumly, we stared at the headline.

The Bergman Love Story
The only story personally approved by Ingrid Bergman

Here the real Bergman emerges — a woman Hollywood never knew.

Inside were pages of color photos of a beaming Ingrid on the island of Stromboli, posing both with a lean, smiling Rossellini and with the peasants who inhabited the island.

"I love Roberto," Ingrid was quoted as saying. In one photo — dressed in a red peasant skirt, long hair blowing in the wind — she looked wholesome and happy. "One day when I am free, we shall be married," the caption read.

We drank in the words, eager to understand. The author wrote sympathetically of Ingrid's life journey, from the death of her mother when she was two years old to the glamour of Hollywood. Before she became famous, men ignored the shy young woman, except for a doctor ten years older named Petter Lindström, "who she came to see as the answer to her inner longing for surcease from iron-bound restrictions," the article said.

"She was too young to marry," I declared. "He must've tried to control her." I already knew whose side I was on.

We kept reading, hungry for understanding.

People of high position become public domain, the author declared, "which casts idols in the mold of [the public's] own imagination and standards," rendering it futile for any "idol to plead its humanness." And now, "happy with the man she loves, she is struggling to get joint custody with her husband of their daughter, Pia," but he was resisting.

Kathleen nodded slowly, but stayed oddly silent.

"What's wrong?"

"I'm wondering how Pia feels."

I heard a strange note in her voice.

"But we know Ingrid wants her daughter with her, the article says so — she isn't really *abandoning* her."

She nodded again. "I'm just wondering how Pia feels."

She said no more. We kept reading. Ingrid was an artist, dedicated to her work. She would stay in Italy until her divorce was final, she told the interviewer. She would never stop fighting for custody of her daughter.

It was the author's last paragraph that stopped us cold. "I talked with her alone, seated by the charred ruins of an old house on the mountain of Stromboli," he intoned, "as a cloud of sulphur fumes hung over the crater of the volcano."

We closed the magazine. No need to comment on the image of Ingrid Bergman sitting in a cloud of sulphur fumes, teetering on the edge of a bigger crater than any on Stromboli.

"Somebody has to help her," I said.

"To do what?"

I couldn't swim in these waters. "The right thing," I said.

"Whatever *that* is," said my pragmatic friend with a small chuckle.

Christmas was coming, though in Los Angeles you pretty much had to guess the season from store display windows. Either that, or by noting the Salvation Army people jingling bells and smiling every time someone dropped a dime or a nickel into their pots.

Philip and I were an "item" now, in movie language. We saw a lot of films together, necking in the dark. My mother liked him very much, especially after hearing that this handsome captain of the Thomas Aquinas basketball team led his teammates in prayer before every game. On one knee, I told her. We were very proud of him.

Philip and I perused college catalogs together, mostly the ones that interested him. I started knitting him a pair of socks. It was a badge of prestige at school to be knitting your boyfriend's socks, whipping away, with little spools of different colors dangling from your needles.

Truth was, we were preparing for the usual — maybe a year or two of college, but then marriage, the sooner the better. The unspoken challenge was staying a virgin until Philip slipped a wedding band on my finger. After his first year of college, of course.

Come Christmas Eve, as usual, we had our tree up, Bing Crosby was crooning "Silent Night" and "Adeste Fideles" on the radio, and Mother and I were making Christmas cookies, baked ones this time. Everything was exactly as it always was — including the fact that the studio Christmas party was "running late," as my father put it in his usual nine o'clock phone call home. Mother reminded him that Father Nolton would close the confessional at Saint Ambrose in an hour, and he had promised to make it this year, so we could all three take communion together on Christmas Day. Her voice was tensing up. She told him that I had held off going to confession earlier, that I was waiting to go with him; it was a father-daughter thing. Truth was, I let myself be a bargaining chip in hopes of making this annual scenario play out better.

We waited. Nine-thirty. Mother sat now, hands folded, staring at the clock, and I was mad at both of them. I knew exactly what would happen. He would screech into the driveway at nine-forty-five and yell for me to jump in the car, and off we would go, down the hill to Saint Ambrose. He would be drunk, and I would cross my fingers, hoping that if we crashed it would be on the way back, after the priest's absolution.

What kept them together? My mother, with her delicate features and huge eyes, was beautiful; any man would have been drawn to her. I had felt their warm and sensual attachment to each other from the beginning, without words to describe it. My father would watch my mother working in the kitchen, joking and conversing, his eyes traveling over her skin, from the nape of her neck to her slender hands as she ladled onto our plates Friday night's macaroni and cheese. But their rhythms, their personalities, their beliefs — when they fought, I felt like loose electric wires were snaking and buzzing in the air. My job was to dodge them.

"Jesse, get a move on it!" Brakes screeching right on schedule; I grabbed my jacket and ran for the car. "Good girl," Father said with a grin.

I gripped my seat on our wild ride to the church, trying not to watch the road. What was the use of trying to understand my parents? I couldn't figure myself out. It was probably natural that the product of two such confusing people was doomed to be a jumble of contradictions. Maybe that wasn't all bad. I thought of all the roles Ingrid had played, how her essential self always shone through. Even thinking about her was calming.

"Does Ingrid usually come to the Christmas party?" I asked as we skidded into a space in the empty parking lot.

"She did last year," he said. "She's still in Italy. In the dumps about *Joan of Arc,* probably. And *Under Capricorn.* Two bombs in a row."

I felt a familiar thump in my heart. How anyone could have watched *Joan of Arc* and not been transported, I did not know. There was such purity in Saint Joan's face as she looked up to heaven and vowed her dedication to God. No one but Ingrid could have made Joan so believable, so transcending. She made me determined to be good. Well — anything short of renouncing Philip.

"I don't see how anybody couldn't love her movies," I said.

He gave me a loose smile. "Her publicist thanks you."

It dawned on me then that maybe he wasn't going to tell me what was going on unless I asked straight-out. Anything bad for her was bad for him, and that meant for our family, and I was suddenly nervous. I pointed to the cigarette held tight between his teeth. "You can't take that into church."

"You sound like your mother." He pressed the cigarette into the ashtray. Unexpectedly, he put an arm around my shoulder, and pointed to the glittering lights of the city below the sloping hill on which we were parked. "Saint Ann's makes everything simple, right? Just follow the rules and everything adds up," he said.

"Pretty much." I hesitated, and went ahead. "What's happening with Ingrid? Is she really in love with Roberto Rossellini?"

"Jesse . . ." He seemed to be debating

186

what to say. "She's moved on."

"You mean to the island of Stromboli?"

"You read that carefully planted story in *Photoplay*?"

"Yes."

"Did it make you sympathetic?"

"Yes." I swallowed. I might not say that to Sister Teresa Mary, but I could say it to my father.

"Good. That was the plan." He stepped out of the car and waited on the path for me to join him. Even under the weak beam of the parking-lot streetlight, I could see the newly worn creases in his face.

"Is Stromboli as — as dangerous as it sounded?" I asked.

"Depends on whether Rossellini's movie is any good. But, yep, it's a crummy little island with an active volcano that just might cause plenty of trouble." He glanced at his watch. "Now run for it — let's get in there before they close up."

We made it. Last ones in the confessional. Stromboli.

Later in the night, drifting off to sleep, home sin-free and alive, I realized I didn't like the name of the place. It came out like a hollow croak, not the romantic name of a romantic island. Or maybe it was just the way my father said it, inhaling his cigarette, then spitting the island's name out like a piece of indigestible meat.

Mother stood pale in the doorway when I walked in the house the day after Christmas. I could see my father's figure in the kitchen, back turned to me, hunched over the telephone on the kitchen counter, talking in low, tense monosyllables.

"They're sending him there," Mother said, looking shell-shocked. "He came home half an hour ago, after they told him to pack his bags for Italy.

"He wants to talk to you, Jesse. Now, please be calm —"

We both jumped at the sound of his slamming down the phone.

I brushed by her, not listening anymore.

"Jesse, come sit down."

He didn't sound like himself. I moved into the kitchen and sat across from him; he looked very tired. So many times over the last few years, we had sat across from each other like this — me struggling with homework; Father explaining equations and advanced math, helping me with my history homework, shaping explanations so things made sense. I still believed he was the smartest man in the world.

"You've got the picture, don't you, Jesse?"

"I think so."

"Events may be moving too fast."

I wasn't sure what that meant. But I nodded.

"What do you think? Is she still your hero?"

"I . . ." How did I answer this? "Hero" sounded suddenly like a child's word. Was it wrong still to admire her? She had looked happy in the photographs in *Photoplay*. She wasn't some fallen woman, I told myself. But I was still thrown.

He smiled with a touch of melancholy. "You're not sure," he said. "How would you feel if she admitted she was wrong and came home to her husband and child? Would you forgive her?"

"I would feel much better," I said.

"So you see why the studio is sending me over there?"

I saw. But how was he going to convince her to come back? "How will you do it?" I asked.

"I'll reason with her," he said. He stood, obviously unable to sit still, and began pacing. His forehead was damp with sweat. "I'll tell her what she is throwing away — a career, lots of money. What do you think?"

He was asking what I *thought*.

"That's not enough," I ventured. "Maybe

tell her what a hero she is to so many people, and so many young girls like me. Tell her we are shaping ourselves around who she is —"

"It's too big. It isn't tangible."

"If I could only talk to her, I could tell her . . ." I hesitated, realizing my father had stopped pacing.

"Take me with you," I blurted. "I could help."

"Jesse, I can't do that."

"Why not?" I was stuttering with excitement now. It made perfect sense — I was my father's true ally, I could see that now. We thought alike, we shared the same ideas, we could be a team on this —

"No," Mother said, her alarmed voice cutting through the air. "This is not something a girl your age can be asked to do."

Father whipped around, and answered just as sharply. Just this one coil of resistance brought it out of him. "Ingrid likes Jesse," he said. "Maybe she's a good reminder of what it means to be put on a pedestal, a reminder of all the people, young and old, in this country who admire and respect her. It might even sharpen her loneliness for her own daughter —"

"What about Pia? Her daughter? Surely, if anyone could change Ingrid's mind, wouldn't it be Pia?" Mother was clutching the door frame as if to anchor herself against a vanquishing wind.

He shook his head. "Lindström won't let Pia go see her."

"That's awful," I said. "She must be so lonely. How could a father be so cold?"

"They've wrapped that stupid movie on Stromboli. We'll only be there for a few days."

"This is crazy," Mother said. "This is *your* job, not your daughter's."

"The studio will do anything I want if it brings that woman back where she belongs." He turned to me, ignoring Mother, his eyes lit with fierce energy. "You've got a good brain, Jesse. You up for this?"

"Absolutely."

"Sorry to mess up your Christmas vacation."

"Oh no, I don't care, this is wonderful." He had dealt me in and I was dizzy with triumph. Yes, we were partners in this, and if Mother didn't like it, too bad. *She* would be too timid to try something bold. But Kathleen would be impressed, I was sure of that. I might take the rules too literally, but I was *not* timid.

Father shifted his attention back to Mother, whose face seemed shaped of clay.

"Vannie, the knives are sharpening here — and a lot of people will lose their jobs if she stays with Rossellini," he said. He paused a beat. "Maybe even me. Please understand."

She then said the strangest thing: "I'm losing her," she whispered. "To you."

We stared at each other. Mother stood silently behind me, saying nothing. From the living room, the sound of Bing Crosby's voice filled the air, and I knew the tree in the bay window glowed with blue lights, just as it always did. This year, we had piled on a ton of tinsel, and I had only broken one shiny Christmas ornament. Just like usual. Everything was the same.

But not really.

CHAPTER TEN

Los Angeles / Stromboli — 1949
Somewhere around eight o'clock that night, a black studio limo slipped silkily into our driveway. The driver stayed in the car, never turning off the engine, as my parents and I — we'd been waiting on the porch steps — opened the door and climbed in. I remember clutching my mother's smallest Samsonite suitcase tight, running through a checklist of its contents in my mind — an extra skirt, a heavy sweater, a fresh bra — then wondering in a wave of panic if I had brought any Kotex. My period might start early, you never knew, and here we were, already driving at high speed to the airport.

"Mother —" I whispered.

She squeezed my hand. I could feel the skin pulled taut over her delicate bones. "I put some in," she said. "But don't worry, they have drugstores in Italy."

I could tell she was having one of her

headaches, but she insisted on coming to the airport to see us off, which relieved me. The idea of this dizzying trip was suddenly overwhelming.

"Bringing Jesse is ridiculous; you're pulling her into a crazy world and a crazy situation," Mother had protested.

"It's the world that pays for her fancy convent education," my father retorted.

How did this bizarre trip make sense? The truth of it? My father was willing to try anything in one desperate attempt to snatch Ingrid Bergman away from Roberto Rossellini and tuck her back into the heart of an adoring American public. Why? Because he knew that if he didn't get her back she would be eaten alive by that same "adoring" American public. I saw his urgency, and, in my mother's eyes, the growing realization of what was at stake for us. If Ingrid Bergman lost her following, my father would lose his most famous and lucrative client.

Our plane, a fat-bodied silver Pan Am Constellation, sat at the gate, looking very strong and safe, as we said goodbye to Mother and climbed the stairs. A smiling stewardess in navy blue and high heels stood waiting to greet us, pressing postcards with glossy pictures of the plane into our hands.

"To share your trip with your friends," she murmured.

On the tarmac below us, a small group of well-dressed men and women clustered together, grinning, hands over each other's shoulders, as a second stewardess took their photograph. Everybody seemed to be on holiday, but one look at my father's face told me not to treat this as anything other than the dead-serious trip that it really was.

I glanced back just before entering the plane and saw Mother at the gate. Feeling suddenly guilty that she wasn't along for this splendid adventure, I waved. She smiled and blew me a kiss, a gesture that brought to mind the way she had blown soap bubbles into the air to delight me when I was a child. I blew an awkward kiss back, then took my seat and waited for the enormous engines to roar into life and lift us out of all that was familiar.

It wasn't my first flight, and I was a bit out of sorts when the stewardess thought it was, but dinner was elegant — baked lobster served on white china, with crystal glassware for my Coke. Father never stopped smoking, but no one else did, either. Within a few hours, a pale haze hung over the cabin. Maybe it was to get the sting out of my eyes, or maybe it was because of the thunderous vibration of the Constellation's engines, but after the first four or five hours, I fell asleep, not even awakening when we refueled.

A pair of narrow-eyed men in open-necked shirts — one of them wearing a gold necklace — greeted us at Fiumicino Airport. Industry representatives, my father said quickly when I asked who they were as they strode ahead of us out of the terminal. He looked furious.

"Where are they taking us?"

"A quick plane to Naples, then the ferry to that damn island. Rossellini took her back to Stromboli for some kind of cast party. If he thinks we're not following, he's crazy. We're going straight from that airport to the harbor, and straight to a boat that takes us to the fucking island."

He didn't apologize for his language, which made me feel both worldly and daunted at the same time. I looked at him quickly. He needed a shave.

I barely remember the second plane to Naples. But then came a terrifying ride through the narrow, twisting streets of the city to the harbor, skidding past vendors, dodging traffic cops in white helmets who were standing tall on platforms and pirouetting, their commanding arms held high, their bodies as taut as orchestra conductors'. Our escorts ignored them. I gripped the door handle, disappointed that I wouldn't see Rome, at least get a glimpse of the Vatican before we ended up in flames somewhere.

Finally, we were at the harbor. I held tight to my bag as we climbed on board and hoped I wouldn't be seasick. I wasn't. But my period did start shortly after we lifted anchor and headed out onto the Tyrrhenian Sea. And I tried not to cry, because I knew, without asking, that there were no drugstores on the island of Stromboli.

And there it was, straight ahead, the island of Stromboli, a strangely black patch of earth dominated by a mountain — not just a mountain, a huge, looming volcano. I hadn't quite absorbed the fact of the volcano before. But it was real, a monster of a thing, which even now — sending a jolt of fear through me — belched out lazy blobs of lava onto the crater rim.

"Don't worry," the boat captain said, his genial Italian accent doing nothing to break the unsettling imagery. "There hasn't been a major eruption since 1930; nothing to fear."

"Why is the land so dark?" I asked.

"That's the ash from the last eruption. It left the beaches and rocks — nothing much else here — as black as sin."

I shifted uneasily, wishing my father would break away from what seemed like a tense argument with those studio representatives, whoever they were, and come stand by me while we docked. I stared at the black land and wondered, How could Ingrid Bergman, my adored Ingrid, be here, on this desolate island, and what was I supposed to do?

And where could I get some Kotex?

A small knot of Italians with set faces waited on the dock. They reached for our bags, exchanged some cryptic words with Father, and beckoned us to follow them up a path to a long shed-like building covered in metal shingles that flapped nosily with each puff of wind. It sat precariously on the side of the mountain, looking ready to fall down at any moment.

"There he is, the bastard," Father muttered to me.

I could see a figure in the doorway. We were almost there when, suddenly, the sun came from behind the clouds and I could make out quite clearly the restless, handsome face of the balding man straddling the entrance. His features were sharply defined, his skin was tanned, and his lips curled in a lazy smile. Hands at his hips, elbows out. My first impression wasn't of these details, though — it was of the *energy* he exuded. It didn't pour out of him, it *exploded.*

My father's face turned calm and calculating. "Here we go," he said.

This, I knew without asking, was Roberto Rossellini.

"You do realize you're too late," the man said in English as we approached the doorway. His accent caressed the language in a way that gave me a delightful shiver.

"Too late?" My father raised an eyebrow.

"To watch any of the filming of *Stromboli* — isn't that why you are here?" Rossellini said. He sighed theatrically. "What a long way to come just for that, but you Americans are always in a hurry. We wrapped a few days ago; nothing to worry about — it's brilliant! Come, we celebrate. Have some good Italian wine." Stepping aside, he welcomed us in.

The smoky room was crowded with what looked less like a typical movie crowd of cameramen, producers, and actors than a gathering of village people: the men in shabby pants with drawstrings; the women in peasant dresses and kerchiefs. I remembered my father talking about Rossellini's quirky ways of using local people, not professional actors, for his movies.

And then I saw a flash of red. It was Ingrid, in the same skirt she had worn in the *Photoplay* pictures, smiling and waving and looking very happy.

My father saw her at the same time. Without a word, as Rossellini turned aside to trade a joke with an island shopkeeper, Father moved swiftly over to Ingrid, leaving me alone.

"Gabriel," she sang out teasingly, spotting him. "Welcome, my dear. Are you here as a friend or an avenging angel?"

I couldn't hear his reply. When the two of them had vanished through a back door, I glanced swiftly at Rossellini. He looked in their direction, but was seemingly unconcerned as he poured himself a glass of wine.

I desperately wanted to sleep. But mostly I needed a bathroom.

"Toilet?" murmured an elderly woman, watching me sympathetically.

I nodded, clutching my valise with its urgent contents.

I was never more grateful for my mother than when I was able to close the door of an outside privy and fish out the sanitary napkin that would save me from humiliation and total despair.

That's when I heard my father's voice. I couldn't hear the words, but the tension and anger in them shocked me. Who was he talking to? Was he still with Ingrid?

When I came out, he was waiting, hands jammed in his jacket pockets, his face almost ashen.

"What happened?" I asked.

"I think it's over. Dead. Jesus, this is bad." He pulled a handkerchief from his pocket and wiped his brow. His hand was trembling.

I was frightened. He never talked like this. "What do you mean?"

"She says she won't come back. She's besotted with this guy, and once the news gets out, she's finished. There's no saving her from herself."

"Where is she?" I asked.

He pointed up the hill, his voice cracking now. "With that witch hunt going on at home, and now this . . ."

I think he had almost forgotten I was there. What could I do? I squinted against the sun, looked up the hill, and saw a flash of red. Yes, it was Ingrid, all alone, settling herself on a rock.

My father glanced over to the nearby dock. "Get some lunch in the lodge, Jesse. Grab a sandwich — that bastard Rossellini owes us that much." He took a deep breath, visibly strengthening himself. "I'll try to reason with her one more time. Maybe I can get Rossellini to understand what she's throwing away." He paused, staring out over the water. "I'll tell the captain to stick around for a while." He strode quickly toward the anchored boat, which bobbed up and down in a restless sea.

I started to obey, staring after him, my heart thumping hard. This was my father, the strong, confident man who provided the sunlight in my life. But, no, it wasn't — this was someone else, a frightened man. I could feel his fear closing in, claiming us both.

Pivoting, I stared up at Ingrid. A surge of reckless confidence swept over me. Maybe I could help. I turned back and ran up the hill.

She sat on a smooth rock, red skirt spread around her, a slight breeze ruffling her hair, knitting. She welcomed me with a faint smile. "Hello, Jesse; I saw you at the lodge door with your father. Are you still studying Shakespeare?"

She remembered. "Nobody can bring Portia alive the way you did," I said.

"Thank you. But you didn't come all this way to tell me that. I'm sorry you and your father made the trip for nothing." Her fingers were almost a blur as she swiftly worked her needles.

What could I say? What was I supposed to do?

"I knit now, too," I offered. "I'm knitting a pair of socks for my boyfriend."

"My, you're old enough for a boyfriend already?"

"He goes to Saint Aquinas. He's captain of the school basketball team." What was I babbling about? How could I help my father?

Ingrid stopped knitting and slowly let her hands rest in her lap.

"I know why you're here," she said.

I had to do something. "Miss Bergman, you've been my hero most of my life. You mean so much, I've learned so much from you —"

"What have you learned?"

"About grace and kindness; about love and nobility and being brave —"

"And you wouldn't know about any of those virtues without the 'me' you've seen on the movie screen?"

"You are a big part of it. You came to my school, you made us proud; you were a perfect, holy nun. Everybody loves you."

She sighed. "Oh, Jesse. I am no saint, I am an ordinary woman. Don't ask too much of your heroes."

I didn't know what to say. So I blurted out what was left inside my head and heart. "Please come back," I begged. "It's sad that your marriage is ending, but people will forgive you. Please, we need you."

"No, no." She jumped to her feet, suddenly impatient. "Don't you people realize what you are doing? You are asking me to fulfill *your* fantasies, and I can't do that! I'm not some nun or saint, I'm living my *own* life, not yours!"

You people? I was stunned. Who was this? Her face was flushed; her hands were clenched. I couldn't muster a word. Her knitting fell to the ground.

She reached down to pick it up. "Have you noticed what I'm knitting, Jesse?"

I peered closely. I was staring at a tiny garment, like a sweater, all in blue. A sweater. A baby sweater.

I looked up into her eyes, horrified. Surely not.

"Yes, that's what it is," she said in answer to my unasked question. "Tell your father I meant it — his entreaties come too late. Now, go. Leave me alone, all of you." She raised a protective hand, letting it hover over the visible swell of her stomach.

We stared at each other across a vast terrain of experience. Girls got caught, I knew that. We would giggle and count on our fingers when a girl dropped out of school and disappeared, or, at best, married quickly at a Low Mass in the usual white veil and dress, with only parents attending. This was different. A baby, in public, out of wedlock? This was taking a route with no way back. Not Ingrid Bergman. But, yes, it was, and I was having my first glimmer of the fact that absolutes are tricky in the real world. There was no impenetrable mortar holding them in place, no mechanism to define the good and discard the bad, nothing guaranteed to hold beliefs and values firmly in place.

"I still admire you," I managed.

"I imagine that's hard for you to say at this point."

"No. Not really. I — I don't know." I was struggling to absorb what was happening.

"For heaven's sake, just enjoy my movies and be done with it," she said. She pushed back her hair, her eyes sad.

There was nothing else I could think to say, and I backed off, fighting tears.

"Jesse, we probably won't see each other again," she continued. "But be assured, I am happy. I am doing what I want to do and living the life I want to live, and if Sister

Mary Benedict would be horrified, I don't care."

The face of the suffering nun in *The Bells of St. Mary's,* lifted in prayer, asking God to give her strength to accept her banishment from the school she loved, suddenly filled my brain. Would she condemn Ingrid?

"No, she wouldn't," I blurted.

But she wasn't listening anymore.

CHAPTER ELEVEN

Stromboli / Los Angeles — 1949–50

Someone handed me a plate of ravioli back at the lodge, but I had no appetite. I was numbly waiting now for my father to acknowledge defeat so we could leave. I went out on the steps, sat down, and watched the light darkening over this brooding island as the hours passed. What a raw, harsh-looking place it was. It promised nothing, I could see that. Why couldn't Ingrid?

I saw him finally, standing on the path going up the hill, this time with both Ingrid and Rossellini. I couldn't hear their conversation, but when I saw Rossellini offer a handshake and my father turn his back on the film director, I knew we would be leaving soon.

We met at the bottom of the hill. With all my heart, I had hoped in my fantasies to be the one who saved Ingrid, whose plea to the actress would solve everything and make my father happy and jovial again. But she was pregnant, and that meant it was all over, because only a quick marriage solved *that* problem, and clearly she couldn't get married. I wanted to cry. All my parsing out of what did and did not constitute a mortal sin was of no help to me now.

I reached him and stood silently.

"So — you know she's pregnant, right?"

I nodded.

"I told her that kind of thing could be taken care of, but now it's too late for that." Said briskly, flatly. "She's too dazzled by the Italian anyway."

This was my father talking. Abortion. He meant abortion.

"Daddy . . ." I hadn't called him Daddy since I was a very little girl.

He blinked, as if suddenly aware of who I was. "Never mind," he said. He gestured toward the dock, where a deeply tanned Italian seaman was tossing our bags back into the boat. "We're heading home," he said.

I stepped onto the boat and looked back. Ingrid and Rossellini were still standing together on the hill, his arm around her shoulders, two people proclaiming their love. If this were the ending to a movie, it would be a happy one. These two, standing framed against a still-blue sky, ready, surely, for the cameras . . .

I blinked. This was real life.

What were we doing here? And what exactly was my father's job now?

"Let's go," he barked at the captain. The engine sputtered, then caught, and we were on our way. I stared back at the island as long as I could, watching the figures of Ingrid and her lover grow smaller and smaller and finally disappear.

My father was on the phone nonstop at the Rome airport. I curled up into a ball, my jacket over me, and tried to doze in an airport chair, hearing snatches of the conversations. Did he really call Ingrid an ungrateful bitch? No, he couldn't have. I heard him say the studio had to ram *Stromboli* out into the theaters and keep news of Bergman's pregnancy quiet for as long as possible. He talked and he talked and he talked, and his words began sticking to my dreams, like flies caught in a gossamer web. "This is in confidence," I heard him say to one of the most powerful studio heads in Hollywood. "I need your help. Move fast, we'll get the publicity ready — smoldering love, tragic love, whatever. I've got a team working on it already."

Then, once again, he noticed me. What did I want, or need, from him? I didn't know, except that I wanted my jaunty, loving father back.

We were almost home, long hours later. I was coughing; I must have caught a cold. We broke through the low haze of clouds and finally, not a miserable moment too soon, I was peering down on the welcome sight of Los Angeles International Airport.

"Ah, shit," my father muttered. He looked past me, down to the fast-approaching ground. I didn't have to ask. Below us, dozens of small figures — jostling and elbowing and pointing to our plane — were trying to surge out onto the landing strip; a line of blue-uniformed policemen held them back. Our wheels touched the tarmac. I saw now big cardboard signs hoisted by men in clerical collars, by nuns in black habits, by housewives and kids like me, denouncing Ingrid Bergman as immoral, a sinner, a shameful blot on America. . . .

"Commie!" "Go back to where you came from!" "Whore!" The shouts from outside spiraled into a caterwauling that grew louder and louder as we approached the gate.

"Jesus, they think she's on the plane,"

Father muttered. "If she was, they'd stone her."

I learned later that it was Howard Hughes, the powerful Howard Hughes, who — after promising my father not to tell anyone — had gone ahead and tipped off Louella Parsons, figuring that news of the baby would *improve* chances that *Stromboli* could become a hit. That it would destroy her career and destroy the jobs of dozens of people apparently didn't enter his mind.

I was crying now, crying hard. "I want to go home, please, right away." I said it through uncontrollable tears.

I had to hide in the backseat of a waiting limo, doors locked, while my father talked to the press. I couldn't hear all his words, but he was indignant, and at first I thought he was denouncing the attacks, and then I realized — with mounting shock — that he was vilifying *Ingrid,* complaining of how unreliable she was, of how she didn't care about letting her fans down. I covered my ears.

"You shouldn't have taken Jesse," Mother said angrily, grabbing my hand as I staggered, still crying, into the house.

"I didn't think it would turn out this way," Father said. "That damn actress —"

"I listened to you on the radio, denouncing her, from the airport," Mother interrupted. I had never heard this tone in her voice before. "How could you? How could you turn her into some kind of witch?"

My father paled. "Vannie —"

"What's happened to you, Gabriel? Is that what you think — just toss her and her reputation in the garbage? Is that where you are now? What's her sin, Gabriel? Loving a man?"

I was open-mouthed: this was my pious, religious mother? Father stared at her, voiceless. Some shared, bewildering pain was passing between them.

"This has all gotten too emotional," he managed. He turned on his heel, muttered something, and went back out the door, closing it behind him.

I ran for the shelter of my room.

Funny, how a single moment can get glued into your brain. This one was immediately in mine, laced into a noxious package with church and glamour and black islands and the infernal, nonstop, false sunshine of L.A.

Morning came early and harsh. I woke up and made it first to the front door to scoop up the papers. The *Los Angeles Examiner* blared the news I dreaded in a two-inch headline:

BERGMAN LOVE CHILD REVEALED

There was little else but moral outrage on the front page. It poured out, blistering the air. If I put out my tongue, I would taste acid, I was sure of it.

Down just below the fold, the National Legion of Decency proclaimed its horror and indignation; next to that was an interview with Bishop Francis Doyle. It was clear he relished the invitation to condemn, and he lost no time. "This sinful woman has tricked us all," he declared. An editorial from the Boston *Pilot* was reprinted inside: "The Devil himself is at work," it proclaimed. Ingrid Bergman had "openly and brazenly flouted the laws of God."

I now had more than a glimmer of what all this said about people who felt betrayed. America loved Ingrid; ordinary Americans adored her, and she was a protective coating for the movie industry. Yank that protection away, and the wolves, betrayed, dived in.

Mother sat alone at the breakfast table the next morning, hunched forward, her soft pink robe indifferently tied. Her hand kept going to her forehead. I figured she would be back in bed five minutes after I left the house. My stomach twisted — there was nothing I could do about that.

But she had a glass of orange juice waiting for me, with a chocolate doughnut next to it on a plate. A crisp linen napkin was tucked under the coffee spoon. She straightened, obviously trying to pull herself together. Her voice was steady. "You were tired last night, Jesse. So were we. I do want to assure you everything is fine. We've all had a hard week here."

Her words sounded all sanitized and tidied up, a thought that never would have occurred to me before. They offered only one pathway for a response. "I guess so," I said.

"I overreacted last night," she pressed on. "Your father is a good man. He's scared right now. He doesn't know what's going to happen at the studio, and he has to lash out at *something*. We should be understanding."

I wasn't ready for compassion for anybody. "Yes, ma'am."

The new school term began two days later. Walking back into the embracing, safe, comfortable world of Saint Ann's Academy turned my legs to jelly, because the school I counted on wasn't embracing — it wasn't safe. Small clusters of girls huddled together, glancing over their shoulders as I walked down the path to the main square, where my first class was to be held. Nobody smiled; they all just looked away. After all, they knew my father was responsible for embarrassing the school by linking it to a scandalous Hollywood actress. Saint Ann's had been put under the spotlight by Louella Parsons and disapprovingly mentioned in *The Tidings,* our diocesan newspaper. A chill circled my neck, cold and clammy.

Kathleen was waiting outside the classroom. She looked up as I walked in her direction and said, quite calmly, "Jesse, you are not Hester Prynne."

"What do you mean?"

"You haven't done anything. Stand up straighter."

The worst part was, nobody said a word. Even Sister Teresa Mary, who stood by the chapel door in her usual militant mode, eyeing us as we gathered for Mass, didn't seem to notice I had forgotten to cover my head. That should have meant ten demerits at least. I had expected indignation, sorrow, anger — something from her. What was this?

The priest stood facing us all as we shuffled into our pews, his visage stern. Sister Teresa Mary walked slowly up the aisle and stood before him, cheeks flushed, head bowed. She looked oddly frail. She genuflected slowly, whispered something inaudible, then rose from her knees and backed into her usual place in the front pew.

The priest cleared his throat. "We will now pray to Almighty God to forgive Sister Teresa Mary," he said, then turned and began to celebrate Mass.

Forgiveness? How could I have been so stupid? Sister Teresa Mary was being officially *shamed* because Saint Ann's had been shamed. Well, of course, we had all claimed an immoral actress as one of our own. Bishop Doyle couldn't let *that* go unpunished; the way to keep scandal from the archdiocese was to divert its consequences firmly somewhere else. And that "somewhere else" was my school. By lauding a sinful actress, we — all of us at Saint Ann's — had collectively committed the sin of pride.

That's a great catchall sin, the sin of pride.

I lowered my head, ostensibly in prayer, digging my fingernails into the palms of my hands, shaking with anger.

"Your palm is bleeding," Kathleen whispered, nudging me.

"I don't care."

Later, on impulse, I walked past the site of the plaque marking Saint Ann's as the historic location for the filming of *The Bells of St. Mary's*. There was now just a raw hole. What had I expected? The plaque was yanked from the ground, tossed away somewhere. I wasn't surprised; should I be?

Miss Coultrane was sitting alone at her desk when I reached her classroom. By that time of day, the burden of collective guilt, reinforced in class after class, weighed on me like a cloak of cement.

"A hard day, I'm sure," Miss Coultrane said, looking at me from over the glasses that always seemed to rest on her imperious nose.

"Where is everybody?" I said, gazing around.

"I canceled class so you and I could work on your debate prep," she said. "You've qualified for state finals, and you can win if you work hard, Jesse."

"Who would want me now?" I said.

"Jesse . . ." She sighed, hesitated, then continued. "You know I'm not a Catholic, but I've worked for the nuns for twenty years; heaven knows why. They are fine people, on the whole. But this anguishing over Ingrid Bergman is ridiculous. She's an excellent actress, that's all I care about. The rest is her business. And your job is preparing for that tournament."

I felt myself draw up straight. Miss Coultrane, with a few crisp words, had toughened my spine.

At home, life lurched on, strangely calm, for the next couple of weeks. I reluctantly competed in one tournament on the south side of the city that was lightweight stuff: did President Truman harm or help his daughter Margaret's career when he denounced a music critic who said she couldn't sing? I argued (even though everybody knew the critic was right) that the resultant publicity gave her a bigger audience than she otherwise would ever have had. But Miss Coultrane told me not to sneer at any debating opportunity; I would be facing very smart opponents in the state finals, and I needed to use every opening to think fast on my feet.

I gave her my college applications for Stanford and Bennington and asked for a letter of recommendation. She looked at me rather piercingly over her glasses. "Have you asked Sister Teresa Mary?" she asked.

"No."

"Why not?"

"Because she wouldn't give me one unless I applied to a Catholic school."

Miss Coultrane turned to her desk, picked up a pen, and scribbled something. "Here," she said. "Fill out an application for this college and I'll write recommendations for all of them."

I gazed down at the piece of paper she handed me. "Marymount College in Tarrytown, New York?" A Catholic *women's* college.

"Is that far enough away?"

I took a deep, liberated breath. "Yes, I guess so," I said.

She gave me a starchy smile. "Good. I went there myself. A fine school, even if you do end up at Stanford."

"But you're not a Catholic."

"The grandfather who paid the bills was."

Both of my parents made efforts to talk to me during those shaky days, and I would have none of it. They didn't press. But I listened to everything they said to each other.

The studio, the whole film industry, had to back away from Ingrid, Father argued. Did Mother understand the gravity of the situation? Foreign markets were drying up, television was taking over, and the bishops riding *this* train were now fully energized for renewed attacks on "immorality" that could bring the industry to its knees. Did she understand?

"She's not a whore. She's not a bitch," Mother said firmly.

"I know. She is not."

"Don't ever call her that again."

"I won't. Vannie, I love you."

And on that surrender, they made a shaky peace. But Mother seemed to pull back into herself even more after that. The fire she had displayed was gone.

There was more. I realized that one afternoon as I came into the kitchen after school and found my father, sitting at the table, head in hand, muttering urgently on the phone. "They're just fishing, Jerry," I heard him say. I knew who Jerry was — a short, cheery man who played poker with my father and wrote screenplays. "But try to think their way," my father continued. "You know, memos, letters that look bad . . ." He paused and turned. When he saw me peeking at him from around a corner, he muttered something into the phone and hung up.

"What's happening?" I asked.

"Just studio business."

"Is Jerry Feldstein a communist?" I couldn't help it — I blurted this out.

He stared at me. "Where did you hear that? Were you listening to me just now?"

I tried to avoid a direct answer. "People are talking — I know about HUAC."

His lips compressed. "Yeah, there's a witch hunt on," he said. "People implicating neighbors, turning in friends — it's that senator from Wisconsin, trying to turn decent people into outcasts."

I thought of how the rumors going around were expanding; even movie stars were being talked about. An FBI report named actors Fredric March and Danny Kaye as suspected communists, claiming their criticism of America's growing nuclear arsenal as evidence. But there were whispers about everybody — directors, screenwriters, gaffers.

"Were you ever a communist?" I asked, my voice wavering slightly.

He looked at me, studying my face. "Nope," he said. "But even people who have been aren't out to destroy democracy. Don't worry."

His face brightened. He jumped up, grabbing my hand, and said, "Hey, come into the living room, Jesse. Have I got a surprise for you." With a grand flourish, he pointed to a large television set occupying a corner of the room, the largest I had ever seen.

"Just came this afternoon. I suppose getting it is something like fraternizing with the enemy," he said, a bit shamefaced. "But what the heck, we deserve a little entertainment in this house, right?"

Mother walked into the room, looking bewildered. When he reached for her hand, too, I saw concern in his eyes. "Something to keep you awake with us, Vannie," he said gently.

It was a welcome diversion, that big box, and we began discovering things to watch that we all three liked — especially *The Ed Sullivan Show.* We sat each night staring at that magical screen. We were together, I thought. That was good, wasn't it? And we were also relieved of any need to expect anything from each other.

I didn't notice at first that I wasn't seeing much of Philip that winter. He came over once, but was in a hurry, and when I asked if anything was wrong, he said he couldn't afford to miss basketball practice and would see me later. I kept knitting his socks. Kathleen helped straighten out my stitching every few days, but sitting at lunchtime with my needles working and little bobbins of yarn swinging didn't seem quite so special now. It was beginning to feel too much like a chore.

RKO managed to release *Stromboli* in something of a mad scramble, Father reported, vainly hoping they could somehow capitalize on the Bergman-Rossellini romance. But it didn't help. Reviewers hated the movie, calling it "feeble, inarticulate, uninspiring and painfully banal." Their initial criticism was of the film, but when exhibitors wanted out of their commitment to running what they all saw now as a second-rate movie, the spotlight shifted. They argued that the work of an "immoral" woman like Ingrid Bergman should not be shown in the United States.

"She's barely hanging on," Father said over coffee one morning. "Well, I tried to warn her."

The phone rang. He stiffened.

"Jerry?" Mother whispered.

My father listened briefly, let out a curse, and hung up.

"Turn on the radio, Jesse," he said. His face was pale. "Keep twisting the dial until I tell you to stop."

I did as I was told, going from one station through blurred static to another. Suddenly

I heard a high, reedy voice — and the name "Ingrid Bergman."

"Stop there," Father commanded.

"Who is it?" I asked.

"Some righteous senator from Colorado condemning Ingrid on the floor of the U.S. Senate; this does it."

We stood there, all three, listening. It was hard — the signal was scratchy — but it was horrifying.

"Ingrid Bergman has perpetrated an assault on the institution of marriage," the impassioned voice proclaimed loudly. "She is a horrible example of womanhood *and,* I regret to say, a powerful influence for evil."

It was what came next that took my breath away. Yes, there was a punishment, something I could hardly believe.

"Under our law," the voice thundered out, "no alien guilty of turpitude can set foot on American soil. Mrs. Petter Lindström has deliberately exiled herself from a country which was so good to her."

A thunderous clapping could be heard. Indignation increasing, the senator roared out, "If, out of the degradation associated with Stromboli, decency and common sense can be established in Hollywood, then Ingrid Bergman will not have destroyed her career for naught. Out of her ashes may come a better Hollywood!"

My father grabbed the phone, turned his back, and dialed urgently.

"Her ashes?" I couldn't believe my ears. "Who is this?"

His conversation was brief. He turned back to us. "His name is Edwin Johnson. Just happens to be a good Catholic who hates the movie industry. Ingrid has given him an opening to force through a bill that would allow only people who prove their 'moral decency' to work in Hollywood."

"What's happening to this country?" Mother said. "They can bar her from the United States?"

"Looks like it," he said.

We didn't talk. What was there to say? I imagined fog squeezing its way in under the doors, lapping at the windows, swirling through the room. Obscuring everything.

How could so much vitriol be unleashed denouncing a Swedish actress whose one unforgivable "sin" was refusing to play in real life the role of a saint?

CHAPTER TWELVE

Los Angeles, 1950

There was no immediate disaster, no sudden cataclysmic event that changed our lives after that broadcast. My father was not fired or denounced, but our maid vanished. "We don't need her that much," Mother said when I asked one day why she, not Mandy, was ironing my school blouses. Both parents seemed finally drained of talk. They drew into themselves, each separate from the other. We continued, all three, to sit in front of the new television set and watch anything that was on. In silence.

I wanted them to ask me how things were at school, so I could practice my debate skills and slip in the fact that I just might be graduating with honors. I wanted to talk about Stanford and Bennington and Marymount and should I also apply to UCLA? I wanted to see my mother beam with pride and my father slap his knee and laugh and say, "Hey, wow, am I proud of you!"

I knew some of my father's worries, but Mother was a puzzle. She was more remote than ever. She slept later in the mornings, and fixed dinner silently; once in a while, I caught her gazing at my father with some unspoken question in her eyes.

She continued to come in to say good night, but then sat on my bed without speaking. I didn't know how to respond to that. Was something expected of me?

"Do you need to talk about anything?" she asked one evening.

I thumped my pillow and pulled up the covers, trying to sound confident. "That's okay, I'm fine," I said.

"Good night, then." She squeezed my hand and slipped out of the room.

I stared out the window by my bed, thinking of Mother, of God and school and Philip (why hadn't he called?), everything bunched together. I felt like we were all waiting for something.

"Jessica, when the class bell rings, come into my office for a moment." Sister Teresa Mary's black serge habit smelled faintly musty as she leaned over my desk in study hall. I felt caught in its shadow.

"Yes, Sister," I said, startled. What now? I

remember sending a beseeching glance in Kathleen's direction, but she just raised an eyebrow and shrugged her shoulders — her way of saying, You'll figure it out soon enough.

"Come in, Jessica."

I walked into Sister Teresa Mary's office, a very spartan place with a bookcase, two steel filing cabinets, and an old mahogany desk. A crucifix hung on the wall. I had only been in here a few times, once for some infraction back in seventh grade, and nothing seemed different. The desk, though, was buried in a clutter of forms and papers.

"College applications," she said, seeing my glance travel. "And our recommendations. Sit down, Jessica."

I knew it. She wasn't going to approve my applications.

"I'm glad you chose to apply to Marymount," she said, nodding at the nearest stack of paper. "A good school, though far away." She stopped and gazed at me. "Jessica, have you been happy here?"

Had I been? I had never framed the question. And I realized, astonished, for all my restlessness, I knew the answer. "Yes," I said.

"You've been a fine student in your high-school years; don't think I haven't noticed.

Even though you've been through some turmoil lately —"

Please, I prayed silently, don't denounce Ingrid; please.

"— it's not of your doing. I know things have been awkward the past few weeks, for us all." A flash of sadness in her eyes. "But I've decided" — she drew a deep breath — "you should not be penalized. Jessica, the faculty has discussed this. We want you to serve as valedictorian of your class."

"Me?" I gasped.

And then the stern, unbending visage of the principal of Saint Ann's Academy softened into what I had never seen before: a smile.

"Good luck in the Redlands Tournament," she said. "And don't worry about your applications; they're all going out."

I brought that piece of news home and announced it proudly at the dinner table.

"Fantastic," my father said, dropping his napkin. He stood so he could swoop me up from my chair, and gave me a hug so exuberant it took my breath away.

"Jessica, I am proud of you," Mother said, reaching out to me. Her eyes welled with tears.

It felt wonderful. Everything I had been holding back about all the good things, the exciting things that went with soon turning eighteen, rose like the best of surfing waves — exuberant, catching the wind and the light — and I rode it high.

We had a celebratory night. They even gave me one of their golden cocktails, and I thought, I am here, I am being noticed, I am happy, there could be no prouder moment. We were healing, I was sure of it.

The first thing I saw when I walked in from school a week later was my mother sitting at the dining-room table — pounding it with her fist, pulling at her hair, tearing pieces of paper in two, throwing them on the table, as her voice spiraled into a wail. "I knew it would happen," she said in a strangled, despairing voice.

I rushed to her, frightened. "Mother —"

"Look at these," she said, sobbing. "Read these dirty little notes, just read them." She shoved one into my hand.

I was shaking now, having a hard time focusing, but I smoothed the paper out. It looked like a letter, a letter written in bright-lavender ink with lavish curlicues and flourishes. I stared at it, held fast by three words. *My darling Gabriel* . . .

"You see? You see? What did I tell you?"

Tell me? What was she saying? She was

pulling at her hair again, so hard it frightened me. I picked up another piece of paper, then another. They were all to my father — how could that be? — imploring letters. I saw the word "divorce," and my brain at first scrambled in confusion. Then I put them down; tears were blurring the lines. I didn't need to read any more. I knew what "My darling Gabriel" meant: my father was having an affair.

I tried to release Mother's grip on a chunk of her hair, tried to soothe. "Please don't cry," I begged. I was sobbing now, too.

"It's been waiting to happen —"

Father suddenly burst through the front door and strode over to Mother. She pushed him away.

He gave me a quick glance. "Jesse, will you leave us, please?" he said. It wasn't a request.

I grabbed my books and headed for my bedroom, where I threw myself on the bed, unsure if I wanted to cover my head and hear nothing or stand by the door and listen. How many times had I strained to hear their private conversations, always dreading something?

"God is punishing me," I heard Mother wail.

"Vannie, I won't leave you." My father's voice.

She kept crying; I heard her chair scrape back, then a crash; maybe it fell over.

"Vannie, calm down," my father kept repeating. "I would never leave you." I heard him open the hall closet door. "Here, put on your coat, we'll go talk," he said.

The front door opened and closed; the house was silent. They had left. They had forgotten me.

I lay there for a long time, dozing intermittently, afraid to come out of my room. I didn't want to see those letters again.

It must have been hours later when my door opened and Father came in.

"Jesse, you need to know what's going on."

What was going on? I was no child. "I already do," I said.

"Let's take a walk."

We left the house and started walking up our winding road, in silence at first. There were no people out, no cars rushing by, no honking horns. My clothes felt clammy and rumpled from lying on the bed for so long. All I really wanted to do was take everything off, go back to bed, pull up the covers, and think of nothing. The memory of Mother's wailing made me tremble.

Father cleared his throat. "The first and most important thing I need to tell you is, your mother and I will be all right. The affair is over. She found those damn letters in an old briefcase. I thought I had destroyed them, but —"

"Maybe you didn't because you didn't want to." I spat it out; anger was replacing bewilderment.

"I told you, it was over months ago. Finished. I was a fool. She called me when she found the letters. I rushed home to tell her that."

"Why would she believe you? I saw what some of them said." I could hardly believe I was saying these things to my father.

He inhaled noticeably, a kind of scratchy sound, then yanked a cigarette from the pack in his breast pocket. He groped for a match, took his time lighting the cigarette. "It got out of hand for a while," he said.

I started to cry. "How could you do that to Mother? Why did she say it was her punishment?"

His face sagged; it looked goopy, like butter melting in the sun. We rounded the curve and walked slowly downhill. "It gets complicated; when you're older . . . But — Jesse — I'd give anything not to have hurt her."

I kicked at a broken tree branch, hard. I

was infuriated now. He was trying to excuse himself. The entire night felt smothering, like a pillow descending onto my head. I wanted to hurt something, before it hurt me.

"All right, if you need to have a reason, isn't it kind of out there? I've been feeling for a while that your mother and I don't care about the same things. Don't tell me you haven't noticed."

My fury was rising. Of course I had noticed. I felt like I had been noticing all of my life. "You're an adulterer, that's what you are."

"Look, those thunderous biblical words don't always work in real life."

"Well, they work for me." I started to cry.

His voice was tired; he was beyond seeking understanding. "These things happen to people, even people who love each other. And, crazy as it may sound to you, I love your mother, and I believe she loves me."

This was my father? I had always adored him. He was my escape into common sense, the one who saw the tyranny of clerical orations, the one I could count on to stay straight, earthy, and true. Didn't he see what he was excusing?

"If Ingrid is an awful person because she had an affair, and you had an affair, what . . ." I stopped, waiting until my voice might be steady.

"What does that make me, right? You want a better label than 'adulterer'?"

I nodded.

"I don't know, Jesse. I guess that's up to you." He unlocked the front door and stood aside, looking sadder than I could ever have imagined he could look. I wanted to turn around and march away, just stomp out and never come back. But where would I go?

I walked into the dining room. The table was pristine, empty of those letters written in purple ink. I looked around for Mother.

"She's gone to bed," Father told me. "She said she would talk with you tomorrow."

I don't know how I managed to sleep, but "tomorrow" did come. When I walked into the kitchen, there was Mother, apron on, briskly whipping up batter for corn muffins. I wanted to console her, to tell her I loved her, to try to find the right words that would help. "Mother —"

She turned to me, her chin firm and square. "Jesse, I wasn't thinking straight yesterday. Your father and I have worked it out."

Worked it out? "What do you mean?"

Her chin quivered slightly. "Nothing is going to change."

"What do you mean? What about what I heard you say —"

"There will be no divorce," she said firmly. "That is settled."

Her expression never changed. She didn't seem like Mother; she seemed different — oddly stronger, I thought, but not more accessible. If anything, she had retreated back into herself and was looking out, as if through a car window, at people passing by. People like my father.

That's when he walked into the kitchen.

I felt sick to my stomach sitting there, watching them stare at each other. They were exchanging some kind of message, something that would affect everything, I was sure. I wanted not to know what it was. I wanted to be a kid again, to believe in my parents. How did I fit in all of this?

Mother stood and, with a fluttery motion, patted my arm. "I think we've talked enough," she said. "I'll fix dinner. Corned beef hash tonight. Gabriel, one dropped egg or two?"

I looked at my father's confused expression and, for just an instant, I felt sorry for him. That night, I listened as hard as I could to the murmured rise and fall of their voices, understanding nothing. Would I ever have the whole picture? Deeper down, what I couldn't touch yet, was confusion. All my reliance on absolute values wouldn't help me now. I couldn't label the villain.

And why did Mother think she was being punished? What had she done?

Trying not to think about the sadness that now enveloped my family, I threw myself into preparing for the state tournament at Redlands. I gave it every waking moment, except when Kathleen and I huddled together on the tennis-court benches while I told her everything. She listened intently; she did more than listen, she *heard*. With Kathleen, I could cry and bang my fists and declare my parents hypocrites who were depriving me of my security and childhood and —

"You're really not being deprived of any of that," she broke in. "Your mother and father aren't any different than anyone else who makes mistakes."

"Mistakes? How about sins?"

"When did you expect them to be perfect? Didn't you know they weren't?"

"I knew they fought."

"So, okay, now you know the details." She stretched out her legs and sighed. When she spoke again, her tone was subtly different.

"You're going to be surprised all your life by 'the details' unless you think about what it costs to never forgive anybody," she said.

I gazed at her. She was hunched over, the sleeves of her white tennis jacket pulled tight across her shoulders. She gave the illusion, even to me sometimes, of being wholly strong. I knew she was good at hiding her own pain — but there were times when she showed more.

"Kathleen," I said quietly, "are you saying you've forgiven your father?"

She didn't look up. "No," she said.

"Do you think you will ever be able to?"

She glanced sideways at me, a small smile on her lips. "Probably not. But I remember how lost he looked when you were talking with him at the fence. My mother isn't lost, and neither am I. So, not needing him — maybe that's a first step toward forgiveness."

I thought of Kathleen's brisk, ramrod-straight mother with her sunny smile, working the hosiery counter at the May Company. "You've got a brave mother," I said.

"We do all right," she said. "Even saving for college." She gave me a playful poke in the arm. "Don't look so down in the mouth," she teased. "We're both going to do okay."

And I halfway believed her. Kathleen, my

gritty, no-nonsense friend, tossing that brilliant red hair of hers, walking into every situation with the easy, loose gait of a born athlete. With her casual way of poking fun at authority, her acceptance of what was without raging and screaming, she was indeed brave. I hoped she would be my friend for life.

I've discovered, you only need one.

CHAPTER THIRTEEN

Los Angeles, 1950

Ingrid's baby was born on February 2, 1950, at the Villa Margherita Clinic in Rome. For the next two weeks, it seemed like the whole world had gone crazy.

The stories we heard were unbelievable. Hordes of reporters and photographers swarmed the tall iron gates of the clinic as soon as the news was out. Hospital workers, nuns, nurses, janitors — anyone with a scrap of information to offer was besieged. One reporter was even caught trying to climb a drainpipe to get to Ingrid's room. News crews tried every possible ruse to sneak in and get a view of this "love child" of the most notorious couple in the world — even as the nuns stood guard at the towering iron gates, swearing to all there was no one named "Ingrid Bergman" at the clinic. In Italy, the nuns were on Ingrid's side.

Letters poured in, hundreds of them — many denouncing Ingrid as a fallen woman, others congratulatory. The Italians were far more forgiving than the Americans, my father pointed out. They were proud that Ingrid had escaped from punitive America to their country — after the humiliations of World War II, her presence made Italy shine again. In the United States, it was clear Ingrid would remain tabloid fodder as long as her husband refused to give her a divorce: her child was gleefully labeled "the bastard son."

"It's getting more ink than the hydrogen bomb," Father muttered. His expression was still as he read every newspaper and every magazine — I hadn't seen his usual grin for a long time, which was hardly a surprise. And his face was almost gaunt; he was losing weight. We were back to playing roles, acting as if all was normal, even as other things crowded in.

Father wasn't talking much about his status at the studio, but I could tell he was in some sort of limbo. He had other publicity work to do, so I thought maybe studio executives were waiting to see how long it took for Ingrid's "scandalous adventures" to play out.

But there was more.

Kathleen and I were reading everything we could about the Red Scare. Everybody had to be careful. After Humphrey Bogart flew to D.C. to testify in defense of Hollywood liberals years ago, he had been forced by the studio to explain his actions in a *Photoplay* article headlined "I'm No Communist." I couldn't help feeling glad that my father hadn't volunteered his views. But it was strange, the mix of cowardice and bravery swirling around our town.

In an article titled "Let the Hollywood Record Speak," *Photoplay* tried to defend Hollywood with an editorial attacking Senator Johnson, now actively lobbying for his law to control Hollywood morals. They noted, proudly, that the divorce rate in the film industry was significantly lower than in the rest of the nation.

Modern Screen, which we always enjoyed for its gossipy take on the industry, was so nervous about readers pulling away amidst all the charges and whispers that they launched a series called "Why Stars Turn to Prayer." It was a big jump from covering Hollywood divorces. They did squeeze in the breakup of Gloria DeHaven and John

Payne, the lead star in *Miracle on 34th Street,* but noted that the only thing Payne took when he left the house was his Bible. Kathleen and I laughed about that.

Mother was drifting again, and I got used to tiptoeing to her bedroom after school and peeking in, though I knew what I would see — her lying there, a damp washcloth covering her eyes. "A headache again," she would whisper. I would retreat. She always managed to get up before Father came home. I watched him as he watched her, and I wondered, what did he see, what did he want to see?

I knew; I was sure. He wanted her to tell him all was forgiven and wrap her arms around him and laugh again. He probably thought it was enough that he had broken off his affair and that he was sorry. I imagined confronting him — getting angry, as Mother did not seem able to. Betrayal doesn't heal with a quick stitching up, I wanted to say. Maybe what he had done was one of the unforgivable sins.

Oh, righteous anger did feel good. It almost felt spiritual.

Mother. I had to stop myself from hovering protectively over her, and it scared me sometimes, because, in truth, something, some distant, arid space separated us more than ever. I wanted her to be strong, but I didn't want her to go away from me.

"Are you feeling all right?" I whispered one evening when she came in to say good night.

Her cool answer brushed like a kiss across my cheek. "I'm fine, just fine," she said.

It didn't help. I needed to work through the tangles in my heart, and wondered, Were we playing a pretend game? "Right" and "wrong" were just words? I was glad my parents weren't breaking up; but I was afraid.

"You'll have to figure it all out by yourself," Kathleen said the next day.

"I know I'm being self-pitying," I confessed.

"Yeah, well, indulge yourself a little."

"You'd never make it as a nun," I said.

"I'd be a different breed," she replied with a grin.

Philip showed up a week after Ingrid's baby was born. I opened the door and saw him standing there, dressed in a crisp white shirt with his blue varsity sweater, looking uncomfortable. Our phone calls had been brief; he seemed to be having more varsity practice than usual lately. I bit my tongue to stop from saying, "Hey, where have you been?"

We sat on the living room sofa, where we had more than once (when my parents weren't home) laced ourselves together, breathing hard, with me knowing I had to pick exactly the right time to call a halt, because — as every girl knew — boys weren't in charge of that, and if it went too far, well, whose fault was that?

"Do you want a Coke?" I asked.

"No, thanks," he said, then fell silent.

"How did last night's game go?"

"We won."

He didn't look particularly happy, but at least we had opened something of a conversation. We talked about school and how many more games were left, with little pockets of silence in between. Nervous, I began rattling on. I told him I had picked out a perfect dress at the Broadway (white, with a red velvet bolero) that my mother was buying me for the senior prom, which was only a couple of months away. I wanted to hint to him that I really hoped for a wrist corsage — they lasted longer — but nothing I was saying felt appropriate right now. He kept shifting back and forth on the sofa, and darting glances around the room. Anywhere but directly at me.

"That's what I have to talk about with you," he said.

"Well, you need a tux —" I said helpfully.

"I can't go," he said.

"What?" Our date for this big dance had been on the calendar for a couple of months, and we both knew it.

"Look, this whole actress thing —"

"Ingrid?"

"My folks aren't too crazy about me getting pulled into that mess."

"What mess?"

An unnecessary question: I saw it in his eyes. He didn't want to be tarnished by association with the circus of publicity roaring around me, my school, and my family.

"Hey, Jesse, don't make this harder than it is."

It was dawning on me finally. "Make what harder?" I managed.

"We shouldn't see each other for a while. Well, anyway, until this whole thing blows over. It — it doesn't look good to my folks or my coach, either. I'm sorry." He seemed miserable.

In a way, I had known it all the time. How could I be surprised? It had been hovering, waiting to happen. I would not let myself cry. Maybe I was toughening up a little — I didn't know.

But as I stared at Philip, sitting there with his lower lip hanging out, he didn't look like my handsome boyfriend, the popular captain of the basketball team, who prayed before every game, and whom everybody admired and I had considered myself lucky to catch. He looked — I searched for the words, even as I tried to catch my breath — like a scared kid.

So maybe that's why I suddenly felt fed up and angry. It hurt — oh, it hurt — but I couldn't let him kick me down. Enough, enough.

"That means I can't go to the prom," I snapped.

"Yeah, well, maybe another guy —"

"Someone who makes his own decisions?" I stood up.

"What are you going to do?" He really did look scared.

My feet provided the answer. I moved swiftly to my bedroom, picked up my knitting bag, pulled out the half-finished socks and the needles with the little dangling bobbins of gray and purple yarn, and walked back. I held the whole project aloft, eyeing it critically. To be honest, the products of my labor already looked limp and soiled.

"As long as I'm not going to see you again, I might as well give these to you now.

Surprise."

I pulled the still-unfinished sock off the needles and yanked out the rows of knitting, one by one, pulling hard at each strand, until I had only a ball of yarn in my hand. I offered it to him. "Here," I said.

"Jesse, I'm sorry, this isn't my idea," he said.

"You see, *that's* what's wrong. Who runs your life?" As if I didn't know. I tossed the other sock into his lap and turned to open the front door.

"Bye," I said.

He stood, holding the tangle of yarn in one hand, a dingy sock in the other. He looked confused. "I can talk to them again —"

"Don't bother."

"I'm sorry about the dress."

I closed the door firmly behind him.

Philip's exit from my life wasn't as hard as I thought it would be, for the simple reason that now I had a safe focus for my anger. He was a coward, I told myself. When my parents asked about his whereabouts, I told them he didn't want to be tarnished by scandal and I didn't care; as far as I was concerned, he could go jump in a lake, because I wasn't interested in him anymore.

My mother said loyally she had never liked him that much anyway, and my father called him a jerk. In truth, I sensed all three of us were relieved to find a cause to rally around, something simple and clear to share. It felt cathartic to anoint a villain, someone else to denounce with-out inflicting damage to any one of us. Anyway, we were talking again.

I threw myself into preparing for the forensic state finals. I was at last waking up to the realization of how proud Miss Coultrane was that I had qualified to compete — in *two* categories, which was unheard of for a girl, especially one attending a Catholic high school.

"Why weren't there more of us?" I asked one day. I had practiced most of the afternoon, standing behind the battered wooden podium Miss Coultrane had in the corner of her studio as she tossed debate topics at me, making me argue both sides of an issue, pushing me to think quicker, always quicker. She coached me on the techniques, the tricks, what to look for in an opponent. I was getting tired.

"Girls or Catholics?"

"I guess — both."

"Because there are those who don't consider either of them good enough," she said sharply. Then, casting me a swift glance, "Do not repeat that, Jesse."

"No, ma'am."

"You have a quick mind, a clarity to your expressed thoughts, and you can be a winner, I'm quite sure of that."

"Yes, ma'am." I was even beginning to believe it.

The weekend of the tournament was bright and clear — so much so that the University of Redlands buildings seemed to gleam in the sun. Blinking frequently against relentless light, I kept gulping — against my own nervousness. These were just high-school students like me, I kept telling myself, looking at the dozens of finalists striding purposefully through the corridors between rounds of the different competitions. I was the only one from Saint Ann's Academy, and I felt strange, suddenly made conscious by various sideways glances cast my way — the badge I wore identifying my school was large — that I was, indeed, kind of the odd one in this energized gathering.

The early rounds were easy. I placed second in debate and first in extemporaneous. But debate was the big one, and I couldn't go to the finals of both. My closest competitor in the second debate round

(Resolved: Communists should be allowed to teach in American schools) was a stocky high-school junior in glasses from a public school in Southwest Los Angeles. His name was Malcolm something. His hair was dark and tousled, and he looked Jewish. There was a sprinkling of acne on his nose, and a slightly scruffy stubble on his cheeks and chin, but his lively eyes and ready smile lit up his face. He was assigned the affirmative argument and I took the negative, which was a lot easier. (One trick of debate: denouncing is usually easier than defending.)

It was a good match. Malcolm threw himself into it and never managed to sneak in the kind of snide comment Miss Coultrane had warned me to be on the watch for from the boys. When I won, he strode over to me immediately and shook my hand. "Great job," he said. "Congratulations."

"You were very good," I said.

"You were better. Maybe I'll come watch you wrap this up." He turned on his heel and walked off.

It was slowly sinking in: I had qualified for the final round.

By midafternoon, my head was pounding. I kept checking and rechecking the assigned times and rooms for the final competitions posted outside the lunchroom. Periodic changes were announced over a scratchy loudspeaker.

Too overwhelmed to talk to the others, I just kept practicing my breathing.

I checked the board again, fifteen minutes before we were to begin, and then made sure I was within a couple of yards of the debate finals' classroom, never straying more than a few feet away except for a hurried trip to the bathroom.

Suddenly someone was in my face, staring at me through owlish glasses. "Jesse, what the hell are you doing *here*?" he yelled.

It was the boy named Malcolm. He grabbed me by the shoulder. "They changed the room ten minutes ago — didn't they tell you?" he said.

"I never heard anything," I gasped.

"Holy smoke, you're going to miss it!"

"Where is it?" I wanted to cry.

Instead of answering, he grabbed my hand and we ran. I could hardly keep up with him as we rushed through the various hallways, out of one building, into another, me sobbing, Malcolm never slowing down.

"Go," he said, pushing me through a door.

I knew the minute the debate moderator saw me that I was too late. He made a show of checking his watch, and his tone was brusque. "Jessica Malloy, you are one minute past the qualifying deadline. I have assigned your runner-up the challenge of competing in your place."

"I am so sorry. I didn't get the message about the room change."

The moderator's eyes were resolutely stony. "Pity," he said. "But all you young people are supposed to be mature enough to know the rules."

I felt all eyes in the room on me — astonished, unforgiving. The only delighted face was that of the runner-up. There was no recourse; I could see that.

"I have to get out of here," I said under my breath.

"Well, obviously." Malcolm took my hand again, and together we left the room.

"I don't know how I could possibly have —"

"Maybe you didn't. Maybe the announcement was garbled."

"Don't try to make me feel better."

"Why not? You weren't sitting around reading comic books." He shrugged his shoulders. "You finished high in extemp, right?"

"Yes. I was first on the last round."

"Then you qualify for the finals." We walked back to the lunchroom and scanned the posted locations for final rounds. Extemp began in five minutes.

I looked at him, the possibility dawning. If I showed up, I could compete.

"Okay, let's go," he said.

The moderator, a precise-looking woman wearing wire-framed glasses, was reciting the rules as we came in the door. Thirty minutes to prepare a seven-minute speech on a selected topic. This time, as I scanned the waiting group, I noticed a girl from Hollywood High who had won first place last year; she was my most serious rival, and her face dropped in disappointment when she saw me.

The moderator paused, and checked her list. "Jessica Malloy?"

"Yes."

"I understood you had chosen to compete in the debate finals."

"I — was too late."

She looked over at the panel of judges and raised an eyebrow. One of the judges shook his head. "Well . . ." She checked her notes. "According to the rules, you qualify as one of the finalists here."

"Yes, ma'am."

"We're the stepchild competition for you, apparently." She obviously didn't approve. "Well, come up here and pick your topic.

Remember, half an hour. You can consult today's newspapers — in the corner over there — and the encyclopedia. That's all."

I walked forward and dipped my hand into the bowl.

What is justice denied? Define it. Give specific and detailed examples.

I had to think of something that had an authentic heart to it, not just deliver an indignant oration. When I looked up, I saw Malcolm at the back of the room, arms folded, looking expectant: he actually thought I could pull this off. I sat down at the front table with a pen and the index card they had given me, sweating. I couldn't think.

What is justice denied?

Not the punitive kind that Shylock demanded. Certainly, delayed justice was justice denied. What about someone accused of murder and left to suffer in prison without a trial? I looked around at my competitors. Too easy. What about Joan of Arc? Left to suffer a fiery death by the king whom she put on his throne — I stopped, pen in midair. Of course. With immense relief, I knew my topic.

Not Joan. Ingrid.

I wrote fast. Ingrid Bergman was clearly a victim of injustice. She was, right now, the hated fallen woman, condemned by American hypocritical moralists, particularly the powerful bishops of the Catholic Church, and —

Wait. What was I doing? My hand trembled.

I was accusing, by implication, the people who had shaped me, who had taught me what was true and safe — who had given me rules to believe in. And if those rules were stern and unbending, with no in between, they gave a safe framework. . . . I closed my eyes, heart beating hard. Was I denouncing my church? I thought of all the whispered sins I had been able to leave in the confessional, the mix of condemnation and comfort, and I had a sudden desire to talk to my parents — even though they would give me different answers.

I had to find my own. The pieces of what I truly believed were falling into place, and I couldn't ignore that. Maybe condemning Ingrid was supposed to be justice, but it wasn't. She had been attacked by the Catholic Church, abandoned by the movie business, deprived of her American career, and warned by the U.S. government to stay out of the United States. All this, for falling in love and having a baby out of wedlock? No, that wasn't justice. It was self-serving hypocrisy.

A bell rang, and I put down my pen. One last look at my notes. I knew I didn't need this four-by-six card. And I had to tell the truth as I saw it.

"Your turn, Jessica," said the moderator.

I had a sudden impulse to make the sign of the cross. That would have horrified the room, of course.

As I took a deep breath and began, I knew it would be the best speech I ever gave. I raised my voice, making no effort to be contained, pouring out the case against those who had worked so grimly to destroy Ingrid. I decried their harshness, their ignorance. I declared some in the Church power-hungry and said the movie industry was filled with cowards. I had it perfectly organized. I took the entire time allotted, caught up in my own passion, *believing* every word I said. It felt so good, like being released from some prison and being *brave,* and telling the *truth* about the nasty hypocrisy of all those out to destroy Ingrid Bergman. I quoted Jesus's chiding to the Philistines, "He who is without sin among you, let him be the first to throw a stone at her." And I wrapped it up by telling the room of Ingrid Bergman's eloquent rendition of

Portia's "quality of mercy" speech in *The Merchant of Venice* at my own school, and how it opened my eyes to what mercy truly meant.

"Unfortunately, nobody condemning Ingrid Bergman stopped long enough to consult the Bible or Shakespeare," I concluded. "And that is justice denied."

I sat down. The room was silent as the judges stood in single file and made their way into the next classroom to consult.

It took fewer than ten tense minutes for them to reach a decision. I won.

People jumped up, smiling, shaking hands. Malcolm stayed back by the door, grinning widely. I blew him a kiss, feeling giddy with relief and joy. I owed him a lot for his friendship. A fleeting thought — he was sort of cute; too bad he was a year younger and an inch shorter.

I scrambled quickly for a phone; I had to share this news with my parents. The phone rang and rang, but nobody answered. I hung up, frustrated. Neither Father nor Mother was at home. I tried his office, too; no answer.

I called Miss Coultrane next, and she was beside herself. "Jesse, Jesse, you've brought honor to our school," she said. "I'm so proud of you." She almost sounded as if she could cry, and I thought, with a jolt of surprise, that my win was also *her* win; how much over all her years at Saint Ann's had she dreamed of having a pupil bring home a state prize?

There was no time to talk; other people were waiting for the phone. I said goodbye, dizzy with joy, and turned back into the room.

"Excuse me, Miss Malloy." A man in a checkered jacket and bow tie, holding a notebook and pencil, materialized by my side. His eyes were squinty, and he had a tight smile that he seemed to be trying to loosen up. "Hey, great job. Very brave," he said. "Jessica Malloy, right? You're here from a Catholic school, right?"

"Yes, Saint Ann's Academy," I said proudly.

"Pretty big deal, you taking on the Catholic Church. Eloquent."

"Thank you," I said, half listening. The head of the tournament was announcing the time for the awards ceremony; it was thrilling — I would be bringing a gold cup back to Saint Ann's, the first ever in speech for my school.

"Somebody tells me your school is the one where they filmed *The Bells of St. Mary's*?"

"Yes." I looked more closely at him now.

"What does your father do?"

"He works at a movie studio," I said.

"You took them all on." He scribbled fast. "What's his name?"

Why was he asking me all these questions? "Who are you?" I asked.

"I'm a local reporter, just suburban news," he said. "Got a quote for me to expand on what you said?"

"No. Where are you from?" I said, a bit alarmed.

"*Herald-Express,*" he said. "Just trolling here for a graph or two on the competition — got lucky, I guess." He tipped the brim of his hat with a cheerful gesture. "Bye, now, and thanks."

CHAPTER FOURTEEN

Los Angeles, 1950
The rest of that day passed like a dream.
The brightly lit auditorium; the sound of
hastily assembled folding chairs scraping on
the linoleum floor; the dozens of students
gathering for the award presentations, which
began at seven o'clock. The euphoria of
hearing my name called, of walking up the
auditorium aisle, of folding my hands
around a splendid gold cup, dimly hearing
the applause, thanking the tournament
judges — it all pushed back a faint fog of
uneasiness over my brief encounter with the
reporter. Surely, any mention of my speech
would be, at worst, tucked deep in the local
section of the newspaper. A high-school
tournament? The *Herald-Express* barely
noticed that kind of event.

Malcolm sat next to me, applauding hard.
"They'll take it back from you for the
engraving," he whispered. "Don't hold on

too tightly."

"Thank you for what you did," I managed to say.

"You've just won your own Academy Award," he said.

I looked down at my beautiful cup, burnishing it with my fingers. Was this the way Ingrid felt when she won for *Gaslight*? I liked that idea.

And then it was over, and we were all climbing onto separate buses to go back to different districts, where our parents were supposed to pick us up. I lost sight of Malcolm; he was on a bus scheduled to go to another part of town. Nice guy, though he had a strange, prissy name. It was quite likely I would never see him again, because he didn't go to a Catholic school. I felt a twinge of disappointment, but I was savoring the excitement of handing my parents the tape of my speech and telling them the great news.

It was very late when the bus reached my pickup point. Mother was waiting, standing by our new Oldsmobile. I slid from my seat, jumped from the bus, and ran over to her, the gravel crunching under my feet.

"Guess what?" I burst out, and then stopped at the sight of her face. Her skin was ashen, crumpled as tightly as the newspaper she held in her hand. She held it out between us like a shielding weapon.

"How could you?" she said hoarsely. "How could you do this?"

Only then did I see my father standing on the other side of the car, staring at me. He strode forward until we were almost face-to-face.

"Some job, kid. How the hell could you do that?" he said slowly in a heavy voice. His face was dark with anger. "I can hardly believe it. It wasn't enough just to jeopardize me — you took down both sides of the family. And I'm standing here asking myself, What kind of daughter are you?"

My head spun; my knees buckled. Dimly, I realized something — that crumpled newsprint in Mother's hand was the evening edition of the *Herald-Express*.

"Read it," Mother said.

Hands trembling, I took the paper and read swiftly. My parents always said Hearst's evening paper fed on lurid stories and gossip. And, yes, I had provided fodder for its reputation.

The article was double-headlined and prominently placed on page 3.

CONVENT SCHOOL GIRL ATTACKS HOLLYWOOD AND CATHOLIC CHURCH
Tournament Winner Defends Shamed Actress Ingrid Bergman

The story was gleeful, missing nothing, naming my father as the "hustling publicist" who had built Ingrid's career. It called me a "defiant" challenger of my own church, and emphasized the "irony" that my school was the same one that had proudly hosted the making of *The Bells of St. Mary's* — nothing was missed.

Some job, kid. . . . You took down both sides of the family.

I don't remember much of our drive home that night. Crying, I tried to explain. I would never have deliberately done anything to hurt either of them — couldn't they see that?

"Seems to me, you were more concerned with defending Ingrid," Father said. His voice was as sharp as flint scraping stone.

"Jesse, were those opinions you expressed your true feelings?" Mother asked suddenly.

I tried to think of a way out. But anything other than the truth would just take me into some cavern of lies. "Yes," I said.

"You really believe the Church is hypocritical?"

"Not in everything, no, and this was never meant to hurt you —"

"What about me?" My father's harsh voice again, but there was something additional, something raw. His eyes met mine in the rearview mirror, and I was shocked. They were filled with pain. His hands gripping the steering wheel were white. "Am I one of those cowards in the movie business you took down?"

Oh God, I wanted to throw up. "No, Daddy . . ." I pleaded. And I could say no more. As the car rumbled on, with the night lights of the city flashing off the windows, the tension swirled, not between them this time, but between them and me. And with that realization came my old fear of sin, and I felt fully, for the first time, that it had always been waiting to pounce on me. There was no averting it, and there was nothing venial about it — this was surely mortal. I couldn't think straight; my head spun. I had dishonored my mother and father. Maybe ruined Father's career.

"I need to throw up," I mumbled.

"Hold it until we get home," Father said. "You've spewed enough bile for the day."

I threw up. Over everything. Little rivulets

of vomit trickled down the window next to me. My father cursed. We were on the new freeway; he couldn't pull over.

"I'm sorry, I'll clean it up —"

"Never mind, Jesse, I'll take care of it." My mother, her first kind words.

"I'll do it —"

"You need your sleep." I heard an audible sigh. "Sister Teresa Mary wants to see you in her office Monday morning."

"Why?"

"Somebody made sure she got a copy of the paper's late edition."

I kept to myself Sunday and slept little that night, just cried bitterly as I stared into blackness. I should have thought more of my parents before I gave my speech; I should have thought of my school. I had struggled; I had wanted to do what was right. I could make excuses for myself, but I knew the truth: I had said what I believed, but that had proved dangerous. I had pronounced my own judgments, and they were outside the moral framework of my life. Hadn't I committed the sin of pride?

I wanted to talk to Kathleen.

The early-morning *Examiner* ran a longer story, with generous excerpts from my speech, elaborating with a few reaction quotes. Howard Hughes's spokesman said the movie mogul was "surprised" that Gabriel Malloy's daughter would take such an "intemperate" position. The chancery office released a one-line statement from Bishop Doyle, expressing his "regret" that one of his flock would hold such views. Another quote, no attribution: "The scandalous actions of Ingrid Bergman continue to distort the values of the young." And one that brought tears to my eyes from a judge at the Redlands Tournament: "I don't know what the fuss is about," he said. "She won the competition. But, then, I'm a Protestant."

It was not yet seven o'clock as I walked up the path to the front offices of Saint Ann's Academy to see Sister Teresa Mary. There were no students around; it was still too early. A mist lay low over the verdant green lawn. The palm trees that lined the path looked like sentries, standing guard, still and silent.

I had come to love this entrance to my school. This was the place, this soft green lawn, where my class would soon graduate — all of us dressed in white, carrying baskets of fragrant flowers, crowned with floral wreaths. The school orchestra would play "Pomp and Circumstance" as we marched, just as it did every year. Our parents would be sitting on folding chairs, straight and proud.

Well, that was the way it was supposed to happen.

The principal's office this time seemed forbidding. As the school secretary ushered me in, I saw it in bleak detail. The bookcase nestled in one corner of the room had a piece of thick cardboard shoved under one of its wobbly legs to right it. The desk was scuffed from years of wear, the finish worn thin, and the wall behind it, painted a steel gray, held nothing except that imposingly large crucifix, which graphically displayed Christ's cruel wounds. It was the same as before, but I was seeing it differently.

Sister Teresa Mary stood up from the desk as I entered. She looked shockingly small. Her body seemed lost inside the heavy serge of her usual black habit, but her blue eyes were as steady and bright as ever.

"Sit down, Jessica," she said quietly.

Only then did I see Miss Coultrane standing at the rear of the room, hands folded tightly in front of her, a set look on her face I could not fathom.

"Miss Coultrane will join us for a moment, at her request," Sister Teresa Mary said. "Miss Coultrane?"

My speech teacher cleared her throat. "I have taught at this school for many years with great pride," she said. "And I have never been prouder of a student than I am of you. Congratulations, Jessica."

"Thank you," I managed, bewildered. Could this be some kind of offered absolution?

"It seems, however, to be an appropriate time for me to retire, and I wanted to tell you myself, with the consent of Sister." She shot a swift glance in Sister Teresa Mary's direction.

"What do you mean?"

"I have submitted my resignation to Sister Teresa Mary," Miss Coultrane said quietly.

"But *why*?" I was aghast.

She glanced again at Sister Teresa Mary. "Sister will explain," she said. She turned then, with a nod, and brushed past me, touching my shoulder lightly as she left the room.

Sister Teresa Mary, with great effort, pulled herself straighter, as if trying to fill her clothing.

"Jessica, I'm afraid I have bad news for you. You cannot be valedictorian at graduation," she said heavily.

My head reeled. "But — but —" I wanted to ask why, but it was sinking in, and I again felt sick to my stomach.

"Yes, I know this must come as a shock. I did not make the decision. Bishop Doyle has ordered that your name be taken off the list of speakers."

She could not look directly at me.

"But I earned it," I said, voice shaking.

"I know you did." Her tone softened slightly. "My dear, I have taken a vow of obedience. I do not question the authority of the bishop."

"But . . . this isn't fair, you know it isn't fair." I was crying. "Was what I said *that* terrible? Don't you sometimes have different thoughts —"

"If I do, I do not express them." She sighed. "Jesse, maturity means knowing when to speak up — and when not to. You clearly haven't learned that, I'm afraid."

I had to fight back. With something. "I'm not a hypocrite," I began, thrashing to recapture some of the giddy pleasure of speaking out and saying what was true. But it was elusive, disappearing; the taste of it had gone thin. "I had to speak out. . . ." I tried to continue, but with what words? I stopped.

"You've had many good years at this

school, Jessica," Sister Teresa Mary said. "Would you dismiss all of us who have loved and worked for and with you?"

Her spine was stiffening, and the hard edge of authority was moving back into her voice.

"No," I said. I wanted to force her to admit this was wrong. Even when, inside myself, I wondered otherwise. "Please, tell me — do you agree with the bishop?"

She paused a short while before replying, fingering the beads laced around her waist, staring at some point past my head. "Obedience is very important in the Church, Jessica. Not just for nuns and priests — for all of us."

"You don't agree."

She gazed at me, and I saw or imagined a lingering sorrow in her eyes. And I think we both knew, in a fundamental way, we were saying goodbye.

"We will make no public fuss about this," she said. "Your name will be taken off the speaker list on the program without comment. I will do whatever I can to make this a less stressful experience for you. As for my personal feelings — they are not relevant."

So, yes, there was a conflict in Sister Teresa Mary's heart and brain. And she was just as ensnared as I was.

I understood now. My wonderful Miss Coultrane was fighting back by leaving a job I knew she loved. She could do *something*. But there was no protest open for Sister Teresa Mary. That increased my pain, but it gave me the only taste of satisfaction — sour though it was — that I would find in the debacle. Somewhere inside this nun, this symbol of authority, were the unharvested seeds of rebellion that stirred now so strongly in me.

Kathleen was sitting on the entrance steps as I emerged from the building. She looked up; she knew. I wanted to hug her and wail.

"How —" I began.

"Miss Coultrane called me last night," she said with a faint smile. "She told me you would need a friend."

"She's quitting," I whispered.

"I know."

"And I did it all. I've destroyed everything."

"That's crap." She stood up. "Come on, let's go talk by the pool."

That's crap. A lifeline, a balm to my father's charge. If only for those two words, I would have reason to love Kathleen forever.

The school was stirring now with sleepy-eyed students hurrying to class. No one was swimming: too early for that. Kathleen and I had the pool area to ourselves, but I couldn't sit still. So we walked and walked around its edges, going nowhere. How could I make sense of it all? I wept, I ranted, I poured out everything all jumbled together, and Kathleen listened. She never stopped me; she didn't try to explain, defend, or console. If I ever needed someone to just listen, it was that day. I had been on both sides of righteous denouncement now, and I deserved my parents' anger, but surely not the humiliation doled out by Bishop Doyle, unless, maybe, it was God's way —

"Stop." Kathleen shoved her hands into the pockets of her uniform. "If you're guilty of anything, it's being clueless about consequences."

"I said what I honestly believe."

"Sometimes consequences matter more."

I opened my mouth to protest. But what came out was, once again, what I was *really* thinking. "How can anybody become a nun?" I asked. "I think Sister Teresa Mary ruined her life. All those girls going into the convent, swearing obedience to a church that won't let them think for themselves — they're going to do the same thing."

"Well, clearly, the convent just lost *you*. Too bad — I was hoping you would get tucked away and do all the praying for both of us from here on." A hint of a smile played across her lips.

I managed a smile back. We weren't trapped, either of us: that's what she was telling me. "Do you still want to be a lawyer?" I asked. She had applied to colleges in the L.A. area, and it struck me suddenly that I would probably be a long way away from her, no matter where I went.

"Maybe. Representing people who are treated rotten, like you."

I couldn't speak then. But it did dawn on me slowly, as we continued walking in companionable silence, that her words showed the kind of loyalty I would do all I could to give back. Whenever needed.

The news of my demotion swept through the school that day, and I saw what I expected in the eyes of my classmates, both sympathy from friends and some snickering from those who relished a mini-scandal that took down the girl from Beverly Hills. I marched through my classes as stoically as possible, keeping my chin up high, like Ingrid in *Joan of Arc.* I decided I could lose myself in a part, too.

I trudged out at the end of the day, looking forward to nothing more than crawling into bed and pulling the covers over my head that night. As I walked past the other, chattering students, I saw a familiar car pull into the school parking lot. My father was behind the wheel.

He stepped out of the car and we stood there, staring at each other.

He had never seemed so rumpled. His tie was twisted and pulled into a hard, graceless knot, and he looked like he needed a shave.

"Jesse, I was too hard on you," he began. "I want to apologize."

My voice trembled. "You told me I took down both sides of the family," I said, tears coming. "You told me I spewed bile —"

"Yeah, over the top. That was — over the top."

I couldn't move, even knowing there were girls brushing past me who were straining to catch what we were saying, their whispers sharp enough for me to hear.

What did he want? For me to tell him this was all right now?

"I won the first state prize in speech that Saint Ann's has ever had."

"You did. You're good." He looked suddenly so weary.

I still couldn't move. "They won't let me be valedictorian. They took it away from me."

"That must have been Doyle's doing. He's a self-righteous bastard. Jesse, you got caught in something you can't be expected to understand."

"I put you in danger." I could hardly get the words out.

He put out his hands, palms up, and said, "Look, plenty of other things are happening, especially in Washington. Movie people have enemies now on every side. You complicated things, but not by intent."

"You never tell me more; you just hint at bad stuff."

"I want you free of it all."

I didn't answer, just climbed into the car, all the emotions of these two days — all the confusion and humiliation, the fear for my father, all the excitement and the pain of losing an honor I had dreamed of — jumbled together in my head.

Mother was waiting at the front door, holding a handful of envelopes, her smile fixed. "Jesse, you've heard from your colleges," she said.

They both stood expectantly, waiting to see what I would do. My hand trembled as I reached for the envelopes. If they thought

I would open these in front of them, they were wrong. I took the official-looking letters and went right to my bedroom, firmly shutting the door between me and the two people that, right now, I both loved and hated most in all the world.

CHAPTER FIFTEEN

Los Angeles, 1950

I sat on my bed, looking around my room. There wasn't much left here of me. It reflected the decorator who had taken over after we moved — a woman with the husky voice of a Lauren Bacall. Wearing a slash of scarlet lipstick that always looked like it had been applied in anger, she had burst in with authoritative confidence. That quickly intimidated Mother, and I had ended up nodding assent to pretty much anything she decreed.

As a result, my four-poster bed now hoisted high a white dotted-swiss canopy that felt to me appropriate for a ten-year-old. The decorator took down my movie posters of Bing Crosby and Perry Como, but I had rescued them from the trash and stuck them under the bed. The only fight I put up was over the big poster of Ingrid as Joan of Arc. It had been rehung, but right now, as I stared at it, I felt empty.

I realized, even before opening the first envelope, that I didn't belong here anymore.

Stanford University is pleased to report that you have been accepted as a member of the freshman class of 1950. Congratulations.

I sat on the edge of the bed, staring at the official-looking welcoming message, waiting for the wave of euphoria I had expected would wash over me. It didn't come. More slowly this time, I opened the three remaining, staring at each one.

Bennington College. *Congratulations.*

Marymount College. *Congratulations.*

UCLA. *Congratulations.*

Still no euphoria. I should be bursting through the bedroom door, announcing this triumph to my parents, basking in their delight and pride, feeling on top of the world. It wasn't happening.

I sat as still as I could, listening to the Baby Ben clock ticking away on the nightstand, counting the seconds, sorting out my thoughts. I knew within a few minutes what I wanted — and suddenly felt calm.

Which college was farthest away?

A click; the doorknob turned.

"Okay," said my father as the door swung open. "What's the story? Don't shut us out, kid."

"No rejections," I said. "And scholarship money, too."

Mother smiled with that clearly relieved, brittle smile she reserved for good news these days. "Well, congratulations, Jesse," she said. "Maybe —"

"I'm going to Bennington."

"You've decided already? Vermont? Jesse, Bennington is a fine college. . . ." Mother stopped, perhaps sensing anything she said would be coming too late.

"No, I've decided."

Father was staring at me. "You would turn down Stanford?" he said. "They don't admit many women; it's an honor to be accepted. For God's sake, why Bennington?"

"I think it would be a good place for me." I couldn't quite bring myself to tell them the truth, but I knew it with full conviction. I wanted to get as far away from here as possible, and I didn't ever want to look back. I had been given a pole vault, and I was going to use it.

The cloud over my father was not going away. When I caught vague snatches of his conversations with Mother, I heard the word "pinko" a few times, which wasn't surprising. Everybody in the movie business was suspected of being a communist these days. Even Mother was gently told by the unwed mothers' home that her help would not be needed "for a while," pleading "overstaffing." She didn't complain. I didn't try to say anything, but volunteered to do the dishes when I heard the news. Talking wouldn't help.

As for reaction to my Redlands speech? Louella Parsons was happy to stoke the flames. I had hoped she would ignore it, maybe have a little sympathy, claiming my father as a "friend," in Hollywood terms. But it only took her a couple of days to dedicate her entire column to my "scandalous" behavior, quoting generously from the speech. She accused Ingrid Bergman of besmirching the morals of even this young daughter of Hollywood. How uncaring could that selfish woman *be*?

"The tragedy?" Louella, a devout Catholic herself, wrote. "Bishop Francis Doyle had no choice. He had to order Jessica Malloy's removal as valedictorian of the graduating class at Saint Ann's Academy to avert further scandal. A price must be paid."

Father gently pulled the paper from me. "The vultures are gathering," he said.

"They're after me, not you."

"What do you mean? You said she was mad because you didn't give her an exclusive on Ingrid's baby."

"It's gone deeper. She knows how to get on the winning side," he said.

I saw that now familiar tense look on his face, and felt my worries about him resurfacing. At the same time, I struggled to detach. I could do nothing about those worries; I could only remind myself I wasn't going to be swallowed up by them. I would concentrate on what I had achieved, and try to forget how quickly my big honor had turned to dust. I had done something good, not bad. And nobody could take away the speech tournament prize — no bishop or sniping columnist, nobody whispering behind my back; nobody, especially not my parents. Only my father could truly hurt me. And he had already done that.

I was late leaving school a few days later, hurrying for the bus stop, slinging my book bag over my shoulder. My bus was just pulling away. Frustrated, I plopped down on the bus bench. Couldn't something go right?

"Hi." A boy's voice. I squinted into the light.

It was Malcolm, the boy from the Redlands Tournament, his dark hair flung back carelessly, a friendly grin stretching his mouth wide. "I just thought I'd drop by and see how you were doing," he said with genuine casualness. "I kind of got you into all this."

"Yeah, I guess you did." I wasn't giving an inch for anybody.

He sat down next to me. "You were really good," he said. "And you should give the finger to people like Louella Parsons and the rest of that crowd."

I smiled, felt myself relenting. "What's your last name?" I asked.

His last name was Carvello, and he was Italian, and a junior at Dorsey High. He wore a pair of baggy chinos and his hands were short and thick, and he was funny. He made jokes. I didn't have to endure guarded sympathy; he just straight-out said I had been "fucked," just like that, and I wasn't put off at all. We talked about getting into speech work, how much fun it was, about the excitement of winning, about our very different schools. Easy stuff, natural. No pauses, no tension.

My next bus was turning the corner; it would be here in a few seconds. I really didn't want to go.

"Do you want to come up to my house?"

I asked impulsively.

He shrugged and gave me his grin. "Sure, why not?"

The bumpy ride went faster than usual, and I felt relaxed for the first time in a while. I was opening the front door when he reached down and pulled up a postal package half hidden by one of Mother's azalea bushes.

"Did somebody miss this?" he said.

I looked at the return address and took in a sharp breath. "What I won? My cup — they've engraved it?"

He laughed. "Jeesh, how many people forget winning a gold cup?"

"Oh, Malcolm . . ." I wanted to laugh and cry at the same time.

We went inside and sat down in the living room. Mother was in the kitchen, but I didn't want to open this in front of her. I quickly tore off the wrappings and pulled out my dazzling cup, hoisting it up for a critical look.

"Oh God, *it's not real gold*?" Malcolm gasped. "Shouldn't you complain?"

I laughed, tracing the engraved letters of my name with my finger, feeling suddenly, unexpectedly, and happily *proud* of what I had done. When I heard Mother coming into the living room to meet Malcolm, I quickly stuffed the cup back in its box and tucked it behind the bookcase. Malcolm raised an eyebrow, but said nothing. His eyes were sympathetic.

We took a long walk that afternoon, trudging along the lush hedges on winding roads through Beverly Hills. I showed him some of the glamour spots, like the house where Douglas Fairbanks and Mary Pickford had lived, but mainly I told him about meeting Ingrid Bergman when I was a small girl, and why she mattered to me. He said that he understood loyalty, that his hero was Jackie Robinson, and no matter what he was or ever did, Malcolm would never desert him. He told me about his family — too many brothers and sisters, but they were okay — and did I like hot dogs, because if I did, he knew where we could get the tastiest ones in the city, if I didn't mind walking a few miles; they didn't sell hot dogs in places like Beverly Hills. "Probably too much to do today," he said.

And I heard myself respond, "Well, maybe tomorrow?"

We began meeting each other a few days a week after school, doing offbeat things like taking a bus to Chinatown, where he took me into a Szechuan restaurant and introduced me to a duck dish smoked over tea leaves and twigs. "It's from the camphor plant," he told me, as if I was supposed to know what *that* was.

He saw my befuddlement and grinned. "I learned that by reading the back side of the menu," he said.

I realized in the first several days that Malcolm never pretended to know more than he knew, no matter what. We talked school, we talked movies; only when he enthused over baseball did my attention wander. He would laugh at himself for not being as up on chemistry as I was, and tell me he never could keep his shirt tucked in properly, which drove his mother crazy.

"I like the look," I said impulsively.

He gave me an almost shy glance, his expression thoughtful.

Two weeks in, we were swinging together in a neighborhood playground one afternoon, when he silently took my hand. We swung in rhythm — for once, in silence. Comfortable silence.

"My senior prom is coming up," I ventured. "I'm wondering, would you be interested in that?"

"You mean, be your date?"

"Yes."

"Yeah, sure," he said slowly. "But you

should know, my mom's Jewish, which means I am. And my dad is Italian, sort of a Catholic, I guess, but he hasn't been in any kind of church for years." His voice was very matter-of-fact.

"So what?"

"Won't your school disapprove?"

I laughed; I actually laughed. "They can't do anything to me anymore," I said. And I truly began to believe it.

My parents were a little startled when I told them I had a date for the prom. Not so long ago, my dad would have wanted to meet Malcolm first, but that seemed the least important thing as the weeks passed, to them or to me. Oh, they asked about him. I didn't mention Malcolm's role in what happened at the speech tournament. My mother raised an eyebrow when I said Malcolm was a junior at Dorsey High, but neither of them reacted when I told them he was half Jewish. Their focus was on other things. It felt like our house was collectively holding its breath, waiting for something — I wasn't sure what. I would catch snatches of their murmurings, enough to learn they were thinking of selling the house, just in case. Father's face had a pasty look all the time, and it was Mother who seemed the strong one now. But cold. It was as if she had turned to ice.

Malcolm showed up on the night of the prom with a big grin and an orchid in a little plastic box. "My mother insisted," he said as he shook hands with my parents. "Personally, I think roses are prettier."

"Me, too," I said, liking him all the more for not being deferential.

It was a little jarring to see an older man with Malcolm's same cheerful grin sitting in the driver's seat of the car. I tried not to show my surprise when he introduced his father. I hadn't thought about the fact that Malcolm was only seventeen, too young yet for anything more than a learner's permit. I tucked that small piece of reality away to think about later. Malcolm was casual about it, and his father assured us he would disappear the minute he dropped us off.

I had dreamed of prom all through high school. It was always held in the glamorous Beverly Hills Hotel, allowing each year's senior class of convent-school girls to sail through the lobby, peeking around corners to spot various Hollywood stars, feeling resplendent in their ice-cream-hued gowns adorned with net. But I couldn't play the fairy-tale game anymore. I felt I was an actor in a play that was no longer real.

Oh, I had a reasonably good time. Kathleen gave me a quick thumbs-up after I introduced her to Malcolm, telling me in the ladies' room she thought he was more mature than any of the other boys there. Malcolm and I danced past Philip and his new date, and I could see the flush of red around Philip's collar. Good riddance to you, I wanted to shout. There were awkward moments — Malcolm was asked a few times where he was going to college, given that it was the topic upmost on all of my classmates' minds. "Don't know," he said breezily. "I don't graduate until next year." I saw the darting, giggly looks from the other girls when they heard that.

Midnight. The lights dimmed, and the band swung lazily into "Good Night, Ladies." Malcolm pulled me close, so close I could inhale the scent of his body. I felt an unexpected stirring as he placed my hand close to his chest; his fingers resting — no, moving — near my breast. I wanted to press closer.

What was I thinking? I pulled back.

Malcolm gazed at me steadily as the band finished the song. Flustered, I asked if he could bring my wrap from the cloakroom; it was time to go home. He did, tucking Mother's best shawl over my shoulders with gently lingering pressure. "Let's talk," he said.

We tucked ourselves into a shadowy corner of the spacious hotel lobby with its richly dark-paneled walls, his arm now resting comfortably around me, reliving the evening as we waited for his father to arrive. He seemed his breezy self again.

"Do nuns always forbid strapless gowns?" he asked. "I saw a couple of your classmates getting scolded. Seems kind of strange."

"Yes," I said, feeling a little embarrassed. We must have seemed awfully provincial to him.

"If dressing kind of . . . demurely is important, why do they have the prom here?"

We both scanned the room. It was filled with the usual opulence of Hollywood — women in pearls wearing low-cut silk and swinging jeweled purses; men in cashmere jackets, draped languorously against the lobby bar — everything a world of money and sophistication away from a convent school.

"I don't know," I said. "Good question."

"It doesn't work, does it?" he said quietly.

"What do you mean?"

"You and me," he said.

"Why do you say that?"

"We're not very much alike. Your friends think I'm kind of different or exotic, and I think they are." He said it easily, no mockery.

I wasn't sure what to say.

"Look, I got you through your prom, and I know that mattered. I'm glad I could do that."

"Malcolm, I didn't ask you just to get me through the prom," I said quickly.

"I know, and I didn't come over to your house just to see you unwrap your ersatz gold cup. But maybe it's not enough."

He leaned close, as if to kiss me on the cheek, but, in a reflex motion, I drew away. His eyes showed disappointment.

"Malcolm . . ." I paused. I had all sorts of things I wanted to say, but nothing seemed up to his matter-of-fact statement. He was trying to give me a bridge; I had to use it.

"I'm going off to college in a few months," I said. "It doesn't make sense to start anything now."

Just a moment, a pause; an assessment. "I know that. You've got big stuff coming up," he said.

I could have said something about coming home at Christmas, but I wasn't sure if I would. "I like you very much —" I began.

He broke me off. "I'll tell you something,

Jesse Malloy," he said quietly. "We're only talking about right now."

He flashed a grin, then waved to his father, who was now in the lobby, scanning the crowd. "And guess what? I'll even have a driver's license."

I laughed. He was such a relaxed friend. Yet I doubted we would see each other after the summer. It was true, he made me feel like a grown-up when I was with him, not just a girl attracted to a funny boy. Maybe there could be more. But there was no way I would come back to Los Angeles to find out.

Late April floated past in a haze of showers and blooming marigolds, drifting into May. We seniors were wearing saffron-hued cotton summer skirts now, a privilege that was intended to make us feel like grown-ups, to lighten the mood, to build anticipation for graduation. I liked being free of my black dress and tie, but I felt too old for the party atmosphere, oddly free of everybody.

Those last days of my years at Saint Ann's were bittersweet. I wandered the halls and gardens in a mood of nostalgia, trying to knit it all together. I could easily remember that first day, when Mother brought me here, when I dreaded being swallowed up by strange teachers swathed in black. And now, in many ways, I loved this place. It had been a haven, of sorts.

But the nostalgia didn't last. I refocused on the fact that there were no more newspaper stories about Ingrid that featured me, so I could walk into class without feeling sick to my stomach. And I sensed an aura of sympathy from some of my classmates, and even from some of the nuns.

I also felt increasingly impatient with my father. He wasn't the same person anymore, and I didn't bother trying to talk with him more than was necessary. He held his shoulders tight, almost hunched, at the dinner table. There were no lighthearted stories about the stars, no gossip about impending Hollywood divorces. No laughter. Worse, very little warmth between Mother and him.

Still, she spoke in his defense one evening. "Your father is enduring a tough time," she ventured, watching him settled into his living-room chair, staring at the newspaper.

"Well, he *caused* some tough times, too," I retorted.

"He's being targeted by rumors," she said.

"Oh, I heard you talking about 'pinkos,' " I said airily. "He's not a communist — at least, that's what he *says*."

"He has friends who are."

"Like Jerry Feldstein?" I felt that was daring of me. There had been more phone calls between him and Father, though no poker games.

Mother ignored my question, looking away as she spoke. "The rumors could weaken Gabriel at the studio. Your speech just added to the tension."

Was this her version of forgiving him? I didn't know; if it was, it was qualified. I wanted to worry about my father, but even after his apology, I couldn't forget his anger that night in the parking lot. And Mother? Remembering her weeping over those awful letters on the dining-room table made me cringe inside. So much passion, and now she was all locked up, as usual. So I said nothing.

She leaned down, opened the oven door, and brought out a Pyrex dish of baked chicken, then briskly changed the subject. "I haven't heard you mention Malcolm since the prom. He seemed like a nice boy."

"He's too young for me," I snapped.

She didn't ask for more. In a display of righteous superiority, without asking permission, I picked a chicken leg out of the dish and strolled out of the kitchen.

CHAPTER SIXTEEN

Los Angeles, June 1950
I wanted to be excited on graduation day. I had a beautiful new dress meant for frothy strolls through garden parties. Kathleen and I had spent a whole afternoon in the stores, trying on a couple of dozen frocks, giggling and laughing. But our levity had a forced quality, no question.

"Malcolm asked if he could come to my graduation," I blurted at one point, surprising myself.

"What did you say?"

"I said yes, but it didn't mean —"

"Oh, pooh. You said yes because you like him."

"Stop always being so direct."

"Anyway, given the way things are going, it gives you a guaranteed support base of two friends," she said calmly.

"It doesn't matter; I'll be gone in a few months."

A flicker of a shadow crossed her face. "Yeah. I'll miss you."

I busied myself, putting my new dress back on a hanger. "I'll miss you, too," I said.

We stood there awkwardly for a few minutes; this was something we had avoided talking about.

"Friends for life?" I said.

"You got it," she said.

At home, the game continued. Mother's bedroom door would be closed when I walked in from school; I was supposed to knock at five o'clock so she could get up to fix dinner, but not before. We were playing our roles — automatically doing the "pass the salt, please" or "how was your day . . . isn't that nice" stuff. I was aching inside. What came next? I wanted to ask; but I didn't know how. I hated the sight of my father slumped down in his chair night after night, staring into the distance, fingers tight around his always full bourbon glass. If an ax was going to come down on his head, would there be any warning?

"Who are you loyal to, Jessica?" Mother asked suddenly, out of the blue, one day.

"My family, of course," I said, unnerved. How could she believe differently? But I was letting them go, I knew; it was just happening. I told myself my father was the source of the make-believe of our lives, and I wanted — oh, how I wanted — to move on, to get out of Los Angeles and away from all of it. To do that, I had to play out my part on graduation day.

The weather was gorgeous that morning. Mother helped zip up my dress, doing everything she could to chatter brightly and play her part. She would drive me over early to the school, where all the girls in my class, whispering and giggling, would be lining up for their pink tea-rose bouquets.

"On the whole, Saint Ann's was a good place for you; I hope you agree," she said with forced casualness. I nodded. She reached for me in an awkward, unexpected gesture. I let her hug me, a quick hug, breathing in the scent of a soft lilac perfume I had never noticed before.

"Is he coming?" I asked.

"He's waiting for a phone call — you know how that goes. But of course he'll be there. I'm going to get us good seats on the aisle so we can watch you march in."

We had one hour before lining up. Holding my bouquet, I impulsively walked across campus to Miss Coultrane's classroom, hoping to see her and say goodbye. I knew Sister Teresa Mary was presenting her with a plaque at the ceremony, thanking her for all her years of service, and I wondered how Miss Coultrane felt, and if, in her dignified, restrained way, she would welcome my impulse to rage at the injustice that had prompted her decision to leave Saint Ann's.

She was there, sitting behind her desk, quite properly erect. She looked up as I came in, and I had a sense that she had been expecting me.

"Well, hello, Jesse," she said, her face softening.

"Miss Coultrane, I think it's terrible —"

"No, it's not," she interjected gently. "It was time for me to go, anyway. But I'm so pleased you came by. Poor Sister Teresa Mary is determined to give me some sort of voice today, which I appreciate."

"She could have turned down your resignation."

"No, dear, I would have insisted." With carefully manicured fingers, she opened the top drawer of her desk and pulled out an envelope. "Now, I'm wondering — when they present my plaque, would you be willing to accept it for me?"

"Me?" I was confused. The last person welcome on the graduation podium was me, surely. Especially since Bishop Doyle, in time-honored tradition, would preside.

"I've suggested this to Sister Teresa Mary, and she agreed. I've finished out this year of teaching at her request, but it's time for me to leave, not stand around to be congratulated. Will you do that for me?" Her gaze was steady.

"But you are right here —"

"I can't face the ceremony. I hope you will do this."

"I . . ." I didn't know what to say.

She smiled, as if at a joke. "Wonderful," she said. She reached out and handed me the envelope. "My remarks," she said. "Please, don't open the envelope until you are on the podium. And, Jesse" — she squeezed my hand — "Sister Teresa Mary is on your side."

Clutching the envelope, I hurried back to where the girls in my class were lining up. I would trust Miss Coultrane; I always had.

It was almost time for the ceremony to begin. The aisles of folding chairs spread across the lawn were filling up. Mothers in crisp summer dresses and festive straw hats were chattering away, greeting each other; fathers in neatly pressed coats and ties were smiling and shaking hands. Sisters and brothers and grandparents all strained for a peek at the graduates as the school orchestra began playing softly. Bishop Doyle, flanked by clerical aides, emerged from the school, raising his hand in a blessing as he took his seat on the dais. His role would be to allow each girl to kiss his ring as he handed out the diplomas. I could taste the cheerful expectations as I hurried for my place in the lineup, and for a moment, I felt truly part of it.

I was straining for a glimpse of my parents just as the orchestra burst into a well-rehearsed rendition of "Pomp and Circumstance." The line began to move, cadenced step by cadenced step, all of us cradling our tea roses, Miss Coultrane's envelope tucked inside mine. And that's when I caught sight of Mother. Her head was turned toward me, and she was smiling brightly. The seat next to her was empty.

I had no protection from my feelings anymore; no matter how much I pretended to myself, I had wanted, craved to see him out there, proud and smiling. Where was he?

The speeches began; awards were given. The girl who had been tapped to take my place as valedictorian was an earnest history student who gave an earnest speech, talking about God, our lives ahead, and hopes and dreams. She glanced at me several times, and I smiled encouragingly; I had nothing against her, though I was quite sure I would have given a better speech.

As she left the podium, I looked for the tenth time in the direction of where my mother was sitting. My heart jumped. He had come; he was in his seat. Looking worn, as usual. I felt an almost giddy relief and did my best to quell it. At least he had given me his presence.

Graduation was reaching its concluding moments. I saw parents checking their programs, discreetly ready for the pageantry to end, when Sister Teresa Mary came to the podium and announced a farewell award for Miss Coultrane, in honor of her many years of devoted service to Saint Ann's Academy.

Due to Miss Coultrane's unfortunate illness today, Sister announced, the award would be accepted for her by one of her students. She took an obvious deep breath and said, "That would be graduating senior Jessica Malloy. Jessica, will you come up here?"

I wasn't imagining the sudden tremor of surprise among my classmates as I rose to my feet, clutching the envelope, and made my way up the platform stairs. And I wasn't imagining a sudden alertness in the priests flanking Bishop Doyle. I wanted to glance back at my parents for support, but any nerve needed here would have to come from me.

Sister Teresa Mary presented me with the plaque, her eyes unusually bright. I thanked her, cleared my throat, and faced the crowd.

"Miss Coultrane has asked me to convey her thanks," I began.

I quickly opened the envelope, conscious of the rustle of paper being magnified by the microphone. Scrawled across the top of the page, in Miss Coultrane's handwriting, were these words: "This is for you, Jesse. And for Ingrid. Read it all. And tell them it is a lesson in the meaning of mercy. If they take nothing else away from this day, let this be it."

It was Portia's speech.

I did just that, and began, in a shaky voice at first.

"The quality of mercy is not strain'd,
It droppeth as the gentle rain from heaven
Upon the place beneath: it is twice blest;
It blesseth him that gives and him that
    takes. . . ."

A few puzzled glances were exchanged among the parents and relatives sitting there, balancing their folding chairs on the soft grass. A murmur threaded through the group. Everyone at Saint Ann's surely knew about my disgraceful behavior at the Redlands speech tournament. And — especially if they read Louella Parsons's column — they knew that Portia's speech had been misused as part of my recklessness.

An aide to the bishop moved over to him and whispered in his ear. I ignored them and continued reading. Ingrid had brought these words to life for me; she had given them meaning. And Miss Coultrane wanted to remind me of that. I could do this.

" 'Tis mightiest in the mightiest: it becomes
The throned monarch better than his crown;
His sceptre shows the force of temporal
    power,
The attribute to awe and majesty,
Wherein doth sit the dread and fear of
    kings;
But mercy is above this sceptred sway;
It is enthroned in the hearts of kings,
It is an attribute to God himself."

I caught a sudden movement. My father had risen from his chair and was standing, pulled tall to his full six-foot height, a silent gesture of support that set a few people murmuring. I saw my mother, looking horrified, tugging at his jacket. What grandiose statement was this? Of course, here he was, embarrassing her again. He wouldn't sit down.

He and I locked eyes. The big, jaunty smile I knew so well wasn't there, but his eyes told more. For this moment, wasn't this truly my father? My heart leaped. My voice caught for a second, and then I was overwhelmed by a burst of frustration. I wanted to cry out: Where have you been? *Are* you putting on an act? Is this real? *Where are you?* Trying to decide what I believed, I stared at him, unsmiling.

A total silence fell over the crowd for a few brief seconds after I finished. My father lowered himself into his chair, his face an odd muddy gray. Was something wrong? I tried to catch his eye, to smile finally, but he was looking down. Once again, the microphone caught the sound of the rustling of the paper as I carefully folded it and put it back in its envelope. Without turning my head, I could see the bishop murmur to his aide, who then beckoned to Sister Teresa Mary.

I had to say one more thing as I stood clutching the plaque.

"Miss Coultrane is a gifted teacher, and I am proud to have been her student," I said. "She knew all about mercy and kindness. And telling the truth. Saint Ann's will be the poorer for her absence."

There was a scattered burst of clapping as I prepared to make my way back to my seat.

Sister Teresa Mary, looking, I felt, like a woman going to her execution, stepped slowly to the microphone.

"Thank you, Jesse," she said. "Bishop Doyle regrets to inform us that he has been unexpectedly called away. Unfortunately, that means he will be unable to personally hand out the diplomas. Monsignor O'Hara will take over that conclusion to graduation. But he congratulates you all and wishes you a blessed future."

A buzz of surprise. Parents who had endured the speeches and awards, some half dozing, suddenly realized that the bishop's honored presence, usually the capstone of the ceremony, had been taken away. He was at that moment turning his back, but not before casting a steely glare in my direction, making it very clear to whoever was watching just why this sudden change of plans.

I looked over at my parents — saw my

mother putting an arm around Father's shoulders, talking to him. Look at me, I silently pleaded.

Nobody seemed to know what was supposed to come next. The school orchestra launched raggedly into a hymn as everybody whispered. I wanted to get off that stage, to run off. A few uncertain minutes dragged by, and then Monsignor O'Hara, looking befuddled, started handing out diplomas.

A commotion suddenly burst out where my parents were sitting. People were standing, craning their necks. What was happening? Chairs were toppling over. I heard a man's voice shouting for help. And then I heard my mother scream.

I scrambled off the podium, tripping over a flowerpot, then kicking it out of the way. I couldn't see my parents, I heard somebody yell for a doctor, and I tried to shove through the crowd.

"Jesse —" Kathleen, also out of breath, was at my side. She pointed to the street, where a car had bounced over the curb and kept going through the grass, wheels digging into the loam, all the way to the unfolding scene. Two men, a limp figure hoisted between them, quickly deposited their burden gently in the back seat as the driver kept the engine running.

306

"It's my father, isn't it?"

"I think so."

I ran, my legs rubbery. I saw Mother climb into the car; someone slammed the door shut. "Wait for me!" I screamed. But no one heard, and I couldn't get through the crowd fast enough. The car, churning deeper into the velvet turf, roared away.

"They're headed for the hospital. Are you that man's daughter? Come on, follow me, I'll drive you. My car's over there." Who was he? A stranger, somebody's parent. Blindly, I ran after him, Kathleen at my side.

I knew before the doctor approached me in the emergency room. A massive heart attack. I remember crying, crying so hard it hurt my throat. No, this happens in the movies, I tried to tell myself. They took me to the curtained-off room where my father lay still on a gurney. Mother sat next to him, head bowed.

Couldn't I have been given just one last moment with him? Couldn't God have managed that? Instead, weeping, I reached for his motionless hand. All I could do was to watch him turn into nothing more than one of those still, cold statues at Saint Ambrose Church.

Mother looked up as I rushed in, her eyes

glazed with shock. "It happened so fast," she said. "All that waiting — and just like that: fired."

"This morning?"

"It didn't matter, he said." Her voice was choked with tears. "He said you came first today. The heart attack hit right when he stood up for you. The exertion was too much."

"Oh, Mother —"

The tears flooded her cheeks. "You were too hard on him," she said. "You should've been kinder."

The room spun. I heard Kathleen gasp. Covering my ears, I stumbled out of the room. Somebody caught me as my legs buckled — it was Malcolm; he was standing outside the door. Oh God, he had heard this.

"You didn't do anything," Malcolm blurted.

I pulled away from his grasp. Mother was right. He couldn't absolve me of this; there was no absolution. I was guilty.

"Yes, I did," I choked out.

I have memorized every movement, run it in slow motion: the set of my father's chin that fresh June morning, the tired look in his eyes as he stood in support of me. Why didn't I smile? Couldn't I have managed a small one? How wrong it is to be eighteen and decide never to forgive. I have cried a sea of tears, knowing too late the message of love my father had been trying to convey, that of one frail human to another.

Kathleen and Malcolm stood by me at the sparsely attended funeral. There was no Mass. Mother wasn't sure if Gabriel Malloy had ever been baptized, and she couldn't shrug that off. There was no certificate to prove his Catholic credentials, and the bishop was, of course, a stickler for such details. That apparently discouraged the more fervent Catholics of Hollywood, such as Louella Parsons, from attending. And those who had heard the whispers surrounding his firing stayed away, too; guilt by proximity was always a fear.

I saw Sister Teresa Mary and Miss Coultrane standing in the shadows at the funeral home, and felt a surge of gratitude. Jerry Feldstein showed up, looking haggard. His scriptwriting days were over, I had heard. Like others, he wouldn't work in Hollywood again. The room was bursting with elaborate, overly bright flower arrangements displayed on a fake altar, flowers from people like David Selznick, Howard

Hughes, and Gary Cooper. Maybe Cary Grant, too, I never looked at all the cards. I wished I could send Cooper's back to him. He didn't denounce people by name, but he had made it clear he thought communism in Hollywood was a real threat, which kept the shadows building that took down people like my father.

A letter from Ingrid Bergman came, which Mother read and promptly tore up. She stood alone in the church, hard and silent. I kept remembering how she had tugged at Father's jacket, wanting him to sit down. Trying to save him from me.

The weeks of the hollow summer that followed remain blurred in memory. My father's pension from the studio would pay for college as well as supporting my mother, I was told by a very officious studio lawyer. They helped sell the house for us. Slowly, we packed. Mother had decided living in Hollywood was too expensive. With the urging of Father's brother, she decided to move up to Sacramento, where she could buy a nicer house than she could afford in Los Angeles. And I was heading for Bennington College. We shared a sadness, but it was a strange, chilly sharing. We did what we had to do.

Mother went to Mass as usual each Sunday, almost up to moving day. She would stand at the hall mirror to apply her resolutely bright lipstick, just as she had in the old house when I was young. She looked just as fragile, but I was sure she was steel at the core. She always asked if I was coming with her; I told her I was busy.

One Sunday, I did go to Mass — quietly, at the cathedral, alone. I hadn't planned it. I had been walking by when the splendid, soaring Latin hymns of High Mass drew me in, opening all the yearnings for peace and meaning in my heart that would not go away. I sat at the back of that huge, grand church, rosary beads in hand, fingering them, no prayers in my voice or mind. I looked around at the congregation — it was a high-noon Mass, and the church was crowded. Several old people, bent in prayer, sat near me, murmuring their responses, while a young family just ahead struggled to keep four little girls quiet through the lengthy service.

Only as the Mass ended did I realize Bishop Doyle was the celebrant — I was so far in the back of that vast space, I hadn't noticed.

And now, with the organist playing at full volume, he was leading the recessional from the altar, down the center aisle, to the rear of the church. Three altar boys, walking backward, swinging incense burners, led the way. Behind him, the deacon and subdeacon followed in cadenced step. As he passed each pew, people were genuflecting, bowing their heads, and making the sign of the cross. I realized he would brush right past me; I would be expected to do the same.

He was coming closer. Those cold eyes of his fastened on mine.

I couldn't stand it. "Excuse me," I whispered to the people between me and the back exit from the pew. Eyes widened; faces frowned; I was pushing now, shoving slow-moving parishioners out of the way, not even trying to be discreet. I knew, fully knew, I couldn't bend my knee to this man, this representative of the unforgiving God my mother believed in so fervently. That would pile hypocrisy onto sin. I knew I would live with a permanent burden of guilt. And there would always be disapproval, in my mother's face and in my church. I was expected to embrace it. And if I didn't feel there was a place for me in my church anymore, maybe there never had been, all the way back to my reluctance as a child to stand for the pledge to condemn immoral movies.

Bishop Doyle was only three pews away

when I broke free. I glanced in his direction, saw his stony expression, then turned my back and pushed for the door.

I woke up that last night in our house somewhere around three in the morning, unable to sleep. I pulled on a robe and wandered into the living room. It was dark; the furniture was mostly gone, sent with the movers to Sacramento. My bags were packed and by the front door. I stared at them, ran my finger along the living-room wall, realizing all of this would never be tangible again: this house, my parents' dreams, would all exist only in memory for me in a matter of hours.

"I guess you couldn't sleep, either," my mother's voice said quietly, cutting through the darkness.

I started, then saw the burning tip of a cigarette as she released a curl of smoke into the air from her chair by the glass doors leading to the patio. Her profile was etched into sharp relief against the soft glow of a waning moon.

"You never smoke."

"It's a release," she said.

I wasn't sure what to say next.

"Jesse, I want to explain myself better to you," she said softly.

"Please, you don't have to."

"I want to tell you what it was like, working in that ticket booth at Grauman's Chinese. And meeting your father. Will you listen?"

"If it matters to you," I said. There really was no choice.

"It was a job, and I was lucky to have it," she said. "It felt glamorous and important, doling out tickets to lines of people eager to see the most famous movie palace in the world. But it was such a tiny space inside the booth, I could barely move. I thought, for a while, it was worth it." She paused, her voice fading for a moment.

"But all the excitement was on the other side of the glass," she continued. "I took money and smiled until my muscles ached, but nothing was changing. I was memorizing every detail about *them* — but they didn't see *me*. I felt lonely. That sounds vain, I know."

"No, it doesn't," I said quickly. For just a split second, I could envision a young girl from a poor Irish neighborhood outside Boston smiling hopefully out on a world closed off to her by birth and opportunity.

"Gabriel was often in that line, usually with some pretty girl on his arm. He was so handsome and cheerful — I began looking for him, hoping he would show up. He would make a joke as I slipped his tickets under the glass; once he told me I should be in the movies, and I said I didn't want to be, and he asked what time I got off."

"I always thought it sounded romantic," I ventured.

She hardly seemed to hear. "I couldn't believe my luck." Her voice broke; then she went silent.

What was I supposed to say? I waited.

"Things went the way they often do," she continued. "But not like in the movies. Your movie-star heroine knows all about *that*."

Ingrid. She was talking about Ingrid. A realization took root, slowly growing. My devout mother? Who called down fear of God's wrath at the very idea of illicit sex?

"I was afraid, terribly afraid, when I realized I was pregnant. He said he wouldn't desert me. He followed up on that — he was a decent man, and I loved him desperately."

"And he loved you —"

"Who knows? Would he have married me if I hadn't gotten pregnant?"

That shocked me even more. "Of course he would have —" I said.

She cut me off. "Don't pretend, I don't need it. I will never know, but he was a dutiful human being. That's why he married me."

"Mother, I don't believe that. He adored you."

"I didn't deserve him, Jesse. And you should know why." She took a deep breath. "I *deliberately tried* to get pregnant," she said. "I knew it was a sin, but I was willing to risk everything." The glow of her lit cigarette disappeared, scrunched into embers in an ashtray.

"And the fact that he saved me from shame was a miracle, but it didn't wipe the slate clean. I loved him and tried to be a good wife, and prayed for forgiveness. But he could have made a better marriage. I knew, somewhere along the line, there would be a price to pay. My only possible salvation was to make sure nothing like that — the desperateness, the temptation — ever descended on you. I promised myself I would keep you safe."

Until that moment, I don't think I had ever quite realized how much my mother totally embraced her belief in the unforgivable.

"When I learned about his affair, I thought that would settle my score with God. But then you gave that awful speech at the tournament — even that blow wasn't enough."

"Mother" — I couldn't help it — "don't you ever forgive yourself?"

"How? Oh, Jesse, *how*?"

She began crying — in such anguish, I couldn't absorb it. "I lost him, I loved him so much, how do I forgive myself?" I could see her body in shadow; she looked so small and frail, her shoulders heaving.

Maybe by loving me more.

The words were on my tongue, full of my own anguish. I wanted to yell them out, and I tried to form them, but they caught in my throat. I couldn't do that: it would be a slap in her face. I could deal out no more hurt.

I moved to her side instead and embraced her, searching for the right words of comfort. Maybe we could find a way out of what held us both captive; maybe we could reach each other.

She quickly dried her eyes with her hand and then, with just a few words, split the chasm wider.

"God will forgive you eventually," she said. "But you were born under a shadow, and I'm the one who created it."

"Mother, that's a trap; I don't believe it."

Her voice was suddenly calm again. Cool. "I wish you were going to a Catholic college," she said.

"I will be fine," I said automatically. All my words hung suspended — unspoken.

Then, after a silence, she said, "It's time for us to head back to bed. Tomorrow is a busy day." She rose, touched my shoulder, and padded off to her room.

I made no move to follow her.

Later, when the harsh morning sun was high, and the cab-driver was loading my bags, we faced each other one last time on the front porch. I gave her a quick hug goodbye, all elbows and jutting bones, hers and mine, and told her I would come to Sacramento for Christmas. She gave me a stiff squeeze back, and said she would come see me at college.

Kathleen was permanent, I already knew that. But I said a final goodbye to Malcolm after the funeral. He was hurt, I could see that; I couldn't help it. I wanted as few memories as possible, no tethers to this place laughingly called home.

That's all, that's all.

Well, it isn't, really. So many questions still weave through my life. Sometimes I want to find answers, but I'm afraid I will find there aren't any, and that would be worse.

And maybe that is why I am going back.

■ ■ ■ ■

PART TWO

■ ■ ■ ■

CHAPTER SEVENTEEN

Los Angeles, 1959

It was almost disturbingly easy to get time off from my job; obviously, my absence wasn't going to cause a ripple at *Newsweek.* My boss was a bluff, cheerful sort, who called it like it was, usually. "Editors aren't comfortable with single women, even smart broads," he said to me once.

"Why?" I asked.

"Because they'll get married. And then they'll get pregnant."

"So there's not much room for us," I managed.

"You made the copy desk," he pointed out.

"Will I go higher?"

He seemed genuinely astonished to be asked. "Isn't that enough?"

So it was confirmed — I had time off. I typed up a fresh copy of the rejected Barbie piece and stuffed it in the mail to *Life* magazine as fast as I could, sending it off with a version of a prayer.

Then I got down to the business of packing, which brought back some long-forgotten memories.

"Did I ever tell you I tried to pack a year's supply of Kotex when I left L.A. for college?" I said to Kathleen the night before my flight.

"You're kidding."

"I wasn't sure if a small Northeastern town would have drugstores."

"God, Jesse." A pause. A sudden burst of static over the phone line. Or was it a repressed laugh? "You really were a combination of extremes."

Kathleen's comment nagged at me as I boarded my plane the next morning — probably because "a combination of extremes" said it too well. I needed some middle ground. I took my seat and started flipping through the latest *Saturday Evening Post,* scanning the short stories, hoping that one I had sent them would be bought. I fancied it sitting, unread, in some editor's box — where, quite possibly, it would never be read, so that one of those standard rejection slips would just show up in my mail again.

The flight was long and boring. Fortunately, the drone of the Douglas DC-7's engines kept me asleep for most of the trip, letting me dream various floaty scenarios heavy with sunshine and palm trees.

I awoke with a start, my head still tangled in cobwebs, only when the pilot announced we were approaching Los Angeles. I pressed my nose against the window. We were right above a scattering of bright-blue patches. Of course, the pools of Beverly Hills. What perfect, corny timing; it gave me the shivers.

Enough of that. I opened my purse, pulled out a silver compact, and brushed powder over my nose, applying it quickly. And then a flash of memory: Mother's horrified face that day I defied the bishop at Mass, which she called a betrayal. Were memories going to pop up like that all week? I was an idiot to come.

A bounce, a screech of brakes. The question was moot; we were on the tarmac, rolling toward the arrival gate.

Kathleen was waiting, hands shoved into the pockets of a bright-green windbreaker, with a wide grin on her face. How long since we had seen each other? Two years since her last visit to New York? Her face was thinner, her cheeks were less rosy, and her hair was more of a subdued auburn now. But she wore it pulled back into a casual ponytail that bounced and caught the light in perpetual motion. Yes, this was still my ebullient friend.

"I'll bet you're the only L.A. real-estate agent wearing a ponytail," I said, reaching out to hug her.

"If it droops when I show you a house, it means I think it's overpriced," she said with a grin. "God, it's good to see you." She gestured over to the next gate, where an impossibly slender blonde was boarding a plane, waving to a cluster of people shouting goodbye. "That's Betty Hutton, off to Las Vegas. Her last movie bombed; she's hoping for a winning streak. I sold her house for her — got a great price."

I felt better already as she scooped up my suitcase at the baggage claim with an elaborate frown. "Filled with Kotex again?" she asked innocently.

That turned a few heads in our direction. I laughed, delighted in my sudden light-heartedness. Thank you, Kathleen.

Kathleen's car was a sporty white MG convertible. "Wow," I said, truly impressed. We piled my luggage in the trunk, and I slid into the passenger seat, smoothing the soft black leather upholstery with my hand.

"That's what I said when I saw it in the showroom," she said as she maneuvered the car swiftly out of the airport parking lot and onto the road, her foot firmly on the gas pedal.

"You've done all this on your own."

"Right. I like being independent. Great car, isn't it?" she shouted over the rush of wind that came with our quickening speed.

"Yes, but what do you do when it rains?" I shouted back.

"Jesse," she laughed, "you're back in Los Angeles, remember? The land of perpetual sunshine!"

I tipped my head up to the sun, and for just a second I felt Kathleen's exuberance sweep through me; then I caught myself. "A land of pretty harsh sunshine, as I recall," I said.

She said nothing, just reached a hand over to squeeze mine.

"Where are we going?" I asked.

"Home, right now. You're three hours ahead of us — you'll pass out early."

"Where is home?"

"An apartment off La Brea Avenue, near the tar pits. Actually, pretty near the old Charlie Chaplin Studio. It's disgusting what the pinko-haters did, banning him from the country. It wasn't enough to try and kill his movie."

The boycott of *Limelight,* when Chaplin was hounded out of the United States. That was 1952. "I heard that, after HUAC's charges, people yelled at Chaplin in restaurants and even spat in his face," I said.

Kathleen nodded. "Those were awful times here," she said. "I keep asking myself, how did this country let Joe McCarthy take over?" She shook her head. "Did that vicious man ever ruin lives."

I thought of Jerry Feldstein and all the others. "Including the lives of my father's friends," I said. "He was a destroyer."

We sat in silence, remembering. The vigilante senator from Wisconsin had died a couple of years ago, and I had cheered. His power had dribbled away as people began stepping back, finally looking at the cost of all the hysteria over communists and reaching the point of being ashamed.

"It's such an old horror now," I said.

"Not completely. The morality police still hold sway."

"I wonder if the government will relent on Ingrid Bergman. She survived the morality police, that's for sure. They didn't kill her career in Europe."

Ingrid's long absence from the United

States had not stopped her career from flourishing. She and Rossellini had finally married, but only after a bitter divorce and custody fight with the angry Petter Lindström. She and Rossellini made five more films together, none of which gained audiences in the United States.

"She's done all right, don't you think? Movies, the stage — just not here. Other than winning an Academy Award for *Anastasia,* which she couldn't come pick up."

"Thanks to Ed Sullivan. That jerk. She'd be back here by now if it weren't for what he did."

When *Anastasia* was released in 1956, Ingrid was quietly invited back to the States to receive the New York Critics Award. The TV host Ed Sullivan, whose Sunday-night television program was watched by millions, got wind of the impending weekend visit, and in a grandiose gesture decided to let his viewers vote — thumbs up or down — on whether to invite Ingrid Bergman to appear on his show.

"This woman has had seven and a half years of time for penance. Should we let her appear on U.S. television? It's up to the public!" he declared.

An uproar followed: who was Sullivan to launch a national vote for condemnation or praise of an actress? He apologized, but the spotlight of notoriety had been turned on Ingrid again.

Her visit was brief. She fled back to Europe as quickly as she could.

My thoughts went back to Stromboli — to the sight of Ingrid Bergman in her red skirt, standing on that hill, linked to Rossellini. And, yes, to my father's devastation.

All signs pointed initially to a happy union. She had loved Rossellini, that was clear. The U.S. tabloids paid less attention to the two of them as the years went by, especially as she seemed to settle into domesticity — producing twin daughters after they were finally able to marry. Kathleen and I never lost interest, of course, and we agreed at one point that Ingrid's unlikely new family would stabilize.

But the rumors of a volatile relationship came into the open when Ingrid — against Rossellini's wishes — made two career decisions. She would star in *Anastasia,* which meant leaving Italy to film in England — and she also accepted the lead role in *Tea and Sympathy,* a controversial play about homosexuality, which would take her to Paris. Rossellini, the press reported, was furious.

It wasn't very long before we learned that Ingrid and Rossellini were getting divorced.

"So are you disillusioned?" Kathleen had asked in one of our phone conversations at the time.

"Not really," I said. I liked to think nothing could shock me anymore. My own life had seen some turbulence, after all — no need to go over *that*. "I wonder what my father would say."

"He'd probably think it was funny."

"I liked that quote of hers about the divorce — you know the one."

"Yep: 'Italians and Swedes don't mix.' "

And so it came to something that simple. Kathleen gave me a knowing look. "Now, if you and I were fifteen again, we'd be inhaling movie-mag stories on Ingrid and her *new* husband," she said.

"There don't seem to be that many, do there? I guess a solid Swedish film producer named Lars Schmidt isn't quite as juicy fodder as a romantic Italian," I said.

"So, given the fact that we're too grown-up for *that* stuff, I've got an idea for tomorrow."

I was loving the breeze in my hair as Kathleen drove, and feeling sleepy already. "Tomorrow?" I asked.

"Well, how about this? They closed Saint

Ann's ten days ago. But tomorrow there's an auction of artifacts, memorabilia, lots of stuff." She hesitated. "It might feel strange, but —"

"What is Doyle selling off, the desks? The blackboards? The statues and chalices from the chapel?"

"Probably."

"It's that easy to get rid of objects we were supposed to venerate?"

"Yep."

"You're not indignant?"

"I never cared about all that as much as you did." There was a tone in her voice, a hardening around the edges.

"*You* want to go?" I asked.

"Yes."

"Okay. I'm not going to fall apart, if that's what you're worried about," I said quickly.

Kathleen twisted the wheel with one hand, taking a sharp left onto Century Boulevard. "I'm not worried about you — I'm worried about me."

Her apartment was the top floor of a 1930s stucco bungalow with large windows and arched door frames that gave the interior extra grace. It really was warm and inviting. "It's like you," I said, settling in on a bright orange modern sofa and looking around. I nodded in the direction of a large fireplace lined in rust-and-gold Mexican tiles. "Do you use it?" I asked.

"Of course not," she said cheerfully. She finished pouring two glasses of white wine, handed me one, and plopped down on the sofa next to me. "How is your mother?" she asked, looking away as she sipped her wine.

"She's doing fine, I guess."

"Are you heading up to Sacramento to see her after the awards ceremony?"

"I haven't decided. I'm not sure I can take more time off." Which was a lie, of course. Half the people at the magazine would have been hard-pressed to know my name, and my boss had even said to take a few more days if I wanted to. Kathleen would know the truth.

"Well, if you're brave enough to come to L.A., Sacramento shouldn't be too much of a challenge."

"When did I give you permission to see through me?"

"Same time I gave permission to you to do the same. Pretty early, I think."

The silence that followed was safe.

"I feel more comfortable holding her away from me," I said. "But — you know? — she doesn't seem to mind. She does the same when I visit. I don't know if it's a truce or a resolution."

"She and my mother have struck up a friendship; did you know that?"

"No." I was surprised. "How did that happen?"

Kathleen shrugged. "Your mother used to come into the May Company a lot after you left; I guess it was that summer. Mine told me a few months ago that they still write each other, but she shares no details."

A lurch of guilt; I had pretty much frozen Mother out in those months after Father died. I had a sudden image of her standing at the May Company hosiery counter, buying stockings she didn't need, as an excuse to talk to someone sympathetic.

"I can tell you're already building a story," Kathleen said gently. "It may be in your genes, but don't go Hollywood too fast."

I closed my eyes, then opened them again and said, "Your mother was never as devout as my mother. Did that change?"

"No, she treats it all as . . . kind of as a joke."

"What about your father? Has he reappeared at all?"

Kathleen tossed down the rest of her wine in a single gulp and stood. "Nothing much to say. He's out there somewhere. Pizza for dinner, if you can stay awake."

I sighed, eyeing the bedroom door with some longing. No more talking tonight. "I think I'll skip the pizza," I said.

"Good — more for me." Kathleen handed me some toothpaste and said good night.

I don't remember much after that: my first night back in this hostile city was spent in deep and dreamless sleep.

The next morning, we set out early and stopped at a pancake house, where I drank lots of coffee. Kathleen was as bright and bouncy as the day, but I was jumpy, and not just from the coffee. I was beginning to wonder what Saint Ann's Academy would look like without students.

I wasn't sure what to expect. But as we drove into the old parking lot, it was the silence — the suspended animation — that struck me first. The hedges, the palm trees, even the blades of grass and the winding paths, were still. It was as if Saint Ann's had ceased to breathe. Empty. No motion, no sudden movement along those paths, no sound of girls murmuring, no bells ringing. I shut my eyes, trying to conjure up the past.

We parked and stepped out into what felt at first like the flat, still terrain of a cemetery.

"It's not dead until we're out of here," Kathleen said.

"Right."

We walked toward the tennis courts, taking in the sagging volleyball net that nobody had seen fit to remove. We peeked in the building that housed the old study hall and saw it was emptied of desks — probably already auctioned off.

"You're looking a little teary-eyed," Kathleen warned, tugging me toward the tennis court. "I want to see where you were always yelling you were sorry every time you missed a shot."

"I beat you a few times."

"Twice."

We stood at the mesh fence, staring at the old court. It clearly hadn't been used in quite a while. The white paint on the weathered clay had faded, leaving the baseline's location something of a puzzle. But for just a moment, if I blinked, I could hear again the satisfying pop each time a tennis ball met my racquet, feel again that delicious satisfaction of getting one over, clean and fast and low.

"Do you still play?" I asked.

"When I can."

"Same here."

We walked slowly over to the pool, reminiscing about the day when Sister Teresa Mary scolded Kathleen for the unforgivable offense of wearing a two-piece bathing suit. As we rounded the corner, we stopped and stared. The pool had been drained of water, which wasn't surprising. But what was jolting was the sight of jackhammers and other demolition equipment waiting at the shallow end. Two workmen, smoking, sat idly, their legs dangling over the edge of the pool. They were cheerful; greeting us was a diversion from waiting for the signal to smash the pool apart. Maybe today, maybe tomorrow.

We walked on; no lingering here.

"You know what I think?" I said to Kathleen.

"Probably."

"I think the archdiocese didn't give the nuns enough money to fix things up properly because they knew for years they were going to tear down the school. It's always been just real estate to them."

"Cuts a little close to the script of *The Bells of St. Mary's,*" she said.

"You agree?"

"It's plausible. Yeah, I think I do." She stopped, checking her watch. "It's about time for the auction to begin," she said.

"Where is it?"

"On the front lawn. You okay with that?" She looked at me inquiringly.

Well, of course. Where else was there on the school grounds an expanse of space big enough for this kind of event? It was going to be right where, for me, everything ended: auctioneers standing on the steps of the administration building, looking onto the lawn where generations of Saint Ann's graduates had gathered in white dresses with their floral bouquets for the guaranteed tranquil passage into smug and unquestioning adulthood.

So here I was, about to revisit the site of the graduation I had spent nine years trying to erase.

Kathleen's voice cut in abruptly. "Look, you can walk with ghosts or you can attend an auction. Choose one?"

I blinked. "Let's go," I said.

Dozens of people were milling about when we reached the front lawn — a mix of men and women, examining tables laden with artifacts arranged in jumbled fashion, many smoking as they poked away at everything from framed pictures of the Sacred Heart that had once hung in classrooms to well-used Ping-Pong paddles. We spied some of our old classmates. They were eager to chat along predictable lines: Hello, how are you, where do you live now, oh my goodness,

336

you live in *New York*? How glamorous. Married Neddy from Mount Carmel High School, remember him? The twins are almost six years old now. Think I've got another one on the way. . . . Nobody brought up graduation.

"I guess there's something about being almost ten years out of school that makes us all best friends," Kathleen murmured as we moved along.

I ran into one of Miss Coultrane's students; she and I actually shared some real memories of our wonderfully imperious teacher, who had, she told me, died a few years ago. That set me back — I hadn't expected it.

But the real surprise came next.

"Hello, Jesse."

I jumped at the familiar voice and turned around. Standing there, smiling, was a woman with weathered skin who looked to be in her sixties. I wasn't sure at first — she wore a plain navy skirt, some kind of navy cape, and a short veil. But then I knew.

"Sister Teresa Mary?" I blurted.

She smiled. "Good, you recognize me. Not everybody does."

I stuttered out a few pleasantries, and we shared a superficial exchange of information — the type of polite chatter that conveys almost nothing. She asked after my mother, my job, what life was like in New York. I wanted to ask her how it felt to be uprooted from her home, but the crowd was milling around us now, jostling, getting noisier. A couple of former students were hovering nearby, eager to talk to her.

She glanced at them, then said, "Why don't you stop by and see me while you're in town? We've been moved to a school dormitory in the Valley." Her smile turned wry. "It's quite different from here, and needs some fixing up — but we're almost ready."

"Why, thank you, I would like that," I said, startled. And wondered if I meant it.

"Kathleen knows where we are. I'll call you at her house in the next day or two."

I wanted to talk more, but one of the hovering students tapped her on the shoulder and she turned away. I stared after her. So many questions never answered.

Kathleen and I kept wandering from table to table — yes, desks lined in a row, most already tagged by potential buyers. Holy-water fonts from the chapel. The stained-glass windows, though stacked behind one of the tables, were labeled "not for sale."

"Our bishop knows what is valuable," Kathleen murmured.

As she spoke, I spied a dusty bronze plaque propped up against one of the desks. "Look," I said, pointing. I could hardly believe it — I was looking at the plaque installed so long ago as a proud commemoration of Saint Ann's part in the making of *The Bells of St. Mary's.*

"Well, what do you know, they didn't throw it out after all," Kathleen said with a chuckle. "That shameful episode — my, my, they just tucked it away from public view."

It suddenly hit me. "Is this why you wanted to come?" I asked.

"No, but I did wonder about it. I figured if it still existed you might want it." She looked at me expectantly. "And if bidding goes too high, we can pool our money."

Did I really want it? Why? Maybe I didn't want to throw away all the memories; maybe I wanted to hang on to something tangible.

A sudden sound from the newly activated mike. The auctioneer, a middle-aged man with a pencil-thin mustache and bored eyes, cleared his throat and raised a large wooden gavel. The auction was about to begin.

First went the carpets, wall hangings, candleholders, even some old books from the school library. There was quite a crowd now, most of them clustered around the front tables, still fingering through them for overlooked treasures. We saw not a single nun, which was no surprise.

"And now we have here a bizarre memento of Saint Ann's history from the mid-forties," announced the auctioneer, arching a theatrical eyebrow. "Folks, there actually was a time when Saint Ann's lent itself to Hollywood for the making of an Ingrid Bergman movie — before the scandal, of course. And here's a memento of that event, foisted on the good nuns by a fancy publicity campaign."

One of his assistants hefted the bronze marker and handed it up to him. The auctioneer held it high. "It's a pretty dusty piece of metal. Who will give me ten dollars for it? Anybody?"

Maybe it was the sneering "fancy publicity campaign," but I suddenly knew I wanted that plaque. It had actually marked a proud moment, for both me and my school, and I wasn't going to let it get discarded. I raised my hand.

"Ten dollars from the little lady in the back row. Am I bid twenty? Come on, folks, twenty bucks?"

A hand shot up near the front of the crowd. I tried to see the bidder, but couldn't.

"We are off and running, ladies and gentlemen. Give me thirty?"

Hesitantly, I put up my hand again.

The other bidder promptly bid forty.

"I'm in for another ten," Kathleen whispered. My hand went up for a third time. Fifty dollars — I was breaking into a sweat.

No use — the bidder in front never hesitated. I couldn't go higher. Fifty dollars was a fortune; this was crazy.

"Going, going, gone," intoned the auctioneer. "Sold to the gentleman in front for sixty dollars!"

It was all over in three minutes. I felt a bit dizzy at what we had risked, and frustrated. Even angry. So close, and then some stranger grabbed this memory of Ingrid away.

Kathleen squeezed my arm. "Do you see who I see?" she whispered.

I looked up. A man was walking toward us — a man of stocky frame, not very tall, with dark hair. He wore a weathered leather jacket and a baseball cap that shadowed his eyes. There was a faint, unbelieving smile on his lips.

The acne was gone.

"Malcolm?"

"It's me," he said, his voice deeper than I remembered. "And you really are Jessica

341

Malloy. At least, you look like her." His eyes searched my face. "I guess we were competing for that marker."

My thoughts were scrambled. "How did you know I was here?"

"I didn't."

"You were bidding against me?"

"I didn't know who I was bidding against," he said. "And it turns out, hey, it's the girl who left nine years ago. I kind of hoped for a note every now and then; didn't happen."

"I —"

"I know, college, and then I heard you got married and stayed out east. How's New York?"

It was all said very casually, even as I was trying to get my bearings. I could see the boy I had known in his eyes, the boy who had altered my life at Redlands and kissed me at my prom. Just fleetingly. This was a stranger.

"No, I almost got married — that's what you probably heard," I said, instantly embarrassed that I had dropped that piece of information into the conversation.

"Oh." He looked briefly startled.

I tried to say it in an easy way. It was just one of those things that didn't work out, I said.

Kathleen, of course, knew the whole story.

342

A romance with a Yale graduate student — I thought I was in love and he was, too — we even set a date for the wedding. My intellectual, worldly boyfriend thought it amusing that I wanted to get married before climbing into bed with him. So I gave in, afraid he would walk away. Which he did, of course — the wedding date disappeared. We lasted almost a year before he packed a bag one morning, left a note saying he wasn't ready for marriage, and left.

Malcolm and I stood silently for a few seconds, without a script, until Kathleen jumped in.

"I wonder what closet that plaque got buried in for all these years?" she said cheerfully. "God, I love the nuns. They can be so discreetly sneaky."

Malcolm laughed, and I relaxed.

"I'm imagining them peeking through the windows at all this," I said.

"And hopefully getting a good chuckle out of it," he added.

I couldn't picture that, but he was trying.

"Let's get out of here," he said. "Is there a nearby place for a cup of coffee? I'll pick up the — what did the auctioneer call it? — 'bizarre memento' later."

Kathleen and I exchanged glances. Of

course there was, our favorite drugstore, across the street, where all proper Saint Ann's girls had hung out at one time or another — the place where we first bought and devoured our movie magazines.

But it wasn't a drugstore with a soda counter anymore. It was a weary-looking place that called itself the Koffee Kup.

"Oh well," Kathleen said. "We can get burgers."

The booths were shabby and the menus sticky. "What a dump," Kathleen said. She was fully at ease, but, then, she always was. We slid into one of the booths — not too easy a job, since the red plastic upholstery was not only cracked but peeling off.

"What are you doing?" I asked Malcolm. "Are you still in school?" I wanted to ask how he could afford to pay sixty dollars for a nostalgic piece of bronze, but held back.

Malcolm took a gulp of his coffee. "Maybe you still see me as a junior in high school," he said gently. "I assure you, I graduated, went to college, and finished law school. Now I'm gainfully employed, doing fine."

I flushed. That was a bit too close to the point, but, of course, nine years was a long time. "I'm sorry, I'm just trying to catch up," I said.

"And what about you?"

"I'm a copy editor with *Newsweek.* Not the most exciting job, but I'm writing, trying to sell some of my work."

"What are you writing about?"

"Right now, something to pay the bills."

"Is that why you're here?"

"No."

Kathleen and I glanced at each other. "Two reasons," I said. "To see Saint Ann's one more time, I guess. And — to go to the Academy Awards."

He grinned. "So you've been acting or directing on the side?"

"Someone sent me an invitation. I thought it might be a joke, but it's authentic."

He put his cup down slowly. "You have no connections here anymore?"

"None — except Kathleen."

"And, maybe, me."

Kathleen's eyes lit up with interest. "You're an attorney now, right? What firm?"

"No firm, actually," he said. "I'm working in the legal department at Selznick Productions."

"You're in the movie business?" My disappointment was too obvious. How could someone as kind as the Malcolm I remembered work for those cutthroats?

"Not everybody in the business is a sell-out, Jesse."

That brought back immediately a memory of my father laughing during the good times, calling the movie industry our "family business." Not a happy memory.

"Okay, I'll ask the question I'm wondering about. Did you send Jesse that invitation?" Kathleen asked. Our food had come, and she began biting into her hamburger with clear enjoyment. "Seeing as how you work at a studio and it would make a great romantic gesture by an old boyfriend?"

Malcolm laughed, shaking his head. "God, no," he said. "I'm too junior in the department to have *that* power." He looked at me, a quick glance. "But I would have if I could have. If it would've brought you back."

That jumped a few hurdles very fast, which flustered me.

He squirted a blob of catsup on his hamburger and started eating. His hands were large, his fingers stubby. Somewhere in the background, a jukebox was playing a tinny version of "It's Only Make Believe."

There was hope that the lust for hunting moral and political transgressors in Hollywood was losing steam, he said. Plenty of reputations had been destroyed and friendships broken — much done that couldn't be fixed. Movie moguls realized they were being laughed at now, and they didn't like to be laughed at. But the censors were still strong in Washington.

"Even your church is quiet about it lately. Speaking of Catholics, what do you think about your new pope? He's supposed to be quite a reformer. John XXIII, right? Why the hell would anyone want to be the twenty-third of anything?"

I nodded and smiled, still staring at my own burger, not sure I wanted to eat it. "He's not my pope," I said.

"We've both left the Church," Kathleen said helpfully. "We're officially 'fallen away.' "

He turned to me, eyes curious. "How do you feel about that?"

I pushed the burger away. "Perfectly fine," I said.

CHAPTER EIGHTEEN

Los Angeles, 1959

"He's going to call you. Even though you were a bit snappish."

Kathleen and I were sitting in her living room late that afternoon, finishing off a bottle of wine. Actually, I was sitting, and Kathleen was prone on the sofa, her legs propped up on cushions. The sun was setting, sending a soft wash of gold through the room as we talked. We had almost effortlessly bridged the gap that distance had imposed, and I was grateful for that. It felt peaceful to follow each point of light as it touched briefly on my friend's chairs, pillows, and framed movie posters. The life she was stitching together seemed so much more solid than mine.

"I'm not even thinking about him," I said. "Anyway, this isn't high school anymore. I don't need romantic fantasies."

"Oh, for God's sake, don't be so stuffy,"

she said with a giggle.

I relented; Kathleen had a way of pricking almost every balloon I ever launched. "It was strange, seeing him," I said. "He's too much part of all that happened."

Our lunch had been fine — though, as I thought about it, I suspected I had shared more than he had. Or was it just that he listened better? I wondered how it would have gone if Kathleen hadn't been there.

"Maybe that's not fair to him, you know?"

I gestured at the walls. "What happened to that framed poster of Ingrid as *Joan of Arc* you had?"

"Okay, we'll change the subject if you want." She sighed and shook her head, her unruly copper hair catching the golden light. She had never bothered much with the latest hairstyles — no careful pageboy for her. "I hung it for a while, but it opened too many conversations."

Mildly surprised, I raised an eyebrow. "That doesn't sound like you. Conversations between whom and whom?"

"Between me and Ingrid, if you want to know. I looked at it one day and decided maybe both of us were done with phony saintliness."

Just as I started to answer, the phone rang. Kathleen smiled in a maddeningly knowledgeable way and reached for it. I quickly took a deep gulp of wine.

It was indeed Malcolm, and I could see how pleased Kathleen was to be right. Grinning, she untangled her extra-long cord, handed the phone to me, and pointed to the back hall. "I work all day tomorrow," she whispered. "So plan away."

He suggested lunch, which sounded reasonable; I said yes.

"Good, I'll pick you up at noon," he said. "I've got something to show you."

"What's that?"

"It's up at the observatory."

That could only mean the planetarium up in the wilds of Griffith Park. Odd spot for lunch: it was mainly a tourist destination, and usually filled with kids. I had been there several times. "I've seen the stars," I said, a little too briskly. "What is it you want to show me?"

"Something closer to home; you'll find out. We'll eat on the grass; I'll bring picnic stuff."

He showed up precisely at noon the next day, driving one of those strange German cars they called the Beetle. They weren't that popular in New York, but I had already seen a number of them zipping along on the highways here, and couldn't figure out what made such a charmless auto so popular.

"Quit frowning at my poor car," Malcolm said. He was wearing a wrinkled pair of khakis and scuffed shoes. "I know it's dirty, but when I get it washed, it's a pretty decent shade of blue. Great mileage, too."

I laughed and eased myself into the front seat, uneasy about the lack of any normal-sized car hood in front of us. "Where's the engine?" I asked.

"It doesn't need one."

He grinned at what must have been a startled expression on my face. "It's in the rear," he said. "Don't worry, it'll get us there." He nodded to the back seat, where a rattan hamper sat. "And I even remembered to chill the wine."

The road up through the park to the observatory wound in twists and turns through wide swaths of greenery — I had forgotten how spectacular the view of the city was from up there. Slowly, I relaxed. Malcolm was easy to talk to, full of jokes and banter. I didn't feel wary, as I had yesterday.

"Do you have any great desire to go into the planetarium itself?" he asked as we pulled into the parking lot at the top of the mountain.

"Not really. I've been here several times."

"Good." He switched off the engine and pulled the key from the ignition. "What I want to show you is on the west side."

We walked toward the Astronomers Monument — an Art Deco sculpture honoring six of the world's astronomers — at the front of the observatory, and I stopped for a moment. "I loved this as a child," I said. "Copernicus, Galileo —"

"They should've put Einstein up there, too," Malcolm said. "But he was still alive in '34. They decided it was a bit hasty to include him."

"A case of being better off dead?"

He chuckled, and pointed. "Here we are."

In front of us was a large bronze bust crowning a white column. Engraved into the column was a gold star — and a name: "James Dean."

I peered close at the inscription. "James Dean? The actor? What is he doing here?"

"Surprised, aren't you? They shot a big scene of *Rebel Without a Cause* up here early in '55. Then Dean died in that auto crash; instant sainthood."

"And they were ready to either toss or auction off Ingrid's plaque for *The Bells of*

St. Mary's."

"Just another case of being better off dead?" His eyes actually danced.

"You want me to laugh."

He shrugged. "Why not? Contradictions abound; we might as well laugh." He took my arm. "Okay, let's go find a spot on a nice private hillside up here and drink some wine."

We found a place out of sight of the crowds. Malcolm spread a tablecloth, then pulled out two turkey sandwiches, a thick slab of Parmesan cheese, a smaller one of Gruyère, and a package of crackers. Next, he hoisted the bottle of wine. "Is this restaurant okay?" he asked. He actually looked a little anxious.

Everything in me was relaxing. "More than okay."

Stretching out finally on the soft grass, staring up at the small puffs of clouds above us, he told me how he missed his brother, a brother who had moved to Israel. How his father — who had driven us to and from my prom — had suffered a stroke while Malcolm was in law school. He recovered, but never completely, and wasn't able to go back to managing full-time the dry-cleaning store that had been the family's livelihood.

I was more guarded. I told him a little about my years at Bennington, my doomed romance — I could be a bit flippant about it now — which took me to New York; about trying to launch a writing career after the romance was over. He asked what I was writing besides the Barbie-doll piece. I told him about some of the topics, how nothing seemed to jell; how my boring job at *Newsweek* was paying the bills. I tried to make it sound a little lighthearted, but it didn't quite work.

At one point, we fell into silence.

He broke it first. "I've been thinking about the Redlands speech tournament," he said.

"Oh dear, *that.*"

"Your win changed your life. You must have some resentment of me for being part of it."

"No, it isn't important. It's all long ago."

He was persistent. "I've wondered why you cut me off so quickly after your father died."

A vague wave of irritation swept over me. "What are you talking about? It had nothing to do with you. I had to get away from here."

"I know that." His voice was steady. "But something was building between us."

"Oh, I don't think so. How could we have

any future? We were just children."

"I wasn't, damn it. And neither were you."

I sat up. The mood of the afternoon was shifting.

He reached out a hand. "I'm sorry," he said. "I'm too blunt. I have this way of saying exactly what I'm thinking — bad habit."

I took a deep breath. "It's nice to see you again, but, please, don't push."

"Okay." He pulled himself up to a seated position next to me. We were both silent, listening to a pair of quarrelsome hummingbirds in a nearby oak tree darting and jabbing at each other.

"We'll let them quarrel, right?" I said.

"Yep. Better them than us."

But something in me wanted to talk. Slowly, at first. Then more and more. I told him how that summer after my father died had changed me. How I kept feeling he was still in our hollowedout house, how my mother kept pacing at night in the darkness. How I couldn't sleep. How I threw out all the flowers from the funeral because the mixed smell of roses, lilacs, carnations, and everything else made my stomach lurch. The flowers would decay, just like my father would. He was in an unconsecrated grave, and that didn't mean anything to me now, but it did then. I avoided dwelling on

Mother's blaming me — there was no use bringing up that terrible deathbed scene. I said I had decided that heroes were laughable, not worth anything. Even Ingrid Bergman.

"Maybe you expect too much." He said it gently.

"Maybe. What about you?"

"I don't revere anyone."

"Do you even believe in God?"

"Not in the sense of some great guy waiting for me in heaven." He pointed toward the oak tree. "Hey, did you notice? Those two hummingbirds made up and flew away."

Maybe I knew all along it was going to happen. But when he turned toward me then and reached out a finger to touch my lips, it felt natural. I closed my eyes, the scent of the grass and the earth mixing with the scent of his skin, and let myself gravitate in his direction. It was quick, but startling. We almost jumped apart, looking at each other with surprise.

"Wow, a hummingbird kiss," he said. "Want to try again?"

I laughed and shook my head. I had a flash of memory: my father, laughing, kissing my mother, demonstrating Ingrid's artful "hummingbird kiss" in *Notorious*. "That's enough," I said.

He propped himself up on one elbow and looked at me gravely. "Well — I decided at your prom that I would really kiss you someday."

"Like an item on your must-do list?"

I wanted it to sound playful, but a look of hurt crossed his face — and I knew it hadn't quite come out that way.

The kitchen in Kathleen's apartment that night was steamy from a pot of bubbling spaghetti. Frowning, her forehead glistening, Kathleen lifted the pot and drained the water in one quick, expert motion as I finished chopping an onion and tomatoes and flipped them into the frying pan.

"Great, put in some oregano," she said. "We're working pretty good as a team. Maybe we could launch a cooking show."

"Or you could, and I'll write about it."

"So how did it go with Malcolm today?"

"It was good," I said. I struggled with the best way to put it; I was still figuring it out myself. "I think it put some things to rest for him. He seemed touchy about my not saying goodbye."

"Well, you're touchy about a few things, too."

"Sure, but not the same things. Things a lot more important than a high-school romance."

We sat down at the table, now facing two heaping plates of pasta.

"So did he kiss you?"

"Kathleen . . ." I wanted to protest, but couldn't put my heart into it. "A little, okay? It didn't mean anything. And it's sort of private."

She paused, holding a forkful of spaghetti halfway to her mouth. "It never has been before," she said gently.

Which was true, of course. "It's just . . . I've got enough to think about here. He was not expected."

Kathleen shrugged. "You know, I've got something to suggest for tomorrow," she said. "There are some new properties going on the market that I need to check out, and I thought you might like to come along with me. Unless you want to shop for a dress for the Academy Awards."

I had brought a black skirt and a ruffled blouse, but I knew from the baleful look Kathleen had given them when I unpacked that they weren't quite up to the job.

"Or . . ." she added, "we could do both."

"Let's start with your houses," I said, smiling.

"Actually, it's one house," she said. "I got the listing last week. And I may already have a buyer."

There was something odd in the tone of her voice.

"Where is it?"

"Beverly Hills."

I put down my fork. "Kathleen —"

"Look, I told you I would walk through the past with you. My interested buyer is bringing his family by late in the afternoon — let's go before they show up. Let's do it, Jesse."

I closed my eyes. I knew where we were going, right back to the house where my father and mother had shaped the puzzle of my life, with all the small pieces thrown together, everything from the memory of the evening light playing on their golden cocktails to my mother's angry protests when my father took me to Italy on that futile, bizarre attempt to bring Ingrid Bergman back to something called "home." I didn't want to go. That was the last place I wanted to see.

"Jesse?"

I nodded. "Okay," I said.

CHAPTER NINETEEN

Los Angeles, 1959

It was a brilliant morning. I thought of suggesting we take a drive out to Malibu, maybe walk along the sand, get our feet wet in the ocean waters, and forget Beverly Hills. What possible good could come of going *there*? I didn't need to dredge up old memories.

Kathleen shrugged off my objections as we headed out to her car. "Great idea, but I have to check this place out; I have the listing. Remember?" She held up her ring of jangling keys and looked at me with one of those half-smiles I knew so well. "Getting house keys on and then off this ring decides whether I'm able to pay the rent and buy groceries. Would you deny me my livelihood?"

There was no possible answer, except to roll my eyes and get in the car.

Kathleen drove up to the Mary Pickford mansion first, promising an entertaining tour "before we get down to business." So we wound our way through a canyon of villas and mansions and mission-style homes, mixed with a medieval castle or two, while Kathleen kept up a blithe, gossipy commentary on the residents over the years and some of their foibles. The scandals, the marriages, the divorces. We found ourselves at one point behind a tour bus filled with people gaping at the houses. I laughed at a memory — the time Rosemary Clooney's kids got smart, set up a stand, and sold lemonade to the tourists. We passed Jimmy Stewart's graceful Tudor-style home, and Lucille Ball's, and I remembered how, one Christmas, Bing Crosby and his kids had traversed the neighborhood singing carols.

"There's one for the history books," Kathleen said as we drove along Bedford Drive. "Remember Lana Turner's place? It'll be hard to sell after the murder."

Of course. Not too long ago, Turner's daughter had stabbed her mother's mobster boyfriend to death here.

It was no surprise when the tourist bus stopped in front of that house so all could stare and hear the tour operator recount the details. New scandals, always new ones.

Hollywood was good at that.

"The old ones die," Kathleen said, as if reading my mind. "They have to, Jesse. There has to be room for all the new juicy stuff."

She said it lightly, but I knew her too well. "You want me to forget it all, don't you?"

"No, not that. You can't." She turned serious as we came around a final curve and I saw the house ahead of us. "But you can, maybe, drain it of enough sadness to —"

"— say goodbye?" As we pulled into the driveway, a memory flashed: my father, driving home with our brand-new car and parking it in this exact spot. His laugh; the excitement — I inhaled it all once again.

She turned off the ignition. "Let's take a look. Then you tell me."

We stepped into the house. I expected an emptiness, something like the suspended animation I had felt at Saint Ann's. I searched for negatives. Certainly, the carpet looked thin. And I noticed that the marble in the front hall was cracked, and there was a faint smell of chlorine in the air, probably from the pool.

"Looks sad, doesn't it? It's been a rental for a few years," Kathleen said.

But the air held the remnants of my family. And the ghosts crowded forward. If I listened closely, I could almost hear Frank Sinatra's voice wafting from a now invisible Packard Bell. And I could smell a pot roast cooking in the kitchen.

It didn't help to remind myself that once we moved here Mother wasn't all that enthusiastic about cooking.

Kathleen held back while I walked into the living room and stopped at the spot where my father had kissed my mother so tenderly the day we moved in. It was empty and still, waiting for players. I felt like a child peering into a dollhouse, wishing the tiny figures inside were alive.

"You're deep in thought," she said gently.

I told her — the one person who could hear me out more than once. Repeating how closely I had watched them, how relieved I was when I wasn't deciphering the strained times filled with secrets. Did all kids feel that? I had never thought of asking.

"Probably plenty do," Kathleen said. "I didn't. It was just Mother and me. All the drama was over." She paused. "Well, not all of it."

"What do you mean?"

"I've thought more about my father in the past few months, even made a stab at locating him." She started to say something else, then stopped.

"That's got to be a lonely search," I said, surprised.

She shrugged. "I'm not sure I want to find him."

I had a sudden memory of that long-ago broken man staring through the school fence. "You've been saying that if he's alive he's probably under a bridge somewhere."

She didn't answer immediately. "Or somewhere just as bad," she said.

"Maybe run some ads —" I suggested.

She smiled, but shook her head. "I'm better off letting go," she said.

"How come I can't do that, instead of having you walk me through the past?" I said, waving my hand to take in the empty rooms of my family's home.

She grinned and shrugged again. *"Touché,"* she said. We went into the kitchen, which Kathleen said was out-of-date and sure to be demolished by new owners, but all I could remember was a bowl of cookie dough on the counter filled with chocolate chips. "Remember that time we ate the whole batch without cooking it?" I said.

"Amazing we didn't get sick," she said. She ran a finger over the crumbling grout between the kitchen tiles, giving it a close Realtor's eye.

I told her about the evenings I'd spent

watching my parents drink their cocktails, about straining to hear their arguments from my bedroom. She had heard it all before, but she didn't stop me.

"I remember us out by the pool reading our movie magazines," Kathleen said, starting to open the sliding glass doors to the garden outside. "And your mother, sitting at the other end of the pool —"

I surprised myself. "Looking lonely, Kathleen. And I couldn't see it. I barely gave her a moment's thought."

We walked out onto the flagstone terrace.

"How long has this place been empty?" I asked. The house in general had an abandoned feel to it, but the pool — that necessary symbol of status — was usually the last to be let go. Here the water had a brackish smell and was covered with a dull film of leaves.

"Too long," Kathleen replied. "Somebody else's dream of the big time gone bad — I can't remember what movie I plucked that line from."

"You do work at being cynical, but you don't quite carry it off," I said.

"It's protection," she said simply. She glanced at her watch. "My prospective buyer is due soon. I can take you to a coffee shop —"

"I'll wait in the car when they come," I said. I wasn't ready to leave yet.

We went back into the house, and she headed for the bedrooms. I followed, but I stopped first to stare at the dining room, remembering the sight of those devastating letters all bunched and thrown around on the table. I remembered every moment — Mother wailing, Father bursting through the door. Anger pulsed in me again. The fear that had hovered over my young life for so long became real that night.

Enough. I walked on into my bedroom and quickly walked out again. I didn't like remembering how they had forgotten me, how I had lain shut in that bedroom, holding back panic.

"Those letters — everything written in purple ink, right?" Kathleen cut in. "Even for Hollywood, that's over the top — melodramatic."

I smiled. Kathleen wanted to nudge me out of my darker thoughts.

"Very bad taste," I said. "Although . . ."

"What?"

"Every now and then, I wonder — why so many letters? Was she urging him to leave Mother? And what happened to her?"

We turned and walked back toward the center hall; Kathleen gave one glance through the patio doors at the pool. "That's gotta be emptied and cleaned," she muttered, making another note in her notebook.

We were in the hall now. More voices. The three of us standing here after that fruitless trip to Stromboli, Mother screaming at my father, raging at his dismissal of Ingrid. Those exact, uncharacteristic words:

What's her sin, Gabriel? Loving a man?

"What are you thinking?" Kathleen asked.

"That day we came home from Stromboli . . ."

She nodded. "That was bad."

"At least Mother gave me the truth the night before I left."

"Double-shock on that one."

I reached back into my memories. "To find out that her penance was to keep us both in some state of rigid devoutness —"

"Is she relaxing on all of that yet?"

"I don't know. I haven't seen her in a long time. But I'm sure she still believes Father married her out of decency only. And I want nothing to do with her determined misery."

I suddenly had had enough. "Can I get out of here soon?" I asked.

"Well, I'm through with the inspection, and mentally ready to take a bid for a lower price." Kathleen closed her notebook and shoved it into her black leather purse. The two of us stood silently for a few moments, staring around the room.

She checked her watch again. "I hear a car pulling up," she said. "Time for you to get out of here."

I looked around one more time, but the room had somehow tipped. I blinked, my thoughts mixing together, like shards of color in a kaleidoscope.

God is punishing me.

I won't leave you.

"How could she consider herself so unforgivable?" I said.

"Aren't you doing the same thing?"

I had no answer for that. I slipped out the kitchen door and made my way to Kathleen's car. The family coming up the front walk never noticed me, but I had a chance to study them.

The man's open, ruddy face broke into a big grin as he shook hands with Kathleen, then turned and introduced the woman next to him. His wife, I thought, watching now from the car. She glanced around timidly, pulling a much-too-warm fur coat close — her badge, her ticket to a more affluent life. Oh, it brought back echoes. Suddenly a young girl, maybe ten or twelve, came scooting around from the back, jabbering excitedly, clearly having discovered the pool.

They could be us. I slunk down into the seat and closed my eyes.

They were inside for barely fifteen minutes before emerging. I saw the grin on Kathleen's face. A sale? The man was shaking hands with her, and everybody looked happy.

My eye traveled to the wife, who had wandered over to inspect the abandoned flower beds by the side of the house. I remembered them bursting with fat red and white roses, and how much my mother loved them. Oh, I wanted out of this place. Hurry, Kathleen, I urged silently.

The young girl ran over to join her mother. I saw them exchange delighted grins, and I saw something else in the mother's eyes that triggered another memory — of my mother looking that way at me. Was it a true one or just a fantasy? The girl hugged her mother, a quick, carelessly happy hug; when did I stop doing that with my mother? They were sharing the excitement of building a new life in a new home. I shut my eyes again. I let myself remember my mother's warm kisses, not just the touch of her lips cool on my cheek.

It was possible, just possible, that this memory was true.

■ ■ ■ ■

Kathleen's face was flushed as she slid back into the driver's seat after waving goodbye to her clients. "I'm sorry you were stuck here. Forgive me, but — Jesse — this is one of those great moments when I know I'm not going to be out on the streets someday, begging for food."

"You sold it, right?"

"Basically a done deal," she said. Her eyes held extra energy.

"That's great," I said. "You *must* love this — right now you look like you've sold the Taj Mahal."

She laughed. "You bet I do," she said. "Are you convinced now?"

"Okay, I was wrong." I had implored her not to drop out of college in her sophomore year. I had told her it was a mistake, but — in Kathleen's way — she insisted she knew exactly what she was about. School wasn't for her, and that was that.

"Good. No more lectures — we can still be friends," she said now, putting the car in gear and pulling out of the driveway.

"I've never quite understood —"

"Why I dropped out? It's simple — I had no appetite for school after the first two years. It was hard for you to understand, but I wanted to be able to take care of myself." She rapped the wheel with her knuckle. "I wanted not to be . . ." She paused.

"Vulnerable?"

"I told you, begging on the streets. I wanted to build something all my own."

We so rarely spoke of the invisible dividing line that had marked our childhoods. My family was never short of money; I could take it for granted. For Kathleen and her mother, it was different. They weren't *poor,* she'd made clear to me on the tennis court at Saint Ann's; money was just *tight.* It was clear to me then: this was not a topic for conversation.

"I wasn't pretending; it really was better after my father left. He was a major-league drunk — good riddance. I was more relaxed, I guess. I saw my mother as strong, someone who could take care of us both."

"You seemed really strong to me. We never talked much about this when we were kids."

She smiled. "You know the funny thing? I never envied you. I felt luckier — sort of like it was up to me to help you."

"Well, you did. Now you are searching for your father."

She stiffened slightly. "Not too aggressively."

I didn't answer at first, just stared out the window. "Did you really mean 'good riddance'?" I finally asked.

She thought about that for a minute. "No," she said. She swung the steering wheel with extra force as she made a sharp left turn onto Wilshire Boulevard. "I just like to sound tough."

We drank martinis that night. Nice stiff ones.

On my second, I locked Kathleen in a determined stare. "Kathleen, who did that Academy Awards invitation come from?"

"You really think I know?" She looked authentically astonished. "I don't, but I agree, something's going on." She furrowed her brow. "Isn't it kind of a coincidence that Malcolm has such a convenient job at the studio?"

"I don't think he knows how to be devious. He's so — blunt." That bluntness was disconcerting, but I didn't like to think of him as hiding anything. "I'm wondering why he wanted the bronze marker."

"Maybe in memory of you. Why not? Or for the studio. The movie business is always on the lookout for movie props; otherwise, they wouldn't have things like old Model T Fords rattling around on their lots. Could be that someday somebody will use that slab of metal in a movie about Ingrid. Anyway, why don't you ask him?"

I had the opportunity two days later.

The doorbell rang as I was settling into the sofa with the paper. It was Malcolm — just showing up at the door, giving no excuse for not calling first. His hands were shoved in his pockets, which made him look kind of bashful. A false signal.

"I could say I happened to be in the neighborhood, that I was just passing by," he began without preamble. "Actually, I took the afternoon off to take a chance on seeing you. You're not planning to be around very long, so — here I am."

I stared at him, not sure how to respond.

He pulled his hands out of his pockets so forcefully, the lining of one popped out, too. "Look, there's no use trying to take a more sophisticated approach," he said. "There isn't any time. Can I take you to lunch?"

I had planned on a quiet afternoon by myself; I needed a chance to sort out my thoughts.

"Well — you?"

"I've eaten." What was wrong with me?

Kathleen would accuse me of total rudeness. I wasn't sure why I felt wary, why my instinct was to push him away. He stood there without artifice, unlike most men I knew.

"Okay, done checking me out?" he said matter-of-factly. His hands were back in his pockets and he pivoted on one foot, as if to leave. "If you've eaten, we could go ride the roller coaster at Ocean Park." A short silence. "Or hit a burlesque show."

Something loosened in me. I laughed. "Or take a nostalgic ride down to the University of Redlands?"

He looked relieved. "Thank God, you have some sense of humor," he said. "I was getting worried."

"I'll get a sweater." I started to turn back into the house and stopped. "Why did you want that movie marker from Saint Ann's?"

His eyes turned mischievous. "Maybe to have some kind of a gift to give you if you ever came back."

"I'm back."

"It's yours. Happy birthday."

"It isn't my birthday."

"I like banking gifts for contingencies; you never know. Once, I forgot my mother's birthday. Fortunately, I had a Jell-O mold in the closet, already wrapped. Saved my skin that time."

I couldn't help it — I laughed again. Somehow he was the most believable of men.

We drove out Sunset and then up a steep, winding hill that crested at Mulholland Drive. We didn't stop, just kept driving deeper into the Santa Monica Mountains, on the cusp of the Valley. I didn't ask where we were headed. Malcolm drove easily, one hand on the wheel, the other draped over the back of the seat, peppering me with questions about New York, which I kept answering until I realized how little he was sharing about himself.

"So what do you do as a lawyer for the studio?" I asked lightly. "Defend the moguls from those big, bad people on the Hollywood blacklist who still can't get work?"

He didn't smile. "They're still targets for HUAC."

"A despicable group. They've ruined lives by making people afraid to give writers work."

"I'm a newcomer; I do my job. If it's any consolation, the whole bloody witch-hunt is slowly running out of steam. Enough lives destroyed." He closed up, staring straight ahead, both hands on the wheel now.

"So I guess I don't know you, do I?"

"Of course you don't. And I don't know you, either."

We both fell into silence for a few moments.

"Look," he said, "I'd like to talk about that. That's why we're out here, emptying the gas tank. There's no gauge on this car, you know. Up for an adventure if we run dry?"

I started to answer, not sure if this was a joke or for real. But suddenly I smelled salt air. "We're at the ocean?" I asked, surprised.

"Above Malibu. Didn't you drive much in high school?"

I made a face. "I don't like driving, never have — hurtling myself down some road in a car doesn't feel like fun," I said.

He didn't answer at first. The road took a steep turn, and there it was ahead of us — the vast expanse of shimmering blue water and glorious crashing waves of the Pacific Ocean.

I caught my breath. It was splendid and beautiful, and I had forgotten it — forgotten the joy of throwing myself under a wave, breaking through, reaching the lazy, deep swells of water where I could float or swim, answerable to no one.

We were on the beach road now, looking

for a parking place. Malcolm glanced at me, catching in my expression a small crack in the armor. "Ah, you *are* a beach bunny after all," he said. "You'll have to get a driver's license if you come back. Hey, no L.A. girl can stay away from this too long."

"I'm not coming back," I said flatly.

He didn't answer, just swerved into a spot by an empty lifeguard stand. I looked around. On this beautiful beach day, no one else was here.

CHAPTER TWENTY

Los Angeles, 1959
We sat in silence on that deserted beach. I concentrated on listening to the rolling waves break lazily on the shore, a sleepy, peaceful sound, broken every now and then by the sharp cry of a seagull swooping down to the water, searching for dinner.

Wiggling my bare toes under the warm sand, studying my toenails, I wondered vaguely if I should get a pedicure. I lowered my head and let it rest on Malcolm's shoulder. Odd, how peaceful it was just to sit with him, staring at the sea.

"I know I've been making a pest of myself these past few days," he said quietly. "Truth is, I couldn't believe it when I spotted you at the auction. Haven't quite got over it."

"Neither have I," I said. It seemed easy to tell the truth without holding back.

"Look, this is clumsy, premature — anything you want to call it. And I do *not* believe it was an act of destiny." He took my hand and began tracing my fingers with one of his. "Think maybe we've been given some kind of lucky break?"

The words hung there, perilously ahead of their time.

"We've already agreed we don't know each other well enough to make a call like that," I said.

"You said you almost got married at one point. Okay if I ask what happened?"

"It wasn't quite like that." I told him then how I had lived for a year on false expectations, feeling guilty for giving in to my Yale boyfriend, and his leaving anyway. "I don't know why I blurted it out to you; that was stupid," I said.

He lifted my hand and kissed it, leaving a thin layer of sand on his lips. "Maybe it felt like an impediment? Compulsive confessing? You Catholics don't let go of guilt easily."

"Maybe. Don't overanalyze."

He nodded. No probing, no further questions on that, for which I was grateful.

"Anything you want to ask me?" he asked.

"Have you been in love?" I said.

"In nine years? Yes, a couple of times," he said. "Nothing that lasted, but I learned things."

379

"Like what?" I wanted to tease a little.

"Build a better road map for what I want," he said. "Which brings me back to you."

"It's too soon. Isn't this where we started?"

He smiled. "I know, you're heading back to New York in a few days, and that's that. But I'm bringing it up anyway. At least as a hypothetical."

A hypothetical. I looked at him, feeling an odd tug. Maybe it was just the soporific influence of sun, sand, and sea, but this man was attracting me.

"The fact is, I've never cleared you out of my head. I knew the night of your prom what I felt, and don't tell me I was a kid."

"Well —"

His jaw was set now. "I'm not used to saying something like this flat-out, but I wanted to at least bring it up."

"Yes — as a hypothetical, of course."

He grabbed a fistful of sand and threw it toward the water. "Okay, laugh. I should say I'm sorry, but I'm not."

Nine years since I had seen him. His bluntness was almost calming.

I started to say more. But a seagull made a deep, sudden dive over our heads, coming right down toward us. We both ducked; Malcolm threw both arms over my head to ward off the attack. At the last second, the gull reversed course, shrieking, then climbing high.

"I think he's laughing at us," Malcolm said.

"Maybe he's the reason this beach is deserted," I said.

"We've put our bottoms down on some sacred seagull landing field, that's it."

I giggled. He laughed, an unexpectedly deep laugh.

"Be careful, you'll scare the seagull," I said. I looked into his eyes, so close now. And I saw the boy who had grabbed my arm and raced me over to the tournament finals nine long years ago. The friend who stood by me all through the rockiest months of my time at Saint Ann's Academy. He hadn't disappeared; he was here.

By silent consent, we lay back together on the warm sand. He wrapped one arm around my shoulders, silently cradling my neck. No words, no thinking, no anxiety. I shut my eyes, lulled by the sound of the waves, and dreamed my way deep into the moment. There seemed no reason to pull away.

Something *was* stirring, opening. Something.

■ ■ ■ ■

Kathleen was sitting on the front steps when we got back to her house, holding the quick note I had left for her. Her eyebrow went up when she saw our general state of dishevelment, but she made no joke about it, for which I was grateful. We sat down with her. The atmosphere, this convivial gathering on the front steps, felt good. We talked movies, we talked politics, all lazy in the late-afternoon sun. I hovered at a level of contentment I hadn't reached in a long time.

I was startled when Malcolm glanced at his watch and jumped to his feet. He stretched, and said, all too amiably, "I hate to break this up, but I have to get back to the office."

I felt my face go warm. "So soon?" I said.

He shrugged, his voice casual. "Yeah, I've got to check on a case going to court next week. Hope the rest of your visit goes okay, Jesse."

I wanted to reply with some version of "Don't go yet," but I couldn't come up with anything that might be both significant and offhand. Instead, I shrugged, but it didn't fool Kathleen. I saw her eyes darting from one of us to the other, trying to catch a clue.

"Too bad," she said. She stood, too, and said she was headed for the Farmers Market to pick up some of their great fudge and maybe a few healthy apples, and she'd bring home enough for anybody around when she came back. Then she bounced off down the street, with that same swing to her step that I remembered from the first day I saw her at the Saint Ann's pool. I envied her ability to know just when to exit.

"So — you aren't staying for the fudge?"

"The longer I stay, the more involved I feel. And that's not fair to you," he said. He started to lean down, I thought to kiss me. But he stopped and pulled himself straight again.

I couldn't untangle the words. "I don't know . . ."

"Will you stay longer so we can find out?"

"I can't. I have a job."

"You could if you wanted to."

That stung. No important job was calling out to me, true. "I feel you're pressing me again — a little," I said.

"That's why I'm stepping back," he said. "I've been sitting with you and your friend, happy, enjoying being here — maybe a little too much."

"I enjoyed today," I said.

"Yeah." He drew a deep breath, exhaled

slowly, gazing at some spot across the street, with a faraway look in his eyes. "It was a great day."

It sounded too final, almost somber. Should I say it? *Don't leave, please.*

Before I could form a word, he leaned in swiftly and kissed my forehead. "Keep looking for whatever it is you're trying to find," he said. "We'll catch up at some point."

He turned his back and walked down the path, climbed into his funny little car, and was gone before I gathered my wits to say anything sensible.

I did the only thing I could do at the moment — I sat on the step, covered my face, and let the tears trickle down — over my father's death, my mother's secrets, and Malcolm's abrupt departure. He was gone, I knew it. Why was I so sure? Was I just giving up too fast? No, it was simpler than that. He wasn't a man who would hang around waiting for very long. And I wasn't a woman who trusted herself to move at all. I was stuck somewhere.

"So have a piece of fudge. Some are plain, some have walnuts."

My eyes flew open as I took my hands away from my face. There was Kathleen, thrusting a bag of candy under my nose. I ate three pieces of fudge and poured out to her all the news of that strange day. I told her about Malcolm's — what could I call it? — his effort to press for a connection. What was he thinking? It was too fast. She listened silently, rocking back and forth, speaking only when I ran out of things to say.

"He tossed a lot at you, I guess. If anything comes of this relationship, don't let him in any china shop," she said. "Nice guy, though."

"He brings me too close to bad memories. I don't want to dwell on what happened, not even at Redlands. Whatever was happening, I made it worse."

"When it came to the tournament? Yeah, a little," she said with good cheer. "But it took that bitchy Louella Parsons to complete the job. You weren't out to hurt." Her eyes narrowed as she peered at me more closely. "You've got sand caked in your ears."

I felt my face redden. "It's not what you think," I said. "We just relaxed on the beach, that's all. How could I see anything ahead for the two of us on the basis of a couple of days? It's crazy."

Kathleen reached into the bag for the last piece of fudge. "Sand in your ears indicates you were gravitating in one direction," she said.

We sat in silence. She broke it first. "Look — if it takes your mind off today, I've got a bit of news."

"I don't want any more news."

"Sister Teresa Mary called — would love to have you come tomorrow, if you can."

"Yes — oh, good." I *was* pleased. "I want to do that."

"A chance to understand her better?"

"That's what I'm hoping for."

It was one of those visuals that never go away: Sister Teresa Mary facing the 1950 graduating class, announcing the news that Bishop Doyle wasn't going to hand out our diplomas. It came back: her stiff posture, the strain on her face as she spoke, still managing to project all the sternness and authority that had kept a few decades of students obeying her every dictate.

How much of her life as a nun had been just knowing her part? I thought of her scolding Kathleen for wearing a two-piece bathing suit. And insisting that I apply to a Catholic college. And that awful scene in the school chapel when she bowed to having the blame dumped on her head for honoring Ingrid Bergman and *The Bells of St. Mary's* with that bronze marker.

There was one nagging question about her invitation. "Why would she want to see *me*?" I said.

"Probably not to swap stories about Bishop Doyle, though I hear she has a few. Hit you for a donation? Not likely. I don't know, but, hey, why not? I'll drop you there; I can pick you up midafternoon."

I nodded slowly. "I don't want any more surprises," I said.

Kathleen stood, reached down, and pulled me up. "They come when they come," she said. "Let's go see *The Three Faces of Eve* — you know, the one about a woman with three personalities? It's showing in one of those arty movie houses. She can't figure out who she really is, maybe some similarities there? Joanne Woodward won for best actress last year. We can get pizza afterward."

"I've seen it."

She never missed a beat. "I've got a better idea, then. Audrey Hepburn in *The Nun's Story.* She flees the convent. Not exactly the same as the convent leaving her, but you get the parallel."

I nodded again. Kathleen was not going to let me brood.

CHAPTER TWENTY-ONE

Los Angeles, 1959

The dormitory was a nondescript stucco building with long narrow windows set back on one of the arid fields of the San Fernando Valley. It looked as if it had been abandoned. Which was true. Kathleen told me it had once been part of the compound of a private school that pulled out of the Valley for a fancier location. Hard to imagine it as a convent, I thought, as we entered from the north side. Straight ahead was a hall that stretched the length of the building, a hall so long it disappeared into darkness at the end.

"You've been here?" I asked Kathleen.

"I stopped by with my mother. Curiosity, I guess." She held the wheel steady, checking her gas gauge.

"It was definitely a different perspective," she went on. "I was so busy defying them — a lot more than you, but I know you felt much the same — I never thought of nuns as ordinary women. That silly part of the habit the little kids used to think was attached to their heads?"

I laughed; yes, I remembered. It turned them all into the same woman, some with a few more whiskers on their chins than others.

"Sister Teresa Mary looked pretty conservative at the auction," she said. "But her order shocked the archdiocese by voting to shed the habit entirely — probably as a way of thumbing their collective noses at Doyle. Wow, when I heard *that,* I was too curious to stay away. I never heard of a group of nuns doing that before."

"Neither have I."

"So I wanted to see how that changed them."

I smiled. "You wanted to see if they were being treated right — I know you. So what did you find out?"

She pulled into a parking space and yanked on the brake. "No fair sharing test scores; we'll compare later."

In silence, we both stared at the building.

"It's a dump, but it has possibilities," Kathleen said.

"Welcome," a tiny woman with short-cropped hair said in a soft voice. She wore a large, shapeless gray sweater. A pair of wire glasses rested on her nose. She looked vaguely familiar. "It may not look like it, but this is our reception room," she said with a smile. "You're here to see Sister Teresa Mary, I understand."

Kathleen nodded, and then said to me, "I'll leave you here now. Be back in about an hour."

"You aren't staying?"

"No, she obviously wants to see *you*. Anyway, I've got some property to look at." With that, she flashed a bright smile, turned, and left.

The woman in the wire glasses beckoned to me; I followed her as we started down the long narrow hallway. There actually was a conference room, she said, which the nuns expected would prove quite useful; that's where they could meet with family and visitors. There was a small space that was being refitted as a chapel, which was a great relief, she said, sighing. "We miss our chapel at Saint Ann's."

I looked at her sharply. "Do I know you?"

"Of course you do, my dear. I'm Sister Margaret Elizabeth. I was the school librarian."

I flushed red. "I'm sorry —"

"Don't be. Nobody recognizes us out of our habits."

We turned a corner, and I heard a familiar voice.

"Welcome, Jesse."

I blinked. Away from the auction crowd jamming the school lawn, wearing no veil at all, Sister Teresa Mary looked unnervingly ordinary. She could have been someone's pleasant grandmother, though she still had the penetrating gaze that saw everything. She stood as erect as ever, but her face was definitely more weathered. She wore what looked like the same blouse and skirt she had on at the auction. And, yes, she had hair. There it was, totally uncovered, salt and pepper in color, slightly curly in texture. The only thing that marked her as a nun was a small crucifix hanging from a chain around her neck. But none of that quite touched on what I was trying to identify.

She reached out her hand and smiled. "It's good to see you, Jessica," she said. "You came back."

"Just for a week," I said, a touch hastier than I needed to.

"I see. But you came, at least partly to see Saint Ann's again, right?" She gestured toward a chair. "Please, sit down."

I did, looking around at the same time.

"This is quite a different environment from Saint Ann's," I said. I was still trying to put my finger on something about her that had changed.

"Yes, indeed. That's what got my back up. The bishop thought we would go meekly into exile," she said. She smiled with clear satisfaction. "We surprised him. We packed up all those serge habits in a big box and sent them to the chancery office. I'd love to have seen his face when they opened it."

And there it was, what I was searching for: not just an atmosphere of defiance; Sister Teresa Mary was *enjoying* her act of defiance.

"Was it a hard decision to give up the habit?" I asked.

"Yes — and no. We decided, all of us, as a community — that it was our job to serve God in the way that was right for us." Her voice was firm, but not in the same way I remembered.

"Can the bishop . . . Will he try to stop you?"

"I doubt it. We have accepted our move to this new home — no complaints, no entreaties. Now we will shape it."

"What will you do?" There was no school anymore for this teaching order of nuns. No girls to educate.

She looked at me, a steady, clear-eyed gaze. "We will do neighborhood ministry until we hear what our new official role is."

"I admire you."

Her face softened. "You know, when all authority was stripped away, I found strength."

I could hardly believe I was having this conversation. But I could ask directly: "Sister, I'm wondering why you wanted to see me, after all that happened, and all I did."

"Definitely not to censor you or offer some magnanimous forgiveness," she said dryly. "I'm done with that role."

I blinked.

"I read your Redlands speech. I can't speak for what you said about the movie industry, but you were right about the Church. Power-hungry bishops? Yes."

"That's not what you said when you told me I couldn't be valedictorian. I never understood why it was a good thing for me to keep quiet about what was true."

"You know now and you knew then, I had to abide by the bishop's orders."

That relentless hammer of obedience — I remembered last night's movie, *The Nun's Story,* and Audrey Hepburn's struggle with obedience — something she questioned so much she felt forced to leave the sisterhood. "There is a new movie —" I began.

"Yes, I've heard of it."

"I saw it last night." Still vivid in my mind was the final scene, the camera following the small figure of Audrey Hepburn walking slowly down a long corridor toward the outside world she had renounced years before.

Neither of us said anything for a few minutes.

"You were publicly punished for shaming Saint Ann's when the Ingrid Bergman scandal broke," I said, choosing my words as carefully as I could. "How could you accept that?"

She looked at me, eyes steady, then reached up and fingered the crucifix. "I knew there had to be some resolution. And I was the logical one to confess."

"You weren't guilty of *anything.*"

"God writes straight with crooked lines."

"Sister" — how could I say this? — "isn't that just an easy way to justify an injustice?"

"At that time, my pledge of obedience to the bishop was paramount." A faint smile flittered across her face. "Audrey Hepburn's nun spent years putting obedience first, I'm told. Gave it a good try."

"Are you telling me . . ." My eyes widened.

"No, Jessica. I'm not leaving my order." She reached for my hands. "But I no longer feel the need to obey Doyle on all things. I've known that since he walked out on us at your graduation, but the closing of Saint Ann's made me see it plain. My promise of obedience now goes directly to God." She loosened her grip on my hands, but still held them. "You don't have to give everything up, you know. Kathleen told me a little about your struggles. Go past what you need to abandon, and concentrate on what matters."

She was suggesting discarding dogma selectively — deciding that all those rules and prohibitions that had shaped my life were part of a buffet all along, that the guilt and fear of being bad could be tossed, like shrugging off a heavy coat. And somehow that would open a path back into the church.

I couldn't talk for a moment. And then I was swept with compassion for this aging woman holding herself ramrod-straight. She had been a powerful figure of authority in my life, and she was trying to offer a helping hand. But all the terms we used to describe ourselves had changed too much for that to happen.

"That doesn't work for me," I said. "It

would make me lonelier than I am."

"Why?"

"Because it would be replacing one fiction with another. I don't even know if I believe in God anymore."

"That must be hard to say."

I wanted to say, *Not anymore.* But it would've been only partly true.

Sister sighed and pulled herself up even straighter in her chair. "At least drop some of that burden of guilt I hear you carry around," she said softly.

At that moment, Sister Margaret Elizabeth appeared in the doorway and announced that the nearby parish priest who was to bless the space and offer a Mass in their "new home" had arrived.

"Oh my goodness, that's wonderful," Sister Teresa Mary said. She rose with a smile, smoothing down her unfamiliar blue skirt, and turned to me. "Will you join us, Jessica?"

I hesitated. In the silence, I could hear the flapping of a broken venetian blind behind me. I saw the chipped paint on the baseboards. Mostly, I sensed the determination of these women to pull it all together again, to relocate themselves — to build a new familiar.

"I hope you understand I can't go back

—" I began.

"I understand. But you can say goodbye, can't you?"

A pause. "I guess so," I said.

The new "chapel" was dispiritingly barren. There were folding chairs, not pews, and the altar seemed constructed of packing boxes covered with old altar linens. But I recognized the tall, graceful silver candlesticks that had adorned the altar at Saint Ann's.

"How —" I started, turning to Sister Teresa Mary.

"How did we get them out of the old chapel? I stole them," she said matter-of-factly. "Just hid them under a blanket and tucked them into a suitcase before they did inventory."

I couldn't help it — I giggled. Score one for the nuns.

The young priest seemed in a hurry; he glanced once at his watch as a dozen or so nuns quietly filed in, took their seats, and opened their missals. He recited a few prayers and blessed the space with a sign of the cross, then turned to the altar, without presiding over the ritualized ceremony that was the usual way the Church conveyed ownership.

The Mass was also clearly going to be wrapped up in record time. This felt disrespectful to me, but Sister Teresa Mary kept her head bent as she serenely murmured the familiar responses, seemingly undisturbed.

This was the Church stripped of music, incense, and the lengthy rituals that had defined the faith of my youth. Stripped to its underwear, I told myself.

And then — a beat of my heart skipped — I heard a pure, soaring voice lift and swell from the back of the room.

"That's Sister Mary Francis, our last novice here," whispered Sister Teresa Mary. "She is very gifted."

The young nun was singing the "Ave Maria." Her voice rose, filling the stale air of that pedestrian space with something — what? — that lifted me with it, lifting away everything that hurt, releasing it all for this one moment, leaving me free to feel a sense of both relief and loss. Even the priest seemed to slow down. His hands, rising in what was clearly intended to be a quick blessing of the Eucharist, seemed to tremble and then hold steady until that glorious voice faded away.

I looked around at the small group of

women. And, for just that moment, I saw what held Sister Teresa Mary. This shabby room, right here, was the quiet heart of her religion, where belief and loyalty held true — a heart that didn't obscure with pomp and pageantry, that didn't rely on control and fear to give it strength.

I felt tears on my cheeks — tears of recognition of what faith could be — and, yes, relief. I could let go of it now. I could let go of it, but respect what it held for Sister Teresa Mary and the other women in this dilapidated excuse for a chapel. I didn't have to feel thrown out; I could *walk away.* I could let go of it all now, truly.

I felt a gentle pressure and, looking down, saw Sister Teresa Mary's hand cup mine. "You're crying," she murmured.

I smiled and said, "I'm just saying goodbye."

Kathleen was waiting in the driveway when I came out of the building, waving to get my attention, pointing to her watch. Sister Teresa Mary and I shook hands quickly.

"Jessica —"

"You're the last person on earth who calls me by my full first name," I said.

She smiled. "And I will continue to do

so," she said. "Was this visit helpful for you?"

"Yes, it was." I hesitated. "And if I am ever back in L.A. —"

"No promises necessary," she said.

"— I will come again." I turned and walked quickly to the car.

CHAPTER TWENTY-TWO

Los Angeles, 1959

Kathleen was munching from a bag of Hershey's Kisses as I climbed in, and waved her own goodbye to Sister Teresa Mary.

"Eat," she directed. "You look like you could use it."

I picked out one kiss and carefully unwrapped it from its silver foil. I had always loved these elegantly wrapped chocolates. As a child, I had once opened a bag and lined them up on the floor, creating my own royal court, all gleaming and proud. I left them there when it was time for dinner, then forgot them and went to bed. Mother was not happy when Father walked into the room that night and ground chocolate into the carpet.

I unwrapped a second piece of candy, popped it into my mouth, and told Kathleen the story.

"That wasn't as bad as when you left the

dead snake in the garage for three weeks. Remember? The one you brought home from camp that you were going to boil, so you could make jewelry from the bones?" She shivered. "You did some weird things."

We were good at this, finding refuge in shared memories before facing the present.

"So what did you think of the nuns in their new home?" Kathleen finally asked. By now, we were heading out of the Valley, back toward Sunset.

"They're brave." Staring out the window, I wondered how strange it must have felt for Sister Teresa Mary to bare her head for the first time in decades. "I hate the place, but they are brave."

"I've offered to try and help them find a better location, but no response from the archdiocese."

"I joined them for Mass."

She glanced at me, raising an eyebrow.

"I'm glad I did. I understand them better now." I told her how freeing it had felt to let go. I groped for the right words, but I didn't have to work at it; she knew.

"Sounds good," she said quietly.

We rode for a while in comfortable silence, and I found myself drifting into a doze.

Two days until the awards ceremony. I

would soon be due back in New York.

The reality of time racing by hit me that night as Kathleen and I ordered dinner at a small Mexican restaurant near her apartment. It was a place full of light and cheer, with sombreros tacked on the walls at wacky angles and posters of dancing girls, smiling brightly, clicking their castanets in silent, frozen harmony.

"You've been staring at that menu a long time," Kathleen said. "I can vouch for the enchiladas and tostados, if you're having trouble making up your mind."

"I have to go back in a few days."

"Will you be glad to get out of here?"

She said it casually, and I tried to answer the same way. "I'll miss you," I said.

"So nothing changed?"

Running a finger over a grease spot on the menu, I thought about that, wondering. Had anything changed? I had walked back through old memories, touching them as briefly as I would touch a hot stove . . . but there was that moment at Mass.

"Some things, yes."

She was studying me almost sorrowfully. Or so I imagined. "Maybe you haven't gotten to the heart of it."

"Please don't say you mean Malcolm."

"I don't. But now that you mention him —"

The waiter came, sparing me the need to reply. By the time we ordered, I had figured out what I wanted to say. "I think I should say goodbye to him," I said.

Kathleen was dipping chips into salsa, munching with relish. "Then call him at the studio," she said. "As for the awards — you still don't want to buy a dress?"

"I'm not so sure I want to go."

"That's what you came for, isn't it?"

I caught her eyes squarely. "Do you know more about this than you're telling me?"

This time, she didn't act surprised that I asked. "Nope," she said.

"It feels like some kind of — I don't know — public-relations stunt or joke, or even a flat-out mistake."

We jointly mulled that one over as we finished off the salsa.

We were both tired when we arrived back at Kathleen's home. She peered into the mailbox by her darkened front door, grumbling about needing a light there so she wouldn't someday thrust her hand in looking for mail and get bitten by a snake.

"Do you have snakes here?" I said, a bit alarmed.

"No, I just think about it. Ah, something." She pulled out an envelope, glanced at the return address, and frowned.

"Anything for me?" The words just slipped out.

"No," she said. "Nothing from Malcolm."

I slept restlessly that night. I had wondered, coming out here, how I would fill over a full week in this rock-hard place I bewilderingly once called home. Now I felt that I was running out of time, that I had missed something. Questions kept buzzing in my head.

At three in the morning, I gave up and switched on the bedside light. I opened the drawer and took out the Academy Awards invitation, and then I stared alternately at it and the ceiling until, exhausted, I fell asleep around seven.

"Jesse?" Kathleen was gently shaking my shoulder. "Hey, Jesse? Wake up, it's eight o'clock. A phone call for you from New York. Somebody from *Newsweek*."

I stumbled across the room and reached for the phone.

"Jesse, is that you?" The line wasn't very clear, but I recognized the voice of Mabel, my boss's secretary. An envelope had come to the office addressed to me, she said. She reminded me that when we had lunch together a few weeks ago I had told her I was hoping to sell an article, and she figured, well, *Newsweek* could afford a long-distance call; maybe it was something I might want to know about before I came back.

"What's the return address?"

A slight sound; maybe she was flipping the envelope over.

"*Life* magazine," she said.

Just another rejection, I told myself. But maybe . . . I shut my eyes. "Would you please open it?" I said.

This time, unmistakably, I heard the envelope being ripped open.

"Well, they like it," Mabel said.

"Is the word 'regret' in the message?"

"No. They want to buy it. Isn't that nice?"

Laughing, I grabbed Kathleen and hugged her; I thanked Mabel effusively, and then thanked her again. She seemed a bit astonished, but pleased she had called. I collected myself enough to get the name of the editor I needed to contact, and finally said goodbye.

Then I turned to Kathleen, grinning. "It's going to be published. I can't believe it —"

"Why not believe it? You've sold a piece about a doll nobody's heard of yet and that's going to get attention. It's a *success,* and there will be more of them." She shook her head, clearly exasperated. "What did that guy you lived with *do* to you? You've been writing since high school; you didn't just win speech tournaments, you wrote short stories and you talked about writing a novel someday. And you stayed with him for almost a year? *What happened?*"

"I've asked myself that a lot. I think I was just an idiot, wasting too much time feeling sorry for myself." The truth, plain and simple.

"Well, dump *that* question," she said. "I'm sorry for snapping at you. It's what you do now that matters."

"I've got two stories out to *The Saturday Evening Post,*" I said. "They're pretty good; we'll see." I heard a new buoyancy in my voice.

"Fantastic! Hey, you're on your way. Keep writing."

"Right this minute? Can we have our coffee first?"

She grinned. "You never could pass up caffeine."

CHAPTER TWENTY-THREE

Los Angeles, 1959

I called the studio. A click, a transfer, a receiver lifted — and I heard Malcolm's voice. "Look, you're probably busy —" I started.

He interrupted, a brisk, work quality to his voice. "That depends, I guess. Are you calling to say goodbye?"

"No," I said quickly. "I wanted to share some good news."

He seemed pleased when I told him — asking me questions about when it would run, and when I told him they were introducing the doll at the National Toy Fair this year, he actually laughed. "Perfect timing — you're on your way," he said.

He wasn't taking the lead, so I did. "I would like to see you again," I said, adding, "to say a proper goodbye."

"Well . . ."

For a frozen moment, I thought he might say no.

"This afternoon, this evening, or both?"

I laughed. "Just maybe I've had enough of beaches, all that sand —"

"Dinner, then. At one of the best restaurants in town."

"Which one?"

"I haven't figured that out yet."

"What's your favorite?"

"Pink's Hot Dogs. Sorry. But you and I, we're going deluxe."

I laughed again, hung up, and glanced at Kathleen, who was staring out the window with an odd expression on her face. It was gone so quickly I barely registered it; in fact, I wondered if I had imagined it.

We shopped that day; I was more light-hearted than I'd been about it for a very long time. Kathleen coaxed me into trying on some Oscar-worthy gowns in Bullocks, but I couldn't see past the daunting price tags.

"Okay, I'm not giving up." She disappeared from the dressing room and came back ten minutes later with an armful of blouses, all creamy white silk and edged in lace. "And a black skirt," she said, tossing one my way. "I have one just like it at home,

409

but let's see how it looks with the top."

I plucked out one blouse and pulled it over my head; the silk molded to my body, and I was already in love with it. The sleeves were sheer, so light they seemed to float by themselves. It was perfect.

I laughed and twirled in front of the mirror, suddenly thinking: my mother must have done this, at least once, and at this very store, and had she felt the way I felt now? Maybe this was where she had bought her dress for that glittery night when we all three attended the Academy Awards. I could see it again: Mother's beauty, my father's genial exuberance, all framed against the color and light of a fairy-tale moment. And that brought back, even more vividly, my memory of Ingrid Bergman that night. How awkward I had felt, stumbling into a private conversation between her and her husband. And how gracious she had been, surely knowing I was mortified. I could hear her voice again — calm and soothing. If she hadn't been my hero before, she would have become my hero then.

"You look gorgeous," Kathleen said. She collapsed into one of the chairs, grinning. "Good thing, because I'm shopped out." She glanced at her watch. "I have an appointment to show a house in about an hour, but there's plenty of time to get you home."

"No," I said, surprising myself, "I think I'll just walk around this part of town for a while. Maybe look at some of the old places we went."

"You and your parents?"

"Yes."

"Okay. Remember this isn't New York; it's too far to walk home. I'll pick you up at three o'clock, in front of the store?"

"Sure, I'll be here." I had a sudden restless desire to be alone. To walk the streets, look around, maybe remember a few good things.

I said goodbye to Kathleen and wandered to the front of the store, stopping abruptly at the perfume counter. It was as magical as I remembered: mirrored glass trays filled with dozens of elaborately designed crystal bottles lined counters that sparkled under the glowing chandeliers. I inhaled deeply — and realized I was inhaling Mother. She loved perfume. It made Father sneeze, so she didn't wear it in the evenings. But when I was a child, she would dab her favorite scent on in the mornings, even before my father had backed all the way out of the driveway to head for work. Then she would wink at me and put a tiny drop behind each of my ears. When did she do that? How old was I? I remember feeling very grown-up. And now I couldn't remember what scent she had loved.

A brisk wind stirred to life as I left the store and walked down Wilshire. I pulled my raincoat tighter, and remembered how uncertain Mother had been about the mink coat Father gave her that first Christmas in our new house. She had pulled it from layers of frothy tissue and held it up, eyes wide.

"But, Gabriel," she almost whispered, "it doesn't get cold enough here for a mink coat."

"That hasn't stopped every woman in Beverly Hills from owning one," he said with a grin. We coaxed her to try it on. When she did, it enveloped her. She looked like a mountain bear.

"Where did you go, Vannie?" he teased.

She giggled from inside that ridiculous coat. So she had a sense of humor, at least sometimes. Maybe there were more instances, but I had tuned them out. Memories are like that, I had read somewhere. If they don't fit your storyline, they vanish from your mind. An unsettling thought.

It felt good, walking and thinking; it felt good not to be on a cold subway platform, waiting for a late train. It felt good to be spending time with Kathleen. And it felt good to know I was looking forward to dinner with Malcolm tonight.

I kept walking; moving one foot after the other had a way of making life seem less shadowed. I passed a delicatessen my father used to praise for its tongue sandwiches, which made Mother shiver. I peeked in the window; it was full of people, mostly men and old ladies, and they all were eating some kind of sandwiches, probably either tongue or pastrami, which sounded good to me. My father took us here once in a while on Sundays after Mass. Mother would sit quietly, munching on a bagel with cream cheese, while I tried to pretend I loved tongue. It was best smothered in mustard.

I actually reached for the doorknob, then hesitated. Anyone who lived in New York *knew* West Coast delis were inferior, always had been been, always would be. It made me smile to think how my father used to wave his sandwich in the air and scoff at "East Coast snobbism." I didn't want to risk finding out East Coasters were right.

I finally stopped daydreaming and glanced at my watch. Almost three o'clock — time to hurry back.

"So how was it, strolling around the soulless heart of your old hometown?" Kathleen said. She had that bright look in her eyes that I knew meant she probably had closed a sale while I was thinking about bagels and pastrami.

"Do you remember my mother's mink coat?"

She laughed. "That fur thing where you couldn't see her eyes? I sure do."

"She ended up using it as a coverlet on chilly nights."

We laughed together, and in that blithe mood, we climbed into the car, drove away, and somehow decided to pay one final visit to Saint Ann's Academy.

"Why not?" I said.

"Why not, indeed?"

It wasn't quiet this time. We could hear from somewhere the dull, rhythmic thud of a wrecking ball hitting masonry; closer to us, the whine of electric saws and shouts of workers. "Listen," Kathleen said as we walked up to the tennis courts. "If it wasn't so atonal, it might be music."

We could both smile at that as we stared again at the abandoned court. It was, if anything, crumbling even faster now than at the beginning of the week, Kathleen pointed out. But, surprisingly, it didn't trigger in me this time the same sharp sense of loss. One goodbye had been enough.

"Let's see if the auditorium is still intact," I said.

"You're nostalgic for *Pride and Prejudice*? You were quite good as Mr. Wickham."

"No, I want to take a last peek at Miss Coultrane's classroom."

We walked over to the auditorium, which seemed to be sagging into its foundation, though no demolition equipment was at work yet. Most of the seats were gone. It was peaceful, wandering the space, remembering.

"Remember how Ingrid Bergman fascinated everybody when she came here?" I said. "She was amazing, totally invulnerable. Beautiful, and always gracious."

"I never understood why she fell in love with Rossellini," Kathleen said.

"She must have thought he was a great filmmaker — otherwise, why would she have made more movies in Europe with him?" We were falling comfortably into our old gossipy mode, but without our beloved movie magazines to feed it.

"Maybe he's the only director she *could* work with after everything," Kathleen mused. "I read Ingrid and Rossellini were always short of money. Did you hear what he said when they broke up?"

I lifted an eyebrow inquiringly.

"He said what nobody understood was, she always felt like a bird in a cage — she *wanted* to be without roots."

We were walking into Miss Coultrane's classroom now; I hesitated. "Does that describe me, too?" I said.

"A little."

As I stared around the room, I heard other voices — my own, my classmates', Miss Coultrane's. Where would she be if she had lived? Probably still sitting in that graceful spindly chair of hers in some other school, spending her time teaching young girls how to *enunciate,* how to use words to build confidence, how to grow. I stood at the open door of the basement classroom; Ingrid's remembered voice came through, true and clear. The thrill of hearing her *become* Portia for just a few brief moments — Miss Coultrane and I had shared that.

"Miss Coultrane believed in me," I said. "I was lucky to know her."

Kathleen squeezed my hand; she didn't try to reply.

We backed out of the school parking lot in silence. Suddenly Kathleen pulled on the brake, stood in her seat, and shouted, "Goodbye, Saint Ann's! We won't forget you!" A dump-truck driver shoveling dirt and other debris into the truck bed stopped and stared at us, startled. We drove away, relishing the wind in our hair, shouting out the Saint Ann's alma mater, or at least most of it; we couldn't remember all the words.

Malcolm appeared at the door in a suit and tie, looking startlingly put-together. He thrust forward a bouquet of tea roses and said quickly, "These aren't for you, they're for Kathleen. And my mother didn't pick them out this time."

"So I don't get an orchid in a plastic box?" I teased.

"I like roses better."

We stood there for an awkward moment, grinning at each other, replaying that long-ago scene.

"Okay." Kathleen came up behind me and opened the door wider. "Good to see you. Those are for me, you said?" Smiling, she reached for the bouquet. "Thanks, Malcolm. I love tea roses. Have fun this evening."

"Pushing us out?" Malcolm said as I rushed back in to grab a jacket.

"Just remember your curfew and be home by midnight." She gave us both a grin and shut the door.

It did feel strangely like a first date. I kept stealing glances at Malcolm as we drove, expecting to see somebody different, somebody not at ease in good clothes, somebody trying to — what? — impress me? But that wasn't happening.

"You haven't asked where we're going," he said.

"Where are we going?"

"Well, at first I leaned toward something like the Polo Lounge, or Chasen's, but I don't like to do a lot of celebrity watching. And it would look like I was trying to impress you, which is ridiculous — you've probably been in those places dozens of times, starting when you were in diapers."

"Not quite," I murmured. I couldn't restrain a smile at the idea of my proper mother making me eat my spinach at the Polo Lounge.

He glanced quickly in my direction as he swung left onto La Ciencga. "Then I thought of concentrating on the food. I remembered how much you liked hamburgers, so I figured, what about a good steakhouse?" He pointed out the window. "So here we are, Lawry's Prime Rib."

I knew the place; it was still painted in the familiar salmon pink and green that had made Mother roll her eyes a few times, but I had always liked it. It held no bad memories. "Perfect," I said. "My father loved it."

The booths were as cozy as I remembered them. We ordered drinks, and as we scanned the menu, to my astonishment, I was talking again. I told him about the nuns, about the memories triggered by the buyers of my old home, about actually beginning to believe I could break out professionally —

"You had stopped believing that?"

Had I? "I think so."

We ordered the prime rib and a second round of drinks, and I talked more — about New York, about peeking in the window of an old Wilshire Boulevard deli, about my new blouse, about Mother's perfume — I'm quite sure I stopped long enough to eat dinner.

"I'm sorry," I finally said. "I'm talking too much."

"No, you're not. You're bringing yourself up-to-date."

"You make it easy to feel safe." These words, coming from my own lips, didn't quite astonish me.

"Jesse" — his voice was suddenly tender

— "are we ready for each other?"

I took a deep breath. "Maybe we are," I said.

"Is that an invitation?" he asked quietly.

I thought about it, gazing at him. What was I resisting? The answer was so simple.

"Yes," I said.

His arm slipped around my shoulders — steady pressure, pulling me close. The heat of his body mixed with the heat of mine. He released me gently, signaling for the waiter with his other hand. "Check, please," he said.

We only made it as far as the car.

We were barely seated when he took me in his arms and kissed me, deep and full. I felt myself relax into him, holding back nothing of what I was feeling. In a lazy, delicious way, we began exploring each other without hesitation.

"Not the best of places for this," he said.

"It's high school, I guess," I murmured, but neither of us pulled back. Nothing seemed to matter — not the infernal gearshift stick, not the bucket seats — nothing.

"I've waited for you for a long time," he said.

Maybe I had been waiting, too. I held on tight, touching this man, this unexpected lover, and, really, the gearshift stick didn't get in the way at all.

It was at least ten minutes before either of us spoke again. Then, slowly, reluctantly, we began untangling ourselves. He kissed my face gently. "I guess that takes care of high school," he said. He looked out the window, almost as if seeing the other parked cars for the first time. "In a parking lot, no less. Good thing nobody called the police."

I didn't answer right away. Then, "I'm wondering if we did it to prove we could."

"Maybe," he said, curling a strand of my hair around his finger. "Does it matter?"

I thought about that, and felt a release. "I guess not," I replied.

He stretched, smiling lazily. "Now that we're adults, what comes next?"

"I don't know," I said.

"I do. I want to make real love to you — you know, in a real bed."

I couldn't resist a laugh. "I'm not against that," I said.

"I'll be in New York in a few weeks on business," he said. "Maybe, if you feel the same way then . . . ?"

"Oh, don't be so proper," I said. I reached over and kissed him lightly on the lips.

"I could be just getting your signals better, but I have the feeling you want to ask me a question," he said.

"So you're clairvoyant." I studied his face. "Okay, here it is — if you knew why I was invited to the Academy Awards, is there a reason you couldn't tell me?"

"I was wondering why you didn't push on this," he said. "The answer is, I didn't know. I think I do now, but I can't tell you."

"Why not?"

"You'll find out tomorrow."

"Is that ominous?"

"No. If it were, I would warn you."

"You are maddening, you know."

"Of course I am — I'm a lawyer." He turned on the engine and put the car in gear, then looked at me, his familiar grin in place. "If you aren't too annoyed by now, are you still up for meeting in New York?"

So — did I trust him? *Decide.*

"Yes."

He smiled.

"Okay — and I trust *you.*"

CHAPTER TWENTY-FOUR

Los Angeles, 1959

I slept late the next morning, deeply, without dreams. When the sun finally crept through the half-closed blinds and forced my eyes open, I lay there for a while, reviewing the night before, allowing myself to remember it all without unease. It had felt right then, and I knew it, and it felt right now. No counterforce, no guilt, was pulling me apart.

It took me a while to notice the silence. Usually in the morning Kathleen would be clattering around the kitchen, frying bacon, making toast. I rose, pulled on a light bathrobe, and went searching for her. She wasn't in the kitchen, though a plate of sweet rolls and a pot of coffee awaited me. "Hey," I shouted out, "I just wanted to let you know, I snuck in *way* after curfew last night."

I glanced at the clock — it was past noon.

Of course, Kathleen was probably at work; what was I thinking? Then I spied a note sitting next to the sweet rolls.

"Must have been quite a night," it read. "Back at five to drive you to the theater. Wear eyeliner."

It was obviously a busy day for Kathleen, I thought, a bit disappointed. Okay, now I could churn over what Malcolm knew that he wasn't telling me, and that did trigger unease. After breakfast, I scanned the morning paper, finding not a hint of Academy Award news. Tomorrow it would dominate. I started packing for the trip back to New York, then wandered outside, plucked an orange off of a tree. It had never seemed amazing to eat oranges and apricots out in the backyard when I grew up here, but it did now. I settled into a lawn chair and peeled the orange, slowly letting myself realize that I was going into something alone tonight with no idea why I was there. And that took me back to my cautionary common sense — why was I doing this?

I paced. Pulled on some jeans and went for a long walk. Where was Kathleen? Maybe she was staying away on purpose?

But there she was, on the porch, when I came back, obviously looking for me.

"Where have you been?" she said sharply.

"It's a good thing I got back early. It's almost three; we have to leave here no later than five, and you haven't started getting ready at all."

It was the scolding tone in her voice that did it. I was up on the porch by then, facing her squarely. "You know something you aren't telling me about tonight, and I want to know what it is."

She stepped back, looking genuinely startled. "You don't need to confront me like that," she said.

"Well, what's going on? You've been gone most of the day, a pretty important day —"

"Jesse, stop. I've been doing a lot of driving and thinking, and not just about you and your mysterious invitation."

I took a deep breath and mentally stepped back. This was, after all, my best friend. "Okay," I said, "I'm sorry. Can you tell me about it?"

She was silent for a moment, then reached in her pocket, pulled out a crumpled envelope, and handed it to me. When she spoke, her voice was heavy. "I think I've found him," she said.

"Found who?" But I knew who the minute the words left my mouth. "Your father? You found your father?"

She nodded. It had been a crazy idea at

first, she said: just make a request for information through Social Security. They would contact him and convey her interest. Nothing would come of it, she was convinced.

"But then this came."

I glanced down at the bedraggled envelope, noting the shaky return address. "And this is his reply?"

"Yes."

"Wow."

"It isn't much of a message. I've been walking around with it in my pocket for weeks." She looked at me a bit shamefacedly. "You came back here to face your past, and I was still avoiding mine."

"Glad to have been your inspiration," I said gently, handing her back the letter. She looked exhausted. "So — what happened today?"

"A lot of driving, mostly."

She told me how she had cruised the streets of one of the city's worst slum districts, vainly trying to locate the address on the envelope — and then saw it, a crumbling stucco building with broken shutters next to a liquor store.

"It was awful — looked like some kind of group flophouse," she said. "I lost my nerve."

"You just sat there in the car?"

She nodded. "Watching a few people go in and out of the place. I kept wondering —"

"— if one of them was your father."

She closed her eyes; a tear trickled down. "I probably wouldn't recognize him if I saw him."

We sat in silence. "If you go back, I'll go with you," I said.

She shot me a grateful look. "Thanks," she said. "I don't know if I will. Maybe he wouldn't want me to. But I'm going to get him out of that awful dump. Into some decent rest home, I hope. Maybe I'll see him then."

"The cost —"

"I can afford it." She lifted her chin proudly. "You got to me, you know — when you faced the nuns, walked through your old house, and stood on Saint Ann's front lawn — with all its memories — you really were tackling *your* past. I had to act on his letter, or I was a coward."

No words were enough; I reached out and hugged her.

"Don't go weepy on me," she admonished, her voice almost regaining its usual bounce. "I'm feeling fine." She jumped up, suddenly in full efficient mode. "And you've got a big evening coming up."

For just those few moments, the Academy Awards had vanished from my brain. I scrambled to my feet, flustered.

"I think it's time to get dressed, okay?" She gave me a small smile. "Just so you're not running out the door naked when it's time to leave? Give us a little time to talk."

My heart stumbled, a few extra beats. "So you do have something to tell me."

"Yes."

"Kathleen, don't let me down," I whispered, feeling tears forming.

"No way," she said. "But this one you will navigate on your own, and you'll do it well."

Her skirt fit perfectly — all floaty chiffon, three layers of deep midnight blue, not black, that twirled even better than the skirt in the department store. I began to relax when she teased me about my evening with Malcolm. I liked repeating his name, just to hear it.

"Here," she said, as I was adjusting my stockings, clipping them to my garter belt. She pulled a pair of glittering earrings out of her jewelry box. "They aren't real diamonds, just rhinestones, but they're my favorites. I like how they dangle."

So did I. We were almost done.

"Is the eyeliner on straight?" I asked.

"Perfect."

And then I was ready to go.

"You look beautiful," Kathleen said. Slowly she poured us each a glass of wine and gestured toward the porch. "We've got ten minutes. Go sit down, I'll be right back." She vanished for a few seconds into her bedroom, then joined me on the porch, holding a sealed envelope.

I tried to make a joke. "*Another* envelope? At least it looks in better shape than your father's."

She ignored that. "Okay," she said, keeping her voice light. "My instructions for you were, please don't open this until you are in your seat in the Pantages Theater."

"Who is it from?"

"Your mother."

I opened my mouth, but at first no words came out. "What does it say?" I managed.

"Haven't got a clue. But you'll learn why you are here." Her eyes were solemn but gentle as she handed me the envelope.

Just my name, no address — and it was my mother's handwriting, a bit shakier than it used to be. I felt sudden apprehension. I hadn't seen her in over a year. "Is she sick?" I asked. "How did you get this?"

"Through my mother. And, no, I don't

think she's sick."

My fingers trembled. I wanted to get it over with and open the damn thing — right now, here — so I could deal with whatever surprise it contained. All my instincts told me it wouldn't be good.

"Kathleen —"

"Don't. Do it her way, please. I promised you would." She stood. "Time to go."

"You shouldn't have promised for me." But I slipped the letter into my purse and followed her down the steps and out to the car.

We almost got to the intersection of Hollywood and Vine before we were stopped by a line of police. Their job was clearly to keep the lane leading directly to the front of this splendid theater open for the limo drivers carrying the usual array of glittering stars.

I had always loved the Pantages Theater. Its jewel-box interior was one of the magical places that had fed my enthrallment for this land of make-believe. But the electricity that fueled that thrill was here, outside, in the bleachers. The fans. Their numbers swelled with every passing minute, all of them craning, peering, straining for a glimpse of those glamorous beings they paid homage to every year. I saw thirteen-year-olds, dazzled, bouncing up and down, clutching rolled-up copies of the latest *Photoplay* magazine, hoping against hope someone famous would take a second to scribble his or her name and give them a keepsake for their grandchildren.

"Remember when we did that?" Kathleen said.

"We were foolish."

"No, we weren't. We were young."

A cop blasted on his whistle, gesturing us away. Kathleen squeezed my hand. "Better jump out," she said. She pointed to a theater side entrance. "I'll follow the show on TV — and I'll pick you up when it's over, right here." Then she gave my hand a quick squeeze. "You'll see it through," she said.

I smiled, then opened the door. So — here I was. Back home.

It took me more than half an hour in the admissions line to make it up to the brisk ticket taker, who scrutinized each name, matching it to his master list then waving us through. Definitely not the glamour entrance afforded my parents and me back all those years ago. With an usher's guidance, I climbed three sets of stairs, wondering if my seat was going to be in the last tier, the one where a few heads already seemed to graze the ornate ceiling. It turned out to be just below that.

I settled into my seat, wondering about those around me, many flushed, trying not to look disappointed that they would need binoculars to see the stage. Who were they? Cousins, nephews, business associates, deal payoffs — but what couldn't be taken away from them was that they were *here.*

The orchestra began playing a medley of vague show tunes, the kind of filler music that didn't herald much of anything. I looked over the banister and realized why: the majority of the stars due to fill the orchestra seats were still arriving; nothing would happen for a while.

Okay, I told myself. It's time. I took Mother's letter out of my purse and opened it. Her handwriting was precise, and a faint trace of her perfume managed to waft off the page. I scanned it quickly, heart thumping. Two words jumped out: "Ingrid" and "homecoming."

I caught my breath. So it was happening: Ingrid was coming back. It took effort, but I forced myself to read slowly, from the beginning.

Dear Jessica,
    Some young publicist thought inviting

me to a "homecoming" event for Ingrid Bergman would be a magnanimous gesture, though he cautioned that her return had to be kept secret until the last minute. I wrote back, telling him he was mistaken. She was too much part of the scandal that harmed my husband to be a friend. I wanted no favor from her.

I briefly closed my eyes. I didn't want Mother's voice in my head anymore; I didn't want her judgment. I didn't want the *contradictions*. I was pulling out of all that. But I couldn't stop now; I went on reading.

But you were a fan. Always. You thought of her as perfect in every way, and I told him the invitation should be sent to you. At his request, I agreed not to tell you about the big surprise in advance.

Mother

Not even a perfunctory "Love," before her signature. I started to crumple the note in my fist — but then I saw a long postscript on the back.

I cannot put this pen down yet. I have for too long left you to assume you shared blame for your father's death. The truth goes deeper, and it's time to tell you that.

Yes, as you wondered, your father once was a member of the Communist Party. Please, don't be shocked. He was an idealist, an enthusiastic supporter of a strong labor movement. He quit within a year, but that didn't matter to the red-baiters. When his friends were put on the blacklist, the strain of trying to help them without destroying his career and your trust in him was too much. That, more than anything else, I now believe, was what killed him. Not the Bergman scandal, not your speech at the tournament.

He didn't want you to know. So we both lied. That was a sin. But it was for your protection. Your father loved you and still hoped to make it through. He wanted you to be proud of him again, to remain your hero. I've tried to justify what we did by honoring his wishes.

My head began to spin. Secrets, always secrets. Mother had lived with this one for so long. My eyes went to the final lines.

In truth, I was jealous of what you two

434

shared. I always wanted to be your hero, Jessica. Somehow. But it never quite worked out.

My eyes stung with sudden tears.
I always wanted to be your hero.
Nothing could have been less expected. I could not imagine her saying those words. But in that short sentence, in a new way, I felt her yearning.

I smoothed out the paper, reading again, oblivious to my surroundings. *But it never quite worked out.* And I saw her again at church when I was young, trying to counter the easy connection between Father and me — that delicious excitement I learned from him of thumbing one's nose at authority — with her sense of duty, her rules for safety. Love cloaked in vigilance, nothing less. For my mother, parenting had been the act of saving my soul. Could I break that shell now? Was there a way? I thought of Kathleen's hesitant efforts to reconnect with her father. For both of us, it was hard to take that step.

The show began. The minutes ticked by. When I looked at my watch and saw that most of an hour had passed, I was only half concentrating, waiting for whatever was to come next.

"Miss Malloy?"

I looked up into the face of an usher hovering over my seat, obviously in a hurry, but still trying to extend elaborate courtesy.

"Yes?" I said, startled.

"Would you come with me, please?"

"I'm sorry, am I in the wrong seat?"

"No, no." His eyes flicked with impatience. "We're going backstage; please, come now."

CHAPTER TWENTY-FIVE

Los Angeles, 1959

The usher, swinging his flashlight back and forth, led me down several flights of stairs, through a heavy, unmarked door, past a cavernous supply room, and along a winding corridor that finally burst into the backstage of the theater. Chaos — a cheerful chaos — reigned.

So Ingrid was actually here; she had come back, and that was why I was being taken backstage. But for what kind of encounter? I wondered if I cared. My thoughts kept going back to my father — my poor father, trying not to disillusion me, hiding the truth. So much was explainable now. I could only wish that he could know, somehow know, that I didn't care about his lie — I cared that he had lied to protect me. And my poor mother — choosing to live perpetually in sin?

Familiar faces were everywhere. David

Niven was pacing back and forth in front of me as a short, officious-looking man kept pace with him, alternately glancing at his clipboard and talking rapidly. I couldn't remember: had the actor been a friend of my father's? Maybe not; best to say nothing.

"You're telling me I'm supposed to look informal?" Niven was sputtering. "Did you notice, I'm in tie and tails? Okay, okay, I'll strip onstage."

The comedian Ernie Kovacs stood leaning against a large cardboard backdrop, three cigars sticking out of his mouth. One, I noted, was actually lit.

The tension was heightening as I stood watching. I peeked out from behind the heavy fire curtain and saw why. Before me was the crowded theater; dozens and dozens of Hollywood moguls and stars filled the seats. The recessed platform holding the orchestra was rising slowly from the pit. The musicians struck up the song "Thank Heaven for Little Girls" from *Gigi,* one of the Best Picture nominees. Maurice Chevalier, wearing one of his jaunty costumes, dapper and smiling, wandered among the backstage crowds, humming his hit tune.

A frowning guard suddenly pulled me away from the curtain. "Lady, who are you?

438

What are you doing here? Do you have a pass?"

I jumped, startled, and flushed as heads turned at the sound of his voice. "No, I don't, and I don't know . . ." I began, looking around for the usher who had brought me here. He had disappeared.

His hand firmly on my shoulder, the guard began guiding me toward an exit door. "I'm sorry, you'll have to leave," he said.

"Wait," barked a voice. I looked quickly behind me and saw a short, burly man with thinning hair and a cheery smile peering at me. "You're Jessica Malloy? The girl with the bad haircut, right?"

Only one person here knew about that. "As you can see, it grew out," I managed, my heart suddenly racing.

He turned to the guard, satisfied. "I can take over here — she's authorized," he said. Then a nod to me. "Come with me, okay?"

As we wound through the crowd, my guide — who introduced himself as Burt Kramer — talked nonstop. "I'm handling publicity for this show. A lot of excitement right now, as you can see — it's only the second time we've been on TV; everybody's nervous. Jerry Wald — he's the producer — is telling everybody to shorten their routines out there — five sets of hosts this year, a little overkill, don't you think? — he's afraid we'll run over our two hours; if we do, the network will just cut us off."

"Where are we going?"

"We're here." He stopped at one of the dressing-room doors, pulled out a key, inserted it into the lock, and ushered me inside. The walls were ringed with mirrors and bathed in soft light. Hanging from a screen was a dress, simply cut, with a glittering bodice and a soft-rose-colored silk skirt.

"She's wearing that tonight," Kramer said, catching my glance.

I swallowed hard. "Where is she?"

He glanced at his watch. "She's running a little late, but I'll keep you company until she shows up. Have a seat."

I sank into a chair, trying to put it all together. "Did my mother arrange this?" I asked.

I could have sworn he winced. "Your mother is quite something," he said. "She wrote back to me that she wanted nothing to do with Ingrid. I didn't tell Ingrid that. Look, I heard some of Ingrid's friends tossing around the idea of inviting your mother, so I went with it. It never occurred to me that I could've lost my job, sending that invite without clearing it with Bergman first.

She was irritated, fair enough; the last thing she needed was having all that stuff raked up in the press again. But she said to send it on to you, and if you came, to bring you here." He pulled out a handkerchief and swiped at his brow. "Thought at one point I could lose my job. Already said that, didn't I?" He sank into a chair facing mine.

All that in almost one breath. I found myself rather liking him as the minutes ticked by. The show had long since begun. Even I began to get a little nervous; she couldn't miss this.

"Did you know my father?"

"Admired him from afar. He's famous for hitting the right release date for *Casablanca:* perfect timing." Kramer paused, fumbling for a cigarette. "You don't mind, do you? I can't smoke out there, just in the dressing rooms. I wish she'd hurry up; they're moving fast out there." He paused long enough to strike a match and light the cigarette. "I didn't know him," he said quietly. "But I hear he was a decent man."

"He was. He got caught in her scandal. My whole family did."

"Ingrid wasn't some harlot or anything, you know," he said. "It wasn't all about Rossellini; she was dying to climb out of the box she was in in America. She felt rotten leaving Pia, but that marriage was dust. She learned fast it wasn't going to be easy. She knows the difference between fact and fantasy; her fans don't."

I swallowed hard. "We've learned."

He hardly heard me. "Maybe your father believed in the image more than he should have. Anyway, she wants everything to be authentic. She hates phony back-lot sets. She insists on filming on location every time — not possible. She wants it to be real; nobody else cares."

"How can it be both ways?"

His jaw set stubbornly. "If people still want her to be a nun all her life, they're out of luck."

Ten more minutes went by. Finally, a quick, sharp knock on the door. I jumped up; Kramer was faster. A deliveryman with darting, curious eyes, holding a huge bouquet of roses, started to step into the room.

"Thanks, buddy, I've got them," Kramer said, nudging him backward and reaching for the bouquet. He shut the door and hoisted the flowers onto a shelf. "There will be a whole lot of them," he said. "We've got a lineup of stars ready to toss these beauties at her feet." He grinned. "Ingrid's presenting the Best Picture award. How's that for drama? She's the real star, and everybody knows it. And I'll tell you, tonight was planned very carefully to make her 'welcome home' a huge event. But back here is where the fun is. Did you see Jayne Mansfield trying to struggle into one of the costumes from *Gigi*? And wait until you see the soft-shoe routine Burt Lancaster and Kirk Douglas do; this is going to be quite a night. . . ."

I began to tune out my new friend just as I heard the door handle turn; then the door opened. I stood; I was right this time.

"Hello, Miss Bergman," I said.

She paused on the threshold — an almost magical presence, dressed in a floral housecoat wrapped indifferently with a braided sash. There were fine lines of tension etched on her face, but she was as beautiful as I remembered.

"So you are Gabriel's daughter," she said quietly.

It struck me that she might not remember my name.

"Jessica Malloy," I said.

She smiled. "Yes, the girl —"

"— with the bad haircut," I finished, and smiled back.

"You certainly have grown up," she said.

"I'm trying."

She laughed, and the atmosphere eased.

Burt Kramer was hovering, scanning a scribbled list of notes he pulled from his pocket. "You're the last presenter, Miss Bergman," he said rapidly. "You'll be shown your mark at the curtain; when you're called out, walk toward the podium from the right side of the Oscar statue and —"

"That huge piece of gold-plated cardboard? I'm curious, who gets to take that one home tonight?" she said lightly, as she moved toward the dressing table.

A look of consternation swept over Burt Kramer's face; he obviously didn't have much of a sense of humor.

"No one, at least I don't think so —"

"That's all right, Burt, I'm just kidding. Would you mind leaving us alone for a while?"

"Of course," he said, his voice back under control. A flurry of quick goodbyes and he bustled out the door, staring once again at his batch of notes.

"He's a good man, but he does sometimes remind me of the White Rabbit," Ingrid murmured, running a brush through her hair. With all the mirrors in this dressing room, she managed not to look at any of them.

"Miss Bergman, I'm delighted to see you again, but I am wondering why —" I began.

444

"Why I wanted to see you?" she said, laying the brush down. "A simple reason. I forgot your name, but I had this memory of your lively face as a child, that time Gabriel brought you to the studio. I wondered then if Pia would look like you when she was older." Her voice trailed off.

"I remember you telling me that," I managed.

"Then there was that ridiculous trip you and your father took to Stromboli. You, so confused . . ." She shook her head. "I pushed the truth at you. Wiped childhood off your face."

"I never thought —"

She wasn't really listening. "I wondered a few times," she said with a catch in her voice, "how my daughter reacted when she heard."

I had no answer for that. It was no secret that she had fought long and hard with Pia's father to get reasonable access to her daughter. And it had never been enough.

We sat for a moment in silence.

Now she looked at me directly. "I was too abrupt that day," she said.

I blinked, briefly closing my eyes. "You were caught in a hard place," I said.

"And you came out as my defender and almost got your head taken off. I know."

She sighed and stood. "I better get this thing on." She reached for the dress hanging on the screen, and briefly slipped behind the screen. I heard the rustle of the fabric as it slid over her body. She emerged, brow furrowed. "Too many people thought they knew me," she said. "A movie star is a ridiculous commercial product. You know that now. I didn't realize back then it gave license to destroy. People saw me in *Joan of Arc* and thought I was a saint. You really all became" — she was searching for words — "my enemies."

"But you were never mine."

She seemed off balance for a second. Then: "What I wish people understood?" she said. "Not everything in life has happy endings. That isn't fair, I guess; I fantasize, too. Maybe that's why I've been more comfortable in my screen roles than in everyday life."

What could I tell her about her role in shaping me? I tried. "You were important in ways you couldn't possibly know," I said. "You embodied what I idealized, what I wanted to be true. You were my hero."

"I didn't want to be anybody's hero," she said. "I hope to never have to run from that pedestal again." Her face was grave — open, focused inward. It was not turned up to the light, it was not the pure holiness of Sister Mary Benedict; it held its own.

For just a moment, we both hovered between dreams and reality.

She turned her back to me; the moment evaporated. "Now, just to the mundane: can you help me with this zipper?" she said. "I can't reach it."

My fingers were only a little shaky as I zipped up the dress. Make-believe had always felt to me like a protected world, even though I knew that wasn't true. "Were you angry?" I asked.

"Yes. I was angry at everybody."

"Including my father?"

"Including your father. He was selling the product." She paused. "But he was a good man, and I'm sorry you lost him."

From beyond the door, I could hear a mix of voices, laughter, and music. The 1959 Academy Awards show was moving slowly toward closure.

She smiled gently. "Do let go of me, Jesse. I'm just a person. And I'm reclaiming this part of life as my own."

I returned her smile. "And I am reclaiming mine," I said.

An aide's head popped through the door. "Miss Bergman, it's time."

Ingrid stood to full height and was suddenly transformed. Her skin glowed with color. Her dark hair, casually flipped, was rich with texture; her knee-length dress had become a costume of dreams — lushly sequined silk swirling around this fabled star, now remote, cloaked in her fame.

"Walk with me?" she said.

We left the room and walked past a nervous Burt Kramer, whose look of relief at seeing his charge dressed and ready for tonight's re-entry celebration was palpable; past stacks of boxes and huddled aides, stars tugging at collars, eager for the climactic scene coming soon. We paused at the curtain.

It didn't take long. Jerry Lewis grabbed the mike as the house fell into an anticipatory hush. No jokes, just swift words. "And now, folks, I give you Cary Grant."

The actor, an anticipatory gleam in his eye, bounded gracefully onto the stage. He took the microphone from Lewis and faced the audience, which suddenly crackled with anticipation. The people in their tuxes and glittering jewels beyond the lights leaned forward as one. They knew — the whispers had spread.

"For the past two years," Cary Grant began, speaking slowly in his distinct, always recognizable voice, "I have appeared here as a stand-in for a great actress and a great lady — and tonight I get to relinquish that role." He paused, turned to the stage curtain, and reached out his hand. The theater fell into a hush.

"Ladies and gentlemen," he said slowly, savoring each word, "it is now my great pleasure to welcome back our own Ingrid Bergman!"

"Nine years," I whispered to myself.

A roar of applause filled the cavernous theater — sustained, vigorous applause, hundreds of hands clapping furiously for a star. Ingrid's face lit with grace and triumph. She turned to me.

"Goodbye, Jesse," she said. "Go live your life." She lifted her head and walked out onto the stage, the bodice of her dress capturing every shard of light, a smile on her face as fresh and real as that of anyone triumphantly reclaiming a life.

And I could say it all myself with few words: "Goodbye, Ingrid," I murmured. "You, too."

It was complete now, the necessary goodbyes. Goodbye to Saint Ann's, goodbye to my dreams of a fantasized home. Goodbye to a church that no longer spoke to me. And, finally, quite peacefully, goodbye to Ingrid. I didn't need a hero anymore; I didn't have to face the armor and steel of a fictional Joan of Arc and wonder why I couldn't be better than I was. It felt like my heart was unclenching. I could open the doors: love my father, learn to understand and love my mother, and leave the past where it belonged, in the past. I could — with a little more work — untangle the fantasies of my childhood without fearing the realities beneath.

At least, I could try.

"You look very deep in thought," a male voice said.

I didn't even turn around. Just smiled to myself. "Were you going to be here all the time?" I asked.

"No," he said. "Not until Kathleen suggested it might be a good idea to show up. Didn't know what *that* might mean, so here I am. You okay?"

"Yes," I said, turning to face him fully now, reaching for his hand.

"What next, Jesse?" Malcolm said.

"I'm not going back to New York right away," I said, mildly astonished at the ease of my decision.

"What's your plan?"

"I'm going up to Sacramento to see my mother."

"What decided that?"

"I've held her away from me for long enough. I think it's about time we reached out to each other." I touched her note, secure in the pocket of my skirt. "Actually, she already has," I amended. "It's my turn."

He smiled — his glance easy, almost tender — and started to say something, but the orchestra burst forth, swelling louder and louder. The 1959 Academy Awards Ceremony was coming to an end.

Mitzi Gaynor strode onto center stage and burst into an exuberant rendition of "There's No Business Like Show Business." As the audience joined in, a hidden platform, lined with all the presenters, emcees, and Oscar winners holding hands, standing side by side, rose from below; the hit tune felt as stirring as an anthem, which, I realized, it truly was. It was their anthem. I watched the stars grasping each other's hands, transcending their many made-up selves, their identities as burlesque queens, death-row murderers, lovers, kings, cowboys, and, yes, saints, and saw that, if there were true selves in this world of make-believe, here they were.

And I could cheer them on and walk away now and truly say to them all: Goodbye, and I no longer feel caught with a foot in your made-up world, and you don't want me there anyway.

"Quite a show," Malcolm murmured.

"It always is," I said.

"You look happy," he said.

I turned that over in my mind, slowly, and knew my answer.

"Yes, I am."

ACKNOWLEDGMENTS

Every author has her first readers, the ones who cheer her on and protect her from her own missteps. I've been lucky in the legion of friends who are my support and safety net. Special thanks go to:

Mary Dillon, Ellen Goodman, Judy Silber, Judith Viorst, Catherine Wyler, Irene Wurtzel, and, as always, my agent and pal, Esther Newberg.

Special thanks go to Melissa Danaczko, my amazing editor, who helped with my creative process even while she was busy with her own: welcome to the world, little Adelyn.

ABOUT THE AUTHOR

Kate Alcott is the pseudonym for the journalist Patricia O'Brien, who has written several books, both fiction and nonfiction. As Kate Alcott, she is the *New York Times* bestselling author of *The Dressmaker, The Daring Ladies of Lowell,* and *A Touch of Stardust.*

The employees of Thorndike Press hope you have enjoyed this Large Print book. All our Thorndike, Wheeler, and Kennebec Large Print titles are designed for easy reading, and all our books are made to last. Other Thorndike Press Large Print books are available at your library, through selected bookstores, or directly from us.

For information about titles, please call:
  (800) 223-1244

or visit our website at:
  gale.com/thorndike

To share your comments, please write:
  Publisher
  Thorndike Press
  10 Water St., Suite 310
  Waterville, ME 04901